SAM CRESCENT

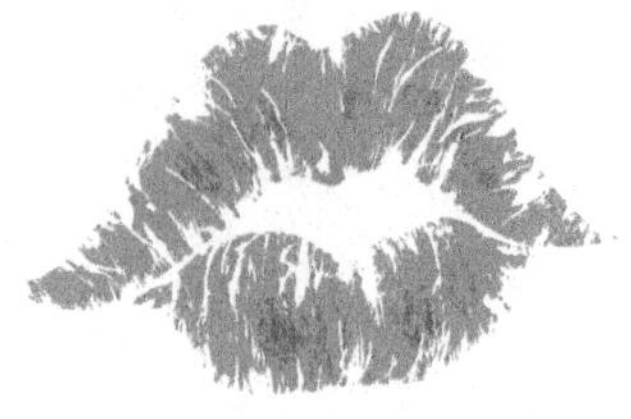

EVERNIGHT PUBLISHING ®

www.evernightpublishing.com

Editor: Audrey Bobak

Cover Artist: Jay Aheer

ISBN: 978-0-3695-0431-9

This is a work of fiction. All names, characters, and places are fictitious. Any resemblance to actual events, locales, organizations, or persons, living or dead, is entirely coincidental.

DEDICATION

To Francesca, thank you so much for asking.

SAM CRESCENT

SECOND BEST

Volkov Bratva, 1

Sam Crescent

Prologue
Aurora

I always knew I was going to die.

My life was destined to end this way right from the start. Staring down the barrel of a gun, pointed at me by my own husband, I was shocked that I was so important that one of the worst men in the Volkov Bratva needed to kill me. The moment I married into this world, my days were numbered. The fact I'd lived this long was a miracle.

Tears filled my eyes, and I hated that they made me look weak.

I wasn't surprised that I was the one on my knees. It took every ounce of strength not to give anything away. Would he kill me if he knew the truth?

I'd never betrayed my husband or Ivan Volkov, the leader of the Bratva, my husband's boss. The moment I'd been with him, I'd been loyal to him, to the entire organization, but it meant nothing now.

My husband wasn't known for his patience, and I was shocked I wasn't dead already. It wasn't like he wanted to be married to me. Like so many things in my life, I was the second-best choice. The real woman he probably wanted was my sister, Isabella. The beautiful one. The one my father couldn't bear to sacrifice to the disgusting Bratva bastards. Me, Aurora Fredo, the second daughter, the ugly one, I was the one he gave up freely. All my life, it had been so easy for everyone around me to pass me by.

I was friends with many but not cared about at all. Kind of crazy. I was the nice one. The one people said was sweet and kind, but didn't give a shit about. I was the one they didn't invite to parties, or they spent more time ignoring me. It was something I'd gotten used to.

My family was worse than that. I was the embarrassment. When we went to dinners, I was placed so far away from them, people had no idea who I was.

Passed over, time and time again.

On my wedding day, men gave their condolences to the man who stood before me.

A peace treaty.

Something new and never before heard of. Ivan Volkov was determined to set about a new era, a modern world for the Bratva, but to do that, for one section of the States he controlled, he needed his head man, his brigadier, Slavik Ivanov, to bring a conclusion to all the bloodshed with the mafia family.

I was the sacrifice in that mafia family.

Our marriage drew peace between the Italians and the Russians, supposedly.

The moment my father placed my hand in Slavik's hand, my fate had been sealed and along with it, this moment.

There were times I thought it would be different.

He'd made me believe I meant something, but like always, I was second best.

I wasn't important.

I wasn't loved.

I wasn't worth anything to anyone.

I'd lived with this knowledge for years. Some days, I could pretend it didn't matter, that I wasn't hurt by it. Then something would happen, a statement, an action, and it would awaken all the wounds I kept hidden.

Now, it was finally going to be over.

I closed my eyes and waited for the inevitable bullet that would finally end my miserable existence and set Slavik free.

Chapter One
Aurora

Ten months earlier

The party was boring.

Women stood in their little groups, gossiping amongst themselves. Some of them glanced in my direction. The Italian mafia-made men mingling with the same version of the Russian ones. I wasn't exactly sure of the full details as to what they were all called. What I did know was Slavik Ivanov, my husband, was like the Capo in his world. Even though we were parted by twenty-one years. He was forty years old, and I was nineteen, but in this world, age didn't matter.

Sipping on my champagne, I held the glass in my hand, counting to ten repeatedly to try to calm my nerves.

I'd been married a week. The event had been a huge success. The press had been there to take pictures and to announce it in the paper. My father hadn't wanted to give my perfect, beautiful sister to such a man, but me, he had no problem. Put my hand in Slavik's and ignored me for the rest of the day.

Even the following morning, I'd done our family proud by bleeding. On our wedding night, my husband had made me bleed. I was sure a lot of virgins did on their first time.

The night itself was kind of a blur.

Slavik and I didn't talk.

No words were whispered or spoken out loud. To anyone who'd look at us, we'd been nothing more than perfect strangers. He hadn't touched me since, which was a blessing. In fact, at night, I slept alone.

The pain had been … well, it wasn't something I wished to repeat.

When we'd gotten to the room, he'd pulled the covers back, tore my dress off with his knife, and I'd lain down and closed my eyes as he climbed on top.

The only sounds in the room had been his heavy panting.

I'd drawn blood on my lip.

Done.

Finished.

No longer a virgin.

The romance books I read were so far off the mark, it wasn't even funny.

Glancing at my husband, I saw he stood with his constant scowl, looking out over the room. I didn't know if he had the first clue of how to smile.

It wasn't my problem. That was the mantra I kept telling myself.

Every single night this past week, he'd arrived home, and each time I saw him, he'd been covered in blood. In our world, it was best not to ask any questions, so I didn't.

Some would call me a coward. My mother had once told me it was all about survival. As women, we were so easily replaced.

In fact, as the men were all cheering at Slavik's virgin, my mother was telling me he'd be bored now and would find other women to deal with his appetites.

What did I have to look forward to? The children he'd grant me unless he killed me first.

It didn't matter. No one cared. I sipped at my champagne and simply waited. This was an engagement party for one of the other bosses' brigadiers or whatever it was he called them. I didn't even know if he kept to these terms as Ivan Volkov was supposed to be taking his Bratva into another era. A modern era of peace, where he set the hierarchy and the new rules and terms for how things were run.

I came from tradition. Where everything was done via the book, including arranged marriages.

Standing at a party, surrounded by a bunch of Russians, well, it was scary. They all spoke English. I knew my husband did speak Russian, or at least I thought he did. Sometimes I'd heard him in hushed tones. I didn't even dare to learn the language for fear of where that would leave me.

Finishing my champagne, I chanced another glance at my husband, and shame washed over me when I caught sight of a barely dressed woman hanging around him. Her head was tilted back and laughter spilled from her lips. The way she looked so calm and collected around him, I didn't get it.

He was scary as fuck.

Not that I'd say it aloud. In fact, over the years, I'd learned the fine art of saying stuff in my head. I'd even begun to cuss out my parents and tell the boss to fuck off. It was kind of fun. They controlled everything else around them, but not my thoughts. It was the one sense of freedom I got.

A waiter came by to offer me another flute of champagne, which I ignored. I didn't know when the polite time would come to make my excuses to leave. Rather than come with my guard and driver, Slavik had brought us. The moment we'd entered the party, he'd left me here all alone.

This was … humiliating.

A week married and my husband couldn't even be bothered to stand with me. Not that it came as any surprise. I wasn't beautiful. All my life I'd been told I was the ugly one. The ugly, fat sister no one wanted. I had long, brown hair, the tips of which touched the curve of my ass, which again was another issue. I had a weight problem. On a good day, I fit into a size eighteen. I had huge tits, massive hips, a somewhat slender stomach in comparison, and chunky thighs. Even when I dieted and exercised, the curves stayed. It was something I had to live with.

Was it polite to fold my arms across my chest?

It was so hard to not show boredom when that was exactly what I was.

When the woman, whoever she was, seemed to be kissing my husband's neck, I'd had enough of the spectacle and decided to make my way outside. The doors were wide open, and the moment I was out in the fresh air, I took a deep, calming breath.

Tilting my head up to the sky, I saw it was a clear night, which explained the cold. The chill made me realize I was very much alive. Not a single part of me was dead, even though people seemed to pray for my death.

The idea of my marriage being a peace treaty was so fucking lame and stupid. They thought it was going to bring peace. The truth was it now made more people hate me because they couldn't continue their bloodshed.

"It's a nice night out, isn't it?"

The deep rumble of a voice startled me, and I turned around to see none other than Ivan Volkov smoking a cigarette in the shadowed corner, slightly hidden away by the door. I hadn't known anyone else was out here.

"Do you speak?"

"Y-yes, sorry. You startled me."

He chuckled. "The party is not to your liking?"

I quickly glanced at the doors. Everything was an act of survival now. If I said the wrong thing, he'd kill me. If he wanted some entertainment with my screams, he'd kill me. There was no way to win.

"It's wonderful."

"And yet you escape to the cold outdoors." He tutted. His accent was rather nice.

"I just needed some air."

"Oh, please, I saw you in there." He chuckled. "I would have thought Slavik would have known better by now."

Crap! Was I going to get my husband in trouble? Did I care? He had another woman hanging off his arm. Girlfriends, mistresses, they weren't exactly unheard of in our circles. For many, it meant the husbands had other places to go for them to sate their appetite. For others, they were a pest and destroyers of loving relationships.

Love.

I didn't have love.

"He's perfect," I said. Internally, I cringed. I'd long ago developed the mask I wore now. Passive verging on submissive. They didn't know I had my thoughts. How I spoke my own mind. Staring at Ivan, though, I didn't like how he looked at me. It took every single ounce of control not to react.

He saw a hell of a lot more than most.

He chuckled. "You're a little spitfire. It almost makes me upset that I gave you to Slavik."

Pressing my lips together, I averted my gaze, bowing my head just slightly. More often than not, this appealed to men. It had worked to divert their attention.

Not Ivan.

He placed a finger beneath my chin and tilted my head back, looking into my eyes. "Such a shame. Slavik is usually a man who sees so much and yet, he doesn't see you, does he?"

"He's the perfect husband and loyal to you, sir."

"Twenty years old and already know the way the world works. I don't get those mafia men. You see, submissive women have their qualities in the world, Aurora, but the women who know how to bite back, they're the ones who make our blood boil."

Why was he telling me this?

"Maybe one day, when you're not so afraid, we can have a proper conversation, don't you think?" He still had a finger beneath my chin. "And when you're dealing with Slavik, heed my advice."

"Sir," Slavik said, choosing that moment to interrupt.

I didn't jerk back, captivated by Ivan's gaze. I couldn't look away. It was like he was trying to tell me a million different things in his gaze alone, and I nodded. That was all I did.

"Charming." He released me and turned to look at Slavik. "You would be mindful to pay more attention to your wife than the whores who grace this place."

Slavik nodded his head.

It wasn't a warning or an order.

I got the sense Slavik and Ivan were more than just boss and employee. They were friends, which again was odd. Most bosses in our world didn't have friends. They made sure people feared them.

Learning the ever-changing dynamics that now surrounded me was difficult, but it was something I needed to master. Years of being around my own family had given me a lot of chances to watch, to listen, and to find out all the details I needed to survive even my father.

"Come," Slavik said, holding out his hand.

I moved toward his side.

He took my hand in his grip, and I expected us to leave. Instead, he led me inside and took me straight to the dance floor. One quick glance around the room and I saw we'd become the spectacle. I hated anyone's gaze on me, but it was easier to get this over with.

Slavik had been scorned. Would he beat me when I got home?

Once, when I was a child, my sister Isabella had embarrassed my father by playing the role of a spoiled brat. When we got home, rather than punish the perfect one, he'd turned his wrath on me, smacking me so hard I'd fallen into furniture. The blow had caused me to catch the skin across my eyebrow. I still had the scar at the corner of my eyebrow. It had long faded, but if you looked closely, you'd see it. The slight imperfection. I had several marks from old punishments. All of which I had to take as my father wouldn't dream of hurting his precious daughter. The beautiful one.

Some would say I had every right to hate and resent my sister. I didn't. I loved Isabella. It wasn't her fault, but our family's. She'd been raised to believe she was a princess who deserved all the attention, while I'd been taught to expect what I got and to be grateful for it.

With Slavik's hand on my back, the other holding my hand, we danced. The tune was soft, not too slow that it required us to stand close to one another, but not fast enough to create a good distance. Being this close to him terrified me.

I'd heard the rumors of just how deadly this man was. He was feared far and wide. The women gossiped about how he had the ability to tear apart a man with his bare hands.

I didn't even know if that was possible. Fear ran down my back, and I tried to ignore it.

Ivan's words rang in my head about how men liked to have a woman who talked back. Not in my experience they didn't. They liked a quiet, submissive woman who was pretty and spat out sons. There, I'd said it, albeit in my head.

"What was Volkov talking to you about?" Slavik asked.

"I'm sorry?"

"You heard me."

I did, but I was buying time. This wasn't a conversation I wished to have with my husband. How did I get out of this?

"He talked about the party."

"And?"

"Nothing more." I wasn't about to tell him the man's advice.

Slavik's hand tightened at my waist. I didn't know if he was trying to warn me, or if he just had to hold me a little tighter.

"How are you enjoying the party?" I asked.

"It's a fucking party, Aurora. How do you think?"

His harsh tone had me flinching. Of course. I was being treated like a fucking dumb woman. Rather than look into his dark, almost black eyes, I went back to staring at his chest. Had Ivan given me that advice on purpose?

Either way, I wasn't going to use it.

Once the dance ended, Slavik told me that my driver, Sergei, was going to take me home.

Without another word, Slavik kissed my cheek and handed me to Sergei. No doubt he was going to be fucking the woman who had been hanging off his arm.

Against my better judgment, I looked toward Ivan, who watched me. He raised his glass in my direction, and I offered him a smile.

Staring down at the floor, I followed Sergei out to the waiting car. He held open the back passenger door, and I slid inside. The noise from the building seemed to grow louder, but I ignored it.

Parties had never been my thing. The fear of

something bad happening always lingered in the air.

I was growing tired of living in fear. Resting my head back against the car seat, I didn't bother looking back to see the building. Instead, I stared out the window at the passing scenery.

The city in darkness always seemed to offer a sense of freedom. There were more shadows, places to hide. It would be so nice to run, to escape.

Now that I was married, my chances were gone. I was trapped in a loveless marriage to a man who clearly couldn't stand me. My days were numbered. Pressing my fingers to my temples, I tried to massage the pain that began to build.

Showing weakness would get me killed.

Being strong and loyal, that was what I needed to do.

To survive.

To one day earn my freedom.

I had a plan, I just hoped I knew what I was doing.

****

Slavik

The party had long ago ended. Wives were gone. Children were nowhere to be seen. The only people left were men, available women, and whores. Ivan sat at the head, looking like a king, which was exactly what he was. In front of him was the woman who had been hanging off me earlier.

Dana was her name, and he had proof of her treachery. No one could outrun the Volkov Bratva and they certainly couldn't betray it. There were many enemies of Ivan's wanting to take over. They didn't like the new era we all worked within. The treaties he built. The places he ran. The rules he implemented.

I did.

I was loyal to him.

My life was in his hands.

I'd die for this man. I owed him everything, and he knew I'd do anything for him. The moment he told me to marry Aurora Fredo, I'd done so without argument. My wife was different. The truth was in marrying Aurora to me, her father had given us the greatest of insults.

It was known far and wide the second daughter wasn't perfect. To many, she was the ugly, fat let-down. The real prize was her sister.

What Fredo didn't know was Ivan had wanted Aurora from the start. Again, I had no idea why he wanted her, only that he did. What I didn't like tonight was seeing them together.

I didn't love my wife.

Our wedding night had been a fucked-up mess.

My order from Ivan had been clear: consummate the marriage and produce the bloody sheets as per tradition in Aurora's family. I'd done that, and even the memory of it grated on my nerves.

She'd been terrified but duty-bound.

The moment I touched her, I found her so fucking dry, it didn't matter what way I'd taken her, she'd have been hurt. Getting it over with had been a challenge. I'd moistened her up with my saliva, pretending I was getting my dick ready as I'd done it.

I hadn't touched my wife in a week, and it wasn't like she complained. She slept stiffly on her side of the bed, rarely moving. I had to wonder if she slept at all.

Some nights, I found myself watching her.

She had long brown hair, a temptation I didn't allow myself to give in to. It would be so nice to run my fingers through the length, to wrap it around my fist, and to jerk her back against me as I fucked her long and hard. To show her what our wedding night should have been like.

Instead, I watched.

I craved.

But I didn't give in.

That would be pointless. At this time, I didn't even know if I liked my wife. We didn't talk.

I stared at the scene before me, and the truth was my dick was not getting hard.

Dana's face was already covered in cum. As per Ivan's instructions, we'd created an orgy. Fuck to your heart's content, and only when he had Dana where he wanted her would he strike.

That time was now.

One of the soldiers had his dick inside her ass. One of his hands gripped her hair, holding her head to the floor as he rode her anus. All the while, he had his gaze on Ivan, waiting for the signal.

The moment Ivan nodded, the soldier pulled her up against his chest, held her hair tightly, and placed the blade against her throat.

It took her several seconds to realize what was going on. Anger, fear, and sadness all danced across her eyes.

"Volkov, what is the meaning of this?"

"You think I wouldn't find out? First you steal from me, then you hand it straight to our enemies, and now I've got their fucking shit running in my clubs. In my city. You fucking dirty slut. You should know that I would find out. Nothing is ever hidden from me. Nothing."

"No, please. No. I don't want to die. They made me do it."

Ivan got up off his seat and walked down to where Dana knelt. Tears streamed from her eyes.

He got close. "You think I don't know about the

payment? How you're a couple of mil up on takings?"

Dana's eyes closed as the reality of what she'd done and been caught doing finally sank in.

The blade swiped across Dana's neck, blood spilling from the wound. She cupped her neck as the soldier pulled out of her ass.

It was done. The deed was finished.

I watched, and I didn't care.

Greed got people killed. Far too many people were lured into a trap by the green stuff. Dana had taken a bag of our coke, our own special blend that was worth so much more money than she sold it for. Once they got the chemist on it, they adapted it and changed the formula. We'd been made truly aware of the damage when ten people had been found overdosed in our clubs within one night.

This was a new part of Ivan Volkov's era. He didn't want people dead. Dead clients meant product didn't move. He liked to keep people alive.

Again, a new first.

Ivan clicked his fingers, signaling the party was over. Dana's body would be disposed of. Unclaimed. Dead and useless.

"You needed an elaborate party to do that?" I asked, following him out toward his car.

"No, I needed an elaborate party because it fucking entertains me."

I only ever talked to him as a friend when we were alone. The moment we were surrounded by others, I was the loyal subject.

"You know your wife was so fucking bored tonight, don't you?"

"Leave Aurora to me," I said.

Ivan chuckled. "I think I made a mistake in allowing you to marry her. You clearly don't see the wild woman waiting to be unleashed."

This did make me snort. The soldiers were a close enough distance away that I didn't have to play any other role. I could be myself. "Are you sure you're looking at the same woman?"

"Are you sure you're even looking at the right woman?"

This made me pause. "I know my wife. She's submissive. That's what they trained her for."

Ivan clicked his tongue. "There you go again. I have to wonder if I should demote you and keep that wife of yours. Look into her eyes, my friend. You will see."

He climbed into his car, bringing our conversation to a close.

We'd been friends for a lifetime already. Together, we'd grown up on the streets. I'd saved him from being killed more times than I could count.

We had a plan. A goal that would make this city ours. When we were kids, the Bratva were … hot tempered, and in truth, their vision wasn't big enough. They worked small. Petty criminals. They didn't see the big picture.

Ivan Volkov had. He was the big picture, and now, he ran half of the country, which he divided into six areas. I controlled area one. The biggest with the main cities all bowing down to my rule. Ivan only ever dealt with his brigadiers, his main men.

I was aware of the men he sent out to all areas. The spies he used to control everyone. It was how he learned of betrayals, of the greed, and of course, the rats. Everyone was in his pocket.

Even though he was considered the fiercest and most evil person around, he was also fair. If you didn't cross him, you lived. If you showed loyalty to him, then he took care of you.

The moment you turned your back on him, betrayed, or stole from him, well, your days were numbered.

Watching the car leave the parking lot, I stood there as the cleaning crew came. They nodded at me. I was on first-name terms with most people in Ivan's control. I made it my business to know everyone.

I'd always been a firm believer that knowledge was power, and when it came to keeping Ivan in control, I was willing to do whatever it took to keep him there, even marry a woman I didn't trust.

It was late when I arrived home. The guard I'd assigned to Aurora's care stood at the door, waiting for my signal to leave. I gave it to him. There were always guards around. Soldiers. Men designed to help us gain power and to forever grow stronger. They rose up the ranks, claiming to be the best everyone had to offer.

After taking a quick shot of the finest whiskey, I headed to the bedroom. Aurora was still awake, but the moment I entered the bedroom, she closed the book she'd been reading.

When all of her belongings arrived at my penthouse suite, I'd been surprised. She didn't have many.

Books.

She'd had close to three hundred books. All in paperback. I'd gotten the designers in, and one of the spare bedrooms had been converted into a library for her. I'd also granted her a credit card in my name to which she'd not spent a single penny. We'd been married a week, and I'd known other men in my position had been near bankrupt in that time by how wild their wives' spending could be.

I glanced at my wife. She wore a silk negligee that showed off her full tits. I hadn't given myself the pleasure of looking at her entirely, but one day soon, I intended to look to my heart's content.

Removing my jacket, I took my gun with me. I didn't go anywhere without at least two guns and three blades. I was a precautious man. I'd survived this long with them, and I wasn't about to ruin my chances by fucking it up and letting down my guard. I'd seen what happened firsthand to men who got sloppy. They ended up dead, and I knew because I'd been the one to kill them.

Once inside the bathroom, I stripped off my clothes and stepped beneath the cold water of the shower. I didn't like taking hot baths or showers. I liked the shock of the cold. It kept me alive and alert.

Also, I didn't linger too long doing one thing. Men struck during these times. I'd lost count of the number of men I'd taken out while in the shower.

I turned off the water, wrapped a towel around me, picked up my gun, and walked back into the bedroom. With my back to Aurora, I put the gun beside my bed and checked the time to see it was a little after three.

"You need to be careful around Volkov," I said.

I had no idea why I was giving her the warning. If she died doing something stupid, it was on her. I wouldn't take responsibility for her mistakes. She was the enemy. A foreigner to me.

"I didn't seek him out."

Her voice was so low, I only just made it out.

I turned toward her, and she immediately shrank away. I didn't need her fear. "Do as I say."

She nodded her head after a few seconds' hesitation, which pissed me off. While I'd been in the shower, she'd already put the book down and had sunk beneath the covers.

My dick was hard, but I was in no mood to fuck an ice queen.

I turned off my light, removed my towel, and climbed into bed.

The bed shook a little. I was sure she cried, but it wasn't my problem. I had a lot of shit to do over the next few days, but sleep didn't come to me.

My eyes adjusted to the darkness, and I could make out her outline. A sniffle escaped her. Time ticked by, and she finally fell into a fitful sleep. It was while she slept that I moved in close. I didn't touch her, but I felt her body heat and breathed in the heady scent of lemon.

It was just one of the many parts of Aurora I found … intoxicating.

Chapter Two

Aurora

There had to be some kind of survival in never seeing your husband. There had to be. The days turned into weeks, then months, and it wasn't long before I'd been married for a grand total of three months and four days. Yay. I was still alive.

Still alive.

Still ignored.

But it was moments like now that I actually lived for.

On rare occasions, Slavik would demand my presence at parties, social gatherings, and the necessary dinner at a restaurant.

The latter was always the hardest. They tended to be the two of us. He'd look the part but spend the entire time either talking on his cell phone or to a guard. I'd sit and have to listen to his tones of Russian.

I'd thought about starting to learn, but so far, I hadn't pushed my luck. Now these occasions, where we sat for dinner with a group of people, I could get through them. Slavik sat beside me, ordered my dinner, and complimented me. Played the role, saying all the right things. For a short time, I could pretend this was normal.

At least at this dinner party, there were other women. Three of whom I sat close to. They were talking about their latest designer gowns. I had no idea who I wore but they seemed to.

I nodded and smiled, laughed at the right points, and even told a few jokes. Sofia, Irina, and Amanda were all beautiful women. They were destined to be married to three of the other brigadiers under Ivan Volkov's rule. I wasn't sure who they were going to marry, but by the rocks on their fingers, it was a pretty big deal.

"You know, I was thinking we could all do lunch," I said.

In the last four months, other than being with Slavik, I spent most of my time indoors, unless he ordered me to shop.

It would be nice to make some friends in his world.

No one called me from mine. No distant friends or cousins. Even my sister didn't have time for me.

I smiled as the women agreed.

Feeling the need to use the bathroom, I excused myself, feeling happier than I had in a long time. This dinner could be the turning point, where I finally found some people. The bathroom was divided into two sections. One was lit, and the other was in darkness. For some odd reason, I decided to go to the opposite side, shrouded in darkness. I used the toilet, flushed, and was washing my hands when I heard the giggling.

"Can you believe her?"

I recognized Amanda's voice. I stepped back into the toilet stall. Who were they talking about?

"My face hurts from smiling so much," Sofia said.

"Tell me about it. If Slavik wasn't here, I would have been able to ignore her. Do you know what they call her?" Irina asked.

"No, what?" Sofia and Amanda asked.

"The fat Italian. Honestly. People feel sorry for Slavik. I don't know how he puts up with her. He could do so much better. I know my dad tried to get me thrown at him, but Volkov decided the Fredo girl was more important." The jealousy in Irina's voice was clear to hear.

So, where I thought I'd made a connection with these women, it was all an act.

"Did you see the dress?" Amanda asked. "She looked like a cow. All Slavik has to do is say the word, and I'd do anything for him. I heard on her wedding night, Slavik had to cut himself because he couldn't find her pussy through the layers of fat."

It went on and on. Between them using the bathroom, washing their hands, and applying makeup, they continued to insult me. Once they left, I stepped out of the stall. It wasn't the first time this had happened.

I stared at my reflection. My hair had been curled by the male hairstylist Slavik had hired. He'd wanted to cut my hair, but I refused, and so he curled it.

Tonight … I thought I looked pretty. I guessed I was wrong.

Tears shimmered in my eyes as I looked at my reflection, and my smile wobbled. "What did you expect?" I took a deep breath, calming down my nerves, and finally, the tears faded.

Time to go and play a role.

I stepped out of the bathroom and took my seat back at the table. My hand shook as I reached for the glass of water.

Amanda, Sofia, and Irina were back at the table, and I kept my gaze forward.

Slavik's hand brushed mine. I turned toward him as I jerked my hand away from him. My entire body shook.

"What's the matter?" he asked.

"Nothing. I'm fine."

He didn't need to know that another hope and dream had just been dashed. My pity party was my own.

My heart raced and I sat back. I ignored the women at my side and stared across the table. Ivan stared right back at me. I didn't know what to do, and so I looked down at where a slice of chocolate cake waited for me.

It looked delicious with the dark frosting and the moist cake, but I felt sick.

"I ordered dessert for you," Slavik said.

"Thank you, but I'm not hungry." I sipped at my water.

"I don't suppose you've got some news to tell me?" Ivan asked, silencing the table as he talked.

When he spoke, everyone else shut up.

Heat filled my body, and I made sure not to look at Ivan.

"No news."

"So no little babies coming our way? The next generation of good strong men?" he asked.

Babies. We'd have to be having sex to have babies, and that wasn't happening.

"No babies," Slavik said.

"Aw, Slavik, you break this poor man's heart. I want to see more children."

This entire conversation was getting to me.

"May I go home?" I asked.

As I asked, I knew it was incredibly rude of me, but I needed to get away from here. I had to have a break and leave. The thought of staying here, well, I needed distance from the women, from Slavik, from duty.

Gazes turned from me to Ivan, and he nodded. "Of course, my dear."

Slavik clicked his fingers, signaling Sergei, but Ivan tutted. "No, your wife is clearly feeling unwell. We'll talk another time. Go with her."

Ivan's word was law.

So, together, we stood. I made my escape toward the exit. Sergei already had my coat, which I took, grateful.

Slavik came back and held out a small white card.

"Amanda said you needed to organize a lunch together."

I stared at the card for several seconds before I reached out to grab it. Without question, I tore it up and threw it in the trash. I wasn't going to make friends with people who talked behind my back like that. All my life I'd been alone, and I could continue to be so.

Wrapping my arms around my body, I stood outside, waiting for the car. Slavik stood beside me. He was so much taller than me. Muscular as well. From the glimpse I'd gotten of him on my wedding night, I knew he was heavily inked, and he clearly worked out a lot.

I gritted my teeth as the car came into view. Sliding into the back seat, I tried to hug myself against the door, but I couldn't get close enough. Slavik was too close.

He pressed a button that raised the partition, separating us from the driver. We now had privacy.

"Do you want to tell me what is going on?" he asked.

"Nothing is going on. I didn't need you to take me home. I was happy going with Sergei." I sank my nails into my palm as I stared out the window.

Slavik wrapped his fingers around my wrist and tugged me close. "I don't like being ignored."

"You're hurting me."

"And you're starting to piss me off."

Tears filled my eyes. He could so easily break my wrist. I stayed perfectly still.

"I just … I wanted to leave."

"You think I didn't see a difference after you'd gone to use the bathroom? What was said? They went after you but came out first? Are you hiding a pregnancy from me? Tell me."

He spat out all these questions, and I struggled to

keep up. I was terrified, scared.

"What? No. I'm not pregnant. And … I don't want to have anything to do with the other women." I didn't want to tell him the reason why, but when he insisted, I had no choice but to tell him what I heard. I told him every single word.

Afterward, silence fell between us, and I realized he'd released my wrist. I pulled away from him, holding my wrist against me, protecting myself against him. He … frightened me. There was no other word for it, and now he heard my shame.

"You will never be left alone with those women," he said.

Not like I hadn't already planned to ignore them. I wouldn't invite myself to any of their parties, nor would I have anything more to do with them.

I'd wanted friends. Who didn't? But there was no way I was going to impose my presence on people who didn't want me.

My lip wobbled.

I hated this feeling. Gritting my teeth, I tried to ignore the pain. The loneliness. The desperate question of why people didn't like me. It wasn't like I did anything to incite it. At least I didn't think I did. I guessed I was just one of those people others couldn't stand.

"Are you sure you're not pregnant?"

"I've been having my period," I said. "It takes sex to have babies."

I hoped he didn't think that was an invitation.

We arrived back at his apartment building. From what Sergei had told me, Slavik owned this place, and several more. They were his personal investments. It was why if I chose, I could have the indoor swimming pool to myself, along with the gym.

Thinking about the cake tonight, those horrible words the women threw at me, I finally made a decision.

I took a deep breath and climbed out of the car, not waiting for either man to open my door.

Whenever something like this happened, solitude helped me to deal. Keeping the tears at bay was proving to be difficult. A burn settled at the back of my throat.

Staring at my reflection in the metal elevator doors, I had to wonder, was it me? Did I make people hate me? Was being nice a crime? A weakness? Why did people go out of their way to despise me? To hurt me? Or better yet, to avoid me?

I rubbed at my chest where a stabbing pain struck hard.

Stepping into the elevator, Slavik put his hand at the base of my back, but I didn't feel it.

"Do you ever care what people think of you?" I asked.

"No."

I smiled. It didn't exactly reach my eyes. Simple. Direct. To the point. I liked it.

"Do you?"

"I know I shouldn't, but it's kind of hard not to when everyone around you seems determined to hate you."

The bell dinged, and the doors opened.

We stepped out.

Slavik keyed in the code to our apartment.

When we arrived, I often kept my distance, steering well clear of him out of fear of capturing his attention. Today, I wanted to be alone.

I removed my shoes, placed them in the right place, and without another look back, I went to the bathroom.

Door closed and locked, I stared at my reflection

in the mirror and allowed the spiteful words to wash over me.

They were not the first.

"The fat Italian. Honestly. People feel sorry for Slavik. I don't know how he puts up with her. He could do so much better. I know my dad tried to get me thrown at him, but Volkov decided the Fredo girl was more important."

"She looked like a cow. All Slavik has to do is say the word and I'd do anything for him. I heard on her wedding night, Slavik had to cut himself because he couldn't find her pussy through the layers of fat."

"You're a disappointment."

"The ugly one."

"The fat one."

"What can we do to avoid being near her? No one likes her, no one wants to be around her."

I pressed my palms against my eyes as the tears fell, thick and fast. Each one that dropped added to my mortification. I was not liked. I was not loved. My own family didn't care who they sold me to.

"Aurora, open the door."

"I'm in the shower."

"I don't hear it running. Open the door or I knock it down. Two choices."

I splashed my face with water, wiping off the makeup I'd chosen to wear.

"Aurora!"

I opened the door and stepped back. Turning the shower on, I reached for the clasp at the side of my dress and eased it down.

Slavik was in the bathroom, and any other time, I'd have been afraid. There was no fear right now. Just pain and anger. Humiliation.

I hated this feeling.

"What is going on with you?" he asked.

I ignored him.

Was I sporting a death wish?

No one ignored Slavik Ivanov. His reputation for destruction preceded him. Women talked about him with a combination of awe and fear.

With the dress on the floor, I flicked the catch of my bra, followed by my panties, then stepped beneath the spray of the water. I let out a cry as the cold water washed over my body, shocking me to the core.

In the back of my mind, I cursed myself, telling myself that I shouldn't be doing this. Slavik had asked a question, and the least I could do was answer.

Silence.

Gritting my teeth, I closed my eyes and tilted my head back.

I'm fine.

I'm fine.

I'm fine.

The mantra went on and on inside my head. I didn't have much choice. When I was a kid, I had to learn to live with it. My father had hit me for showing weakness. Tears were pathetic and shouldn't be seen on a Fredo's face.

I released a gasp as strong arms grabbed my shoulders and turned me around to face him. Slavik was naked as well, which surprised me. I expected him to leave.

Why hadn't he left?

"Tell me what the hell is going on."

"Nothing! Nothing is going on. Don't you get that? I'm taking a shower."

"I know you're lying to me."

Be the lady. Don't give in.

Old advice and demands rushed forward. The

rules of the obedient woman consumed me, making me feel sick.

"You really want to know?" I asked. I didn't give him chance to answer. "I am sick and tired of being treated like I don't care. Like I don't matter. I tried to make friends and like always, I got shit on. What is it about me, huh? Do I just have *unlikeable* written across my forehead? Do people just enjoy kicking me while I'm down? The only reason they were nice to me tonight was because of you." I took in a deep breath, realizing my mistake and wishing I could take it back.

This wasn't what I wanted. I stepped beneath the spray, waiting for the hit, the punishment. It was destined to come. My mother, when she talked back to my father, always ended up bruised. One time, I had lain in bed, terrified as I heard them. The yells, followed by the screams, the cries, the begs. The following day, I hadn't been allowed to see my mother.

For three weeks she stayed in her room, and when she came out, she sported a broken arm, split lip, and bruised face. That was what we could see.

My mother had taken me and Isabella aside not long after and said we must do whatever we could to not fall into the trap of inciting our husband's wrath.

This was a code I tried to live by.

No blow came.

I wasn't even worth it.

Instead, Slavik left the shower, leaving me to feel far emptier than I ever thought was possible.

****

Slavik

The following day, Aurora's words were still running rife through my mind even as I dealt with the necessary business of incorrect funds at one of our many brothels. We worked it all, guns, drugs, money, pussy, whatever depraved thing men and women wanted and could pay for, we supplied.

We had politicians, government officials, and police officers on our payroll, and all were told to turn a blind eye. Where there was power, we had a hand in it. It was how we always stayed one step ahead.

When a brothel began to lose money, especially a really good one, it meant trouble. Not for Cara, the cute redhead who ran the place. The moment she saw a problem, she called. I didn't like dealing with the small businesses, but Cara was … a friend of sorts.

She sipped at her coffee, dressed in a cute pinstriped business suit. No one would have ever guessed that she loved her job running and participating in a brothel. She was a powerful woman and knew how to manipulate men.

I happened to adore her, as did Ivan, which was why I dealt with her face to face. Cara had been on the streets, fighting for her life. She'd helped to save our lives a time or two, and that meant we took care of her.

She was loyal and we cared for her. Protected her.

"As you can see, the money doesn't add up. We're gaining more clients every fucking day, and that shit doesn't sit well with me." She also didn't dress anything up either. She was fact all the way.

"Are you sure you just can't count?" I asked.

"Cheeky bastard. You think I didn't go over the figures a hundred times before calling you?" she asked. "I get how busy you all are, and I run a tight ship."

I took the file she offered me and started to look through the facts and figures. Just from the quick glance, it appeared they were losing close to ten grand a night—not good. The brothel Cara ran was more … exclusive. Rich men who wanted to live out every dirty little fantasy could have their fun. The women were always beautiful, always ready to fuck. Cara said she didn't deal with crack whores, or women who were desperate. She worked with women who wanted to get paid to fuck. Who actually enjoyed their work. When she ran the idea by Ivan many years ago, I thought she was going to fail. There was no way women would be lining up to want to fuck for money. I'd been wrong. Her club, aptly called Cara's, had proven to be a success. Even if it hadn't been, I was sure Ivan would have seen to it that Cara was taken care of.

Cara put down her coffee and rubbed at her temples. "I'm pissed off, Vik. It means someone is in my business, taking from me, taking from Ivan. I don't like it."

Only close friends called me Vik.

I looked at the figures. "And you've had no new people?"

"No. None. I haven't hired anyone in a year, at least." She sighed and sat back. "The problem I have is the security cameras, they're all in the rooms. I don't have them in our private business. You know that."

"So whoever it is, they're either taking it from the private rooms or up front. You ever thought the girls are giving it away for free?"

She shook her head. "I have to protect them. You know that. I've got guards there. Payment is always secured before any business takes place. You know my rules."

I did. "I'll take this to Ivan. He'll look into it."

"Tell him I'm on his side. That I'll deal with it." Cara sat back. "So, now that business is out of the way. Tell me how your wife is doing."

I rolled my eyes. "Not happening."

"Oh please, you're being an asshole, aren't you? I think I can see it now. You probably don't even see your wife."

I thought about how she spoke to me in the shower. Aurora had been different then. She'd been filled with fire, passion, and pain. I recognized all three. They were emotions I could relate to.

Staring at Cara, I know she'd understand, but when it came to my wife, I didn't understand her.

"This is not a topic of conversation."

Cara ran her finger along her chin, assessing me. I'd never fucked her. A lot of men had, but me and Cara, we weren't inclined that way.

"You know I met her at the wedding," Cara said.

"You did."

"She … seemed nice. Terrified, which is a given. She was being given to you, but I also heard what people were saying about her. What they were calling her."

"I heard as well."

"Yeah, but does your wife know what you did to those people?" Cara asked. "Is she aware that you put a blade in a man's throat because they called her a fat cow?"

"No one disrespects my wife," I said.

"Which again, I find so intriguing. For a man who claims not to care, you seem to do a whole lot of caring."

"Are we done here?" I asked.

She chuckled. "We are, for now." She stood up and held out her hand.

I shook it and then we embraced.

"Take care of yourself, Vik. Don't be a stranger."

"Let me know if you have any more findings about this." I held the file she'd given me, and she agreed.

She left and I paid the bill, leaving a healthy tip.

I turned on my heel and left the restaurant. After heading to my office, which was located at one of our casinos, I sat down and went through the figures. Cara's notes were along the side, and I could see she was trying to work out the problem.

Cara was an amazing businesswoman, but she sometimes didn't see patterns. There was something here, I could see it.

Closing the file, I placed it to one side, handled a few emails, checked over some inventory. Called men to arrange meetings with, and handled my district one. Sergei regularly checked in with me about my wife's whereabouts, and today wasn't any different. He texted me that she was still inside the apartment.

What was different this time was she'd taken a quick detour to the gym, followed by the pool.

She normally sat and read.

My wife's calendar was always empty.

Sitting back, I stared at the text message.

Aurora was hurting.

Her family hadn't been in touch. Everyone she'd ever known had left her behind as if they didn't care about her.

I didn't understand her pain.

My family was dead to me.

Ivan's words about children came back to me.

Getting to my feet, I texted Sergei to let him know I was heading home.

Everyone moved out of my path as I made my way to the car. I climbed inside the back and handled some more business as I was driven to my apartment. I didn't give Sergei any instructions.

After arriving, I climbed out of the car, took the elevator, and entered my apartment, dismissing Sergei with a single look.

Aurora was nowhere to be seen.

I checked the kitchen, living room, dining room,

and then opted for the spare bedroom I'd turned into a library for her.

She sat in a chair, reading a book. Exactly how I found her more often than not. This time though, she wore large clothes. They completely covered her body. Her glasses were perched on her nose, and she did look incredibly cute.

I entered the library.

"Hi," she said.

I stayed silent, glancing around at the bookshelves. When I'd married, I'd been determined to ignore this woman, but each day, I found her invading my thoughts. It was very fucking annoying.

"You like to read?"

"Yes."

It was a dumb question. Anyone could see she loved to read.

Spinning around, I found she now stood, looking at me. Her hands held the book close to her as if it was a protective shield. It wouldn't ward me off.

"We have a duty to produce a baby," I said.

"Oh." She nibbled on her lip. "I didn't think there was a rush."

There wasn't, but the truth was I wasn't used to going without fucking and so far, I hadn't been with any other woman. Again, it was fucking beyond me why I hadn't. We had willing women at our fingertips, and it would be so easy to find a woman.

"Get in the bedroom. Get naked."

I wasn't a good man. I didn't know how to have a wife, or to be nice to a woman.

She was the enemy.

Aurora left the library.

I didn't trust her. For all I knew, she could be running off and telling her dad all of our secrets. The moment I had the thought, I quickly squashed it. There was no way it would happen. All her actions were monitored. There was no way she'd be able to do it without us noticing.

No one had called her.

Her family had cut her off.

So much for a blessed treaty.

Entering the bedroom, I found her lying on her back, naked, staring up at the ceiling. My cock hardened at the sight of her.

It was true what Cara said. Some men on our wedding day and night offered me their condolences. I'd made sure the men knew to keep their opinions to themselves as they'd been unwanted.

When I looked at Aurora, I didn't see a woman lacking. She wasn't a stunning beauty, but she was beautiful. I liked her curves. I was a big man, and I didn't want to break a woman while fucking her. My strength and my appetite had me drawn to fuller women like Aurora.

I enjoyed sex and wanted it often.

I'd gone without for so long, only taking care of my needs by my hand. Several women had offered themselves to me, all of which I'd turned down. I had no interest in sticking my dick into a used cunt.

There was the problem.

Aurora had spoiled me.

Her virginity had been given to me, and now, there was no other pussy I wanted but my wife. The only problem was I didn't exactly know how to have a wife. It was a weakness, and there was no way in hell I'd ever fucking tell anyone that.

I had no weakness. I was fucking strong.

Standing at the edge of the bed, I saw her eyes close, and I couldn't do it. There was no way I could climb between her thighs and fuck her while she looked like she wanted to be anywhere else but with me.

"Come here. On your knees." I clicked my fingers, and Aurora did as I asked. I saw the redness in her cheeks, but I didn't care.

I had to fuck, to spill my spunk inside her willing body now. I had to take her, and the only way I was going to do that was if I didn't see her face.

The moment I touched her, she jerked.

I moved her into place to steady her, and then I skimmed my fingers along her ass, teasing her. When I cupped between her thighs, I found her completely bone dry, and I cursed.

This would hurt, and she'd probably bleed if I took her. With no other choice, I found the tube of lubricant I always kept on hand, spread some on my fingers, and applied it to her tight cunt.

Easing out my dick, I smeared the rest of it across my hard length. I was rock-hard. My need was so great that I wasn't even distracted by her dryness. All I wanted was to fuck.

With the tip at her cunt, I slid inside, and she was even tighter than I remembered. I'd been with my fair share of women, and I'd never known them to be like this. Clearly, they'd been broken in by a lot of men, because Aurora was tight.

I gripped her hips tightly, closed my eyes, and started to fuck her. I didn't go slow, but I took her hard.

Harder than I intended, but it was what I needed.

In and out, I watched her cunt open up. She softened, but I didn't give her a chance to come. At the final point, I slammed in balls deep and spilled my cum into her cunt, flooding her.

Ivan wanted kids, and I was duty bound to give them to him.

My cock was now spent for the time being. I slid out of her and put myself away.

Aurora didn't move.

I stared at her ass, seeing my cum spill out from between her pussy.

"Lie down, put a pillow beneath your ass, and give it half an hour," I said.

My cell phone rang, and without a backward glance, I left the room, feeling like a fucking asshole.

Why did it matter?

Why did I fucking care?

She was my wife, to do with as I pleased, and if I wanted to fuck her throughout the day, she would submit to me.

Then why did it leave a bad taste in my mouth?

Chapter Three
Aurora

Tonight was going to be a disaster.

I don't know why Slavik had agreed to this dinner, but I was terrified. It was the first dinner as a married couple. Nearly five months into marriage, and he finally decided it was time to host a dinner. A private family dinner.

My parents were coming.

Only mine.

He didn't have any parents.

This was going to be a nightmare, but for the past three days, I'd been planning it. Slavik had insisted on a cook. He wouldn't eat anything I cooked for him. Not that it hurt or offended me.

It really did, but I tried not to let it show.

Along with reading, I also liked to cook. What Slavik didn't know was that I'd put myself on a very strict diet. Years of name calling and abuse, and I was done. I wanted to be happy with myself, but I couldn't handle it anymore. That day back in the restaurant had sealed the deal. Those words the women had laughed about. They hurt.

I worked out at the gym every single day. I swam every day. I counted calories, being sure not to go over my limit.

So far, I'd lost a couple of pounds, not that anyone noticed.

I did.

I'd even started to use the scales in the bathroom. They'd been placed in one of the storage cupboards. Now every single morning and each night, I weighed myself. It was difficult, but I tried to keep the weight the same morning and night. I ate little. Drank water, and in all honesty, prayed.

This evening was going to be difficult. In the past, my family had even mocked my attempts to lose weight, which had set me on a spiral of overeating.

I'd be in control. I was a married woman, planning my first dinner party. It would all go well. I was determined for it to work out.

Even as I thought the words, I couldn't help but doubt myself.

Slavik had already returned home. We hadn't talked since he'd come home at lunch and demanded sex.

I had no idea why women enjoyed sex. It was … boring, slightly painful. Whatever he'd put on me before he'd entered me had made it comfortable, but still, I didn't understand why so many women were into it. Why there was even a porn industry.

Dressed in a simple black dress, I looked into the mirror. Was it slimming enough?

Slavik entered. "We're not conducting a funeral. Change."

He went to the bathroom.

Staring at my reflection, I thought I looked okay, but black was for funerals. I wished I had the balls to defy him.

I changed out of the black dress and opted for a white one, instead. This one clung to my curves.

I was about to change when Slavik came out of the bathroom, a towel wrapped around his impressive waist.

Attraction was still new to me, and even though I hated my husband, I did believe I … fancied him, at least a little bit. He was heaven to look at.

The bad boy.

Dangerous.

Deadly.

Shaking out of my thoughts, I saw Slavik was still looking at me. “Wear that,” he said.

I looked down at myself.

The dress went to the knee, and the front of the dress plunged to the top of my breasts. It covered everything but it felt so … sexy, and this was a family dinner.

Rather than argue, I changed the black shoes for a pair of white heels. They stung the backs of my ankles, but I ignored the pain.

Just as I was about to leave, Slavik ordered me to stop.

I turned as he came toward me.

He reached behind my head and I had to give myself a pat on the back for not flinching away from his touch. He released the clip that bound up my hair.

Staring up at him, I waited.

He didn’t give me permission to leave as he walked toward his jacket and came back with a velvet box.

He opened it up, showing off a pair of diamond earrings and a matching necklace. They were both beautiful, delicate.

“Thank you,” I said.

“Wear them tonight.”

“It’s only dinner with my parents.”

“I don’t care. I want them on you tonight.”

I took the box from him, but he stopped me, taking out the necklace. Turning my back to him, he placed it over my head so it lay against my chest, and secured the clasp. Staring in the mirror with him to my back, it seemed intimate. I’d read many scenes where the hero had now kissed the heroine’s neck and drawn her back, where she’d be able to feel his arousal. But he stepped away, leaving me cold and feeling a little stupid.

"Go," he said.

My master had finally released me.

I took the box, and in another room, I put the earrings in. They were very pretty.

After closing the box, I placed it in a cupboard and then made my way to check on the table. Everything was set perfectly. Candles had been lit. Wine sat cooling, ready for the right moment to pour.

The house had been cleaned. Slavik had insisted on a cleaner to come in. There was so much he wouldn't have me do. To be honest, I didn't even know why I was here half the time. It wasn't like he had any use for me. It was very embarrassing.

I checked into the kitchen and the chef who had been hired gave me a wink and promised it would be the best food imaginable. It looked like he was cooking seafood. I hated seafood, but I didn't have the heart to tell him for a fifth time.

The scents alone were making me feel queasy. I wondered if I was pregnant and wasn't entirely sure if I was happy or sad about that.

Bringing a baby into this world seemed cruel. A boy would be forced to train and kill. A girl would grow up to be a bride. Either happy or abused by her husband. This was our life. Did I want to risk bringing either child into the world? Possibly hating one while also dreading the life of another? It made absolutely no sense to me to do either.

I left the chef to his own devices and instead went toward the corridor where Sergei stood, waiting for instructions.

He always lingered. I hoped one day he'd come to see me as a friend and not as a job or obligation.

The smile he offered me was welcome.

I spent all my time with him. What I didn't like

was how often he was around me. A constant shadow.

"You're going to do great," he said.

"Thanks."

The truth was I knew this night was going to be a disaster.

"Relax." Sergei reached out, putting a hand on my shoulder. It was the first time he'd touched me since I'd been married to his boss. On instinct, I jerked back. No one else was supposed to touch me or even be allowed near me. Those were the rules. "I'm sorry."

I didn't have time to completely process the thought as the doorbell rang. I should have waited for Slavik, but my nerves were getting the better of me. Against my better judgment, I opened the door to welcome my father, Franco. My mother, Gianna. My sister, Isabella, and one of my brothers, Cole.

Offering a smile, I stepped back to allow them entry. My hands grew clammy and my heart raced.

"You shouldn't be answering the door," my father said. "Can't the Bratva pay for help? Are they that hard up for cash?"

Before I got a chance to answer, Slavik was there. "We allow our women to have their own minds and know they can answer the door without the need for assistance." He came to stand beside me.

I had no idea how much I needed the comfort, but the moment he was there, I didn't want him to leave.

Our marriage wasn't a happy one, nor pleasant, but clearly something had been going right in the past five months for me to prefer his company to my parents. The idea of Slavik coming home every night didn't make me sick to my stomach.

"What if I'd been your enemy? Your wife would be dead now."

My father had clearly washed his hands of me.

No reference to me being his daughter or a member of his family. I was Slavik's now.

"I have Sergei," I said, speaking up, breaking all the rules. My dad couldn't punish me now. I was no longer his responsibility.

In fact, realizing that, it kind of sent a shiver of pleasure rushing down my spine. They were in Slavik's home now. I belonged to him. His property.

"Please, I'll show you to the dining room."

Slavik took my hand, not allowing me to go far.

"They can find the table. Sergei, make them sit," he said.

I heard the outrage coming from my mother, but I ignored it as Slavik held my hand, stopping me from going anywhere. "What seems to be the problem?" I asked.

"Why are we having fish?"

His question caught me off guard. "Excuse me?"

"Fish. It's being served."

"It's what the chef decided."

"You hate fish."

For a split second, I was speechless. How did he know that? Why did he even care? Licking my dry lips, I looked over his shoulder, but he snapped his fingers. This made me feel like a child.

"You wanted a chef, and he wouldn't listen to me. No, I don't like fish, but he wouldn't allow me to have any choice."

"What will you eat?"

"Bread, or whatever else is around. I won't starve." I had to wonder how many calories were in bread. I hadn't eaten a whole lot today. The moment Slavik told me he'd invited my family to dinner, eating had been the last thing on my mind. The idea of sitting with my family and hearing their judgmental comments was enough to stop me from eating. If he'd told me this at the beginning of the week, I'd have lost a great deal of weight already.

"I don't like this."

"Next time, don't organize a chef and have a little trust in me."

"Why should I trust you?" he asked.

I didn't know what came over me. Hurt? Anger. Irritation that I should trust him, but he can't trust me.

"And why should I trust you?" I glared at him and tugged my wrist from out of his hold, marching into the dining room. The moment I crossed the threshold, the mask was firmly in place.

Dinner hadn't even started, and it was already a disaster. My father had taken my place setting at the head of the table. This was an instant sign of disrespect. I clenched my hands together, twisting them, trying to figure out what the hell to do.

Slavik entered and paused. "I'm not married to you, Fredo. Get out of her seat," he said.

I'd never heard anyone speak to my father like that. I looked at my husband, whose gaze was on my father.

"Pardon me?"

"Are you going deaf as well as being stupid? Get the fuck out of my wife's seat now."

"This sign of disrespect—"

I cried out as Slavik grabbed my father, dragging him out of his seat and placing him firmly in his own. "My house! My fucking rules. Live by them, or I will cut your throat, treaty or not."

Silence rang out and was only interrupted by the chef bringing out the first course. The scent of fish was too much for me, and with a hand on my stomach, I threw up all over Isabella's designer dress.

****

Slavik

"It was a family dinner," I said, not the first time either, and Ivan was still laughing. It would seem my father-in-law didn't take kindly to my threats. "Have you had a chance to look at what I've sent you?" I wanted to get back on track, not discussing the poorly organized dinner.

Aurora had looked tense the entire time. I noticed the way her family treated her with indifference. They didn't care about her. I saw it more clearly now than ever before. They'd given me and the Bratva a daughter they held no regard for.

After my wife threw up on her sister's dress, Isabella had changed into some clothes of Aurora's, which had started a whole conversation about the size difference between the two women. I'd immediately brought a stop to it.

Her sister Isabella had talked the whole time, and while she did, the sound of her voice grated on my nerves. Her family doted on her, though. It was like she'd hosted our party last night, not Aurora. As for the chef, well, he'd gotten what was coming to him. Telling my wife what he'd serve and not listening to her. He'd come from one of our restaurants, and clearly, he hadn't been given the update on who was in charge. I'd enjoyed every single moment of reminding him.

"Yes, I'm looking at it, and it seems to occur during two specific times where the rate of men versus income differs."

I listened as Ivan gave me the few remaining details of the puzzle. All I had to do now was go back to Cara with them and we could run down a list of employees who would have full access to the office, along with the ability to take money. It wouldn't be a hard deal to handle.

“How is the lovely Cara these days?” Ivan asked.

With Ivan being in the tower of power, it was rare for him to see Cara. She was considered under my jurisdiction. Of course, if he actually wanted to see her, all he’d need to do was make a phone call.

“Well, from what I saw.” I’d never been one to make small talk.

“And your wife? Have you started to make babies yet?”

I ran a hand down my face. If Ivan wasn’t my friend and my boss, I’d tell him to go and fuck himself.

“Everything is going well.”

“Don’t fucking lie to me, Slavik. You and I know how important this treaty is. I’ve given you a woman because I know you’ll follow instructions and she won’t be dead within a few years at your hand. This play cannot work without all the cogs working. Get her pregnant and do it soon.”

He hung up and I stared at my phone before pocketing it.

I glanced up at the night sky, taking a final deep breath. The play was the chance to expand, to take more turf. With Aurora as my wife, it made the Italians look weak. They wanted an alliance to stop the bloodshed, as we’d been killing their made men for years. This treaty, however long it lasted, would gain us the power to completely wipe them from our list of enemies.

It was always about ground and money. Two of which always equaled power, and we always wanted a lot of it.

Entering the warehouse, I heard the screams. My men stood waiting for the instruction. The man hanging upside down, blood streaming from several slashes that had been made into his flesh, whimpered, and the almost animal-like sounds he made echoed around the room.

I'd long ago been desensitized to the noises of the tortured. This man had stolen from us. Taken product in the intent to hand us over to the law. We didn't take betrayal easily. He'd also been trying to get out of the country ever since he realized he was the piece in a trap.

"No, please. No. I'll do anything."

I crouched down so we were at eye level. "Who were you going to meet with?" I asked.

After he'd called to try to buy protection for the information he believed he had, he went running to one of our enemies, the Italian mafia. This morning, I got the call from Fredo himself, the man willing to trade secrets. This was why the treaty worked.

"I'm dead anyway," the man said.

I tilted my head to the side, looking at him. He'd already pissed and shit himself. The contents of his body swirled on the floor, creating a stink. I hated weak men. This man was the lowest of the low.

When you swore loyalty to someone, you gave yourself to the cause, and this fucker was everything I despised.

Ivan Volkov was a fucking king in our world, and to all those who turned on him, turned on us, I never showed mercy.

"True, but I can make it an easy death. You wouldn't feel pain. Or I can keep you alive for days, weeks, months, and every single day, you will feel nonstop pain." I tilted my head to the side with a smile. "What's it going to be?"

When I smiled, it terrified people.

I was used to having that effect on people because I rarely found humor in this life. I had no desire for it. I had one set mode and that was to kill. To annihilate my enemies.

He still didn't talk, so I figured it was time to remind him. I'd already plucked his toenails and fingernails, but now I would extract his teeth, one at a time.

Two of my men lifted him, holding him still as I pried open his mouth. He thrashed, trying to get away, but he was no match for our strength. I used the right tool for the job, and within seconds, held a very healthy-looking tooth.

"Please, I'll tell you anything."

"I'm listening." I was sure to keep the sight of the tooth for him to see as a reminder. It worked. He told me all about the knowledge of our treaty. How the Italians had insulted us by granting us a marriage with a daughter they wanted to get rid of and how there was a rumor of a takeover.

Now this was news to me.

He continued to explain the gossip running rife about our enemies, how they were willing to band together with some MCs, and even the cartels had been seen coming and going through their turf.

Once he was done, I had enough to work through, and so the death was clean, precise, and over with. He had given me far more work.

We intended to take the turf away from the Italians. Any attack now would be suicide. I filled Ivan in on the details I'd gained, and along with it, I heard the new anger in his voice. We'd been aware of Aurora's lack of desire, but this went beyond that. We couldn't attack now, but we would be aware, gathering the necessary intel that would be required for us to completely wipe them off the face of the earth.

"What do I do with Aurora?" I asked.

"Simple. I have a feeling if she's as expendable to them as everyone believes, they won't care about her death. We keep her alive. You use her. Host several more of those family dinners. Find out everything we know and play the loving husband. We will hurt them for this."

I agreed and hung up.

My biggest problem … I didn't like the way they'd disregarded Aurora. She was my wife, and it was my duty, for now, to keep her alive, but I had a problem with how they treated her. From the moment the agreed treaty of a marriage was negotiated, I'd seen the way she was handled. How they pushed her to one side as if she didn't matter. Not only that, but even the other night with those women at the dinner table. They couldn't stand to be around her.

I didn't get it. Aurora was sweet. She was kind. I saw it in her eyes even though she tried to hide everything. What I also saw was acceptance. She lived with this, being constantly passed over, ignored.

Arriving at my penthouse suite, I discovered it was empty. No sign of Aurora or Sergei, which pissed me off.

I pulled out my cell phone and dialed Sergei.

"Where are you?" I didn't like this one bit.

"We're at the pool. Aurora wanted to do some laps."

"It's Mrs. Ivanov," I said, hanging up the phone.

I was already heading toward the pool. In the elevator, I rubbed at my temple. I hadn't slept in two days so far. Sleep rarely came to me. I had no trust in anyone around me, and right now between Cara's problem, and now the Italian one, there was no way I was going to relax.

You were killed if you let down your guard, and that was the last thing I was going to do.

The elevator went down to the level with the gym and the pool. I saw the sign posted, stating the pool was closed for the time being.

As I entered, I caught sight of my wife wearing a one-piece swimsuit. She had her arms crossed over the edge of the pool, and Sergei, as far as I was concerned, looked a little too cozy with my wife, which pissed me off.

We'd been married a little over five months, and as I watched them, I didn't like how close they seemed. Anger worked up my body as I stepped into view. The moment I did, the smile on Aurora's lips fell and Sergei stood.

He bowed his head to me. "Sir."

"You can leave," I said.

He nodded. Without another look at my wife, he left the room. Alone with my wife, I saw Aurora move back into the water. We looked at each other.

She wasn't a stunning beauty, but there was a beauty there. I'd had my fair share of fake beauty. There was something about Aurora that called to me.

"I didn't know you were coming home," she said.

"You never do."

Again, small talk wasn't my strong suit.

"It would be wise of you not to flirt with my men."

This had her frowning. "I wasn't flirting."

"You think I didn't see what you were doing?"

She looked to where Sergei had left. "We were just talking. Not everything between a man and a woman has to be about … sex."

My cock twitched. I hadn't gotten the pleasure of enjoying my wife. She'd moved toward the edge of the pool, and as she grabbed the side, I watched as she pulled herself out. I admired the curves of her body. The fullness of her ass. She grabbed a towel.

"If you continue to flirt with Sergei and give him

the wrong message, I will kill him."

She glared at him. "I wasn't flirting with him. He's my … friend."

This made me laugh. I couldn't help it. Sergei wasn't a friend. None of my men were her friends, and if given the order, they would turn on her at a moment's notice.

What I didn't expect was the slap to the face. I captured her hand and pulled her against me. She began to wriggle, and with how close her body was, I had no problem with it. Not that I'd force her. Rape wasn't something I wanted to ever experience.

Staring into her eyes, I restrained her, making her pause with a single hand on her ass. I gripped her tightly, and tears filled her eyes.

"Don't ever fucking do that again."

"Why?"

"I don't like being hit. I tend to hit back."

"Then don't accuse me of doing something I never did. I don't flirt. I wouldn't even know how."

"My men know the rules. You're a job to them, nothing more."

She wore a good mask, but I saw my words had struck her hard. "You think I don't know that? It's all I do know. I'm a job. It's why I don't flirt. Now let me go, or is there something else you want from me?"

Her lips looked really tempting, but my anger was not in a good place. I released her, and without a backward glance, she left. The curves of her ass just begged for me to call her back and show her what real sex was all about. The two times I'd fucked her hadn't been real. It had been mechanical, a necessity and then a release. I wanted her again, but not tonight. I never allowed my hormones to take charge. I was the one who held control over myself, no one else.

Chapter Four

Aurora

For the next week, I stopped talking to Sergei, and I ignored Slavik when he decided to join me for dinner or anything else. We did end up going to two different dinner parties, but like the ones before, I was able to sit without saying a single word.

Dinner invitations were offered, but I declined.

I'd come to the conclusion I didn't want to make friends with Slavik's world. So by the second week after my decision, I sat on the sofa, bored out of my mind. I'd read so many books I couldn't even remember a single title or author. The stories had been great but it was like I hadn't really taken them in.

There was nothing for me to do but stay here.

Sergei stood a few feet away as I stared down at my feet.

I'd already done my workout for the day. According to the scales today, I'd dropped another couple of pounds. Even as my stomach rumbled, I ignored the growl. Eating was done carefully and controlled.

"You need to eat something," Sergei said.

"I'm fine."

"Starving yourself is not the answer."

I lifted my gaze. "You shouldn't be talking to me."

"Come on, Aurora, don't be like that."

"It's Mrs. Ivanov," I said. I heard him tut, and I glared at him. "Do you know what my husband thinks? He thinks I was flirting with you." I laughed. "I'm not going to give him the satisfaction."

I hated him. He was an asshole.

I was so fucking bored. Five months of married

life sucked. Not that being a daughter was any easy feat. Nope. Both sucked.

"You do know he is probably with a mistress right now," Sergei said after a short pause.

This had me looking at Sergei. "What?"

He moved closer into the room. I didn't stop him as he sat down opposite me. I moved my feet out of his room. Sergei had never been like this before, and I quickly glanced around to make sure no one watched. I didn't know why I did this. We weren't breaking any rules, but all of a sudden, this felt way too intimate. Like I shouldn't allow this. Did it make any sense?

I wasn't betraying Slavik, but with his accusations still ringing in my ear, I couldn't help but feel like I was.

Other than my family, I'd never sat down with a man. Rarely talked to one that wasn't my husband or blood related. In fact, Sergei and Ivan were the only two men I'd spoken to in my life.

Sergei put a hand on my foot, and I gritted my teeth, doing everything in my power not to pull away from his touch. My family had drilled into me at a young age that touch by anyone but my husband was bad.

"A man like Slavik has needs. They're important to him. He's not the kind of man who is going to enjoy straight sex. He likes it dirty. He'll find an outlet with a woman who is not his wife."

So my husband of five months was already cheating on me. I should have known. Why did it hurt so much?

"Have you … met her?"

"No. Men like Slavik are never at a loss for female company."

I didn't like the way Sergei rubbed his thumb against my foot.

Quickly, I moved, standing up. "Then I guess I should count my blessings that he's finding his pleasures elsewhere. Excuse me."

I left the sitting room and entered our bedroom where we slept side by side most nights. I wrapped my arms around myself. With my back pressed against the closed door, I slid down and stared at the bed.

Sex always sounded so good in the books, but in real life, I couldn't imagine a woman enjoying herself. It was too … horrible and boring. After the two times I'd had sex, I didn't care for a repeat performance. I hadn't enjoyed it.

Running fingers through my hair, I pulled my knees up to my chest, resting my chin on top.

Time ticked by.

The only passing I was aware of was the fading light in the window shining into the room. I didn't move.

My stomach had stopped growling, and the sickness had also faded.

My marriage was already over. He was screwing someone else. Probably a whole lot of something elses. I shouldn't care. In fact, I didn't care.

Then why the hell did my entire core feel like it was being torn in two? It made no sense. Slavik could go and do whatever the hell he wanted. I didn't care.

The bedroom door was pushed open, and the force had me falling forward. I caught myself before I face-planted the floor.

Slavik entered. "What the fuck is going on here?"

I'd started to notice his accent appeared more pronounced when he was angry.

"Nothing." I got to my feet and kept my back to him.

I didn't want him to see me like this. I had to get myself under control.

When he grabbed my arm, I yelled and told him to leave me alone, spinning around to confront him. I wanted to hit him again, but the last time I did, there was a real threat there. This man killed people with his bare hands. I wasn't a match for him.

"What the fuck is your problem?" he asked.

My hands clenched into fists. Had he been with a woman today? Had he fucked her? Had he enjoyed his time with her?

"I don't have a problem. Just don't touch me," I said.

He glared and advanced toward me. I stepped back. I kept on doing this until the edge of the bed met my back and I stumbled, falling. I tried to get up, but Slavik grabbed my arms, pinning me down. "You are my wife. I will touch you if I damn well please!"

I screamed and tried to pull away.

Anger tore out of my throat, but I was no match for him. It would seem I'd never be a match for him as he held me down on the bed.

"Let me go. Get your hands off me."

"Damn it, Aurora. Stop."

"I don't want you touching me with hands that have been on your whore!" I yelled each word, hoping he'd get the hint and leave me the fuck alone. I didn't even know why I was so angry. It wasn't like we had a normal marriage. I didn't know him, and I didn't like the rumors I'd heard. When I'd been given to him, I'd heard what my father had said. He hadn't wanted to give Isabella, his precious daughter, to this man, but me, he was more than happy to. All it did was drive in deep the hurt of not being enough. I never was.

Now I wasn't even good enough to use for sex.

I felt so … humiliated. I wasn't good enough at anything for anyone.

"What the fuck are you talking about?" he asked.

I cried out as he gripped me a little tighter than what I was used to. His touch had me pausing, trying to capture my breath. None of this made any sense to me. Not my anger or the sense of betrayal.

Mistresses were common in our world. I knew for a fact my father had several. My mother never made a scene.

Tears spilled down the corners of my eyes, and I closed them, hoping to stem the flow and to stop feeling like this. I hated all of this. The pain was more than I could bear.

"Aurora."

"I know you have … women," I said.

"You do, do you?" he asked.

With how he held my arms, I couldn't cover my face. I couldn't hide away, and at that moment, there was nothing I wanted more than to hide.

He wouldn't let me.

"Please, get off me. Leave me alone." I was in control now. I didn't yell but spoke the words calmly.

"No," he said, and this made me open my eyes. "I'm not going anywhere until you tell me what the fuck that was all about."

Why did this have to happen? I felt so embarrassed.

"Can we just forget the whole thing?"

"First, I come home and see my wife has spent most of the day here. I open the door and you were leaning against it. I try to talk to you, and you freak out."

"I know … you have needs. I don't want you touching me with the hands you touched her with." I hated this woman so much. I didn't even know who she was, but I despised her.

"You are my wife. You will do as you're told and

submit to me. You don't get a say, and if I decide to fuck other women, then you will do what all women do and learn to live with it."

His words shattered my being.

They struck me more than any blow could.

"I don't know where you're getting your information, Aurora, but I don't have the time to fuck. Ever since we've been married, you're the only woman I've been with." He pulled away from me.

"What?" I asked.

"You heard me."

I rubbed at my temple, already feeling the headache start. "You haven't been with any other woman?"

Slavik merely glared at me. "And if I was with other women, you'd deal with it."

"So, I can take a lover as well?" I asked.

He grabbed the back of my neck with a snarl and pulled me close. "No. No other man will ever touch you. If you so much as try, I will fucking kill him. Do you understand me? You do that and you'll be signing his death sentence."

Slavik shoved me back, and I landed on the bed. He'd been so close, and it was crazy, but at that moment, all I could think about was the fact we'd never kissed. Not even after the priest pronounced us man and wife. He'd kissed me on the cheek. Even the lack of passion had been something to talk about on our day. People had laughed at how he couldn't even stand to kiss me on the lips. He never had.

Touching my lips, I couldn't believe how I felt.

I hated him, but I'd wanted him to kiss me.

What the hell was wrong with me?

Clearly, the pain and years of being neglected had gotten to me.

How could I even want to be kissed by that kind of monster? Getting to my feet, I left the bedroom. With these thoughts running around my head, the last place I wanted to be was anywhere near when he'd finished in the bathroom.

I hid in the spare bedroom and stayed there. He didn't come to find me. For the rest of the night, I stayed in my special chair, wishing for a life that I knew would never come to me.

****

Slavik

I stood in the dance hall with my wife on my arm, and I stared around the room, checking for any possible attackers. Our enemies would be close. I wouldn't put it past them to try to take Ivan out even while we were in a room full of civilians. Parties like these were unnecessary in my opinion. I saw no reason to mingle with the world who pretended the horrors taking place behind closed doors and in the cover of darkness didn't occur.

Ivan needed his top six men all in one place. This was a political ploy as Roger Hampton, an up-and-coming public figure, was trying to gain popularity by threatening people like Ivan. He promised the public he'd drive out the threat and stop the flow of illegal activities. How men and women would be able to walk the streets without fear.

The truth was it would never happen. Anyone who offered that kind of freedom was a fucking idiot who didn't know what they were dealing with.

Aurora was tense on my arm, but I didn't let her go.

A passing waiter offered us some champagne, but I sent him off before she could reach for one.

Ever since our confrontation about my possible mistress, it had been even more tense between us, which pissed me off. I had a feeling I knew who was responsible for filling her head with lies. The moment I caught him, Sergei would learn to keep his mouth shut. The very fact he'd tried to turn my wife against me made me want to kill him.

My thirst for blood and violence was always close to the surface. All it took was a small switch to make it happen.

"It's a busy night," Aurora said.

We were in the watchful eye now. With the game constantly being played and the power at work, I had to make sure people saw only strength, no weakness. I was a man in control of his wife, the daughter of a Capo.

Leaning down, I whispered against her ear. "Tonight is about business. It's a show of force but also a little reminder to our good friends in charge."

Aurora gasped and tilted her head to look at me. Her long hair had been curled once again. Some of the strands were pulled back and tied at the base of her neck. I wanted to touch it, to run my fingers through the long locks. More than anything, I wanted to hold her hair as I fucked her hard, to finally show her what it truly meant to be my wife.

I pushed all these thoughts down and instead focused on my surroundings. I'd already spotted Ivan, surrounded by his men, charming the fucking asses off of everyone here.

Kissing her cheek, I kept my lips close to her ear. "Mr. Hampton seems to think it is okay to take money from us to help him win his political career, but when it comes to keeping his end of the deal, he seems to have forgotten."

"What was his end of the deal?"

"To look the other fucking way," I said.

We never asked for much from people like Roger,

but what we did expect was for them to honor it.

"Now, we're going to dance and play the part of a doting couple."

"Wait," Aurora said, her hand on my arm. "Why are we here? I mean, you're … you know, and I'm well, no one."

"Sweetheart, didn't you know you married a very powerful entrepreneur? My expertise is expansion. I have casinos, real estate, and an entire investment portfolio." I winked at her.

"Of course you do."

We covered our tracks well. I was known as a member of the Volkov Bratva, but no one would have any evidence. It was what made us so powerful and also untouchable. We were businessmen, nothing more.

Taking Aurora's hand, I led her onto the dance floor. After placing a hand at the base of her back, I pulled her in close. The feel of her soft body against mine was close to driving me insane.

Years of control kept me sharp and my dick soft in my pants.

I checked around the room, noticing the additional guards on the doors. Roger also had a man by his side constantly.

Looking back over at Ivan, I saw he kept his distance. This was always the case with parties like these.

"What do you need to do?" Aurora asked.

"Pardon?"

"You're here to talk to him, right?" She glanced behind her. "I guess you can't get too close to him, can you? He knows who you are. What you're capable of."

"Most people do."

She licked her lips and dropped her hands. "Excuse me."

I frowned as I watched her leave. She'd

abandoned me on the dance floor. Running my hands down my jacket, I checked out her ass. The gown she wore covered her body and yet left nothing to the imagination.

I didn't know how it happened, but each time I looked at her, she got sexier. The curves of her ass and hips called to me. I wanted them in my hands as I took her. Maybe it was time for me to get a woman on the side because right now, all I could think about was sex and fucking my woman.

She moved through the throngs of people, and I finally got my feet moving, following behind her. She broke through the group surrounding Roger Hampton, and I was close enough to hear her speak.

"Mr. Hampton, it is an honor to finally get to meet you in person," Aurora said. "I watched the last talk you did, and it was inspiring. In fact, I was wondering if it would be at all possible to have a quiet word with you. I'd like to consider investing myself in your future."

The smile she gave him was … breathtaking.

Out of the corner of my eye, I saw Ivan closing in.

"Well, thank you," Roger said, excusing himself from the guests. He put a hand on the base of Aurora's back, and I wanted to snap it off. No one touched my wife. "It is always a pleasure doing business with beautiful women, Miss…"

"Oh, I'm sorry, it's Mrs. Ivanov, and you know, my husband would love to have a word with you as well." She grabbed Roger's arm and held her other out to me. "Hello, darling. I told Mr. Hampton you wanted to speak to him about investment. If you will excuse me, I see someone I must talk to."

Like that, Aurora left just as Ivan joined us, along with Andrei, Ive, Victor, Peter, and Oleg. The six main district brigadiers, all present and all joined forces with Ivan Volkov.

The look on Roger's face was priceless.

He turned to run, but Ivan had him, and together, we marched him out of the room, heading toward a private office where no one was around.

I checked the room, Ive and Victor covered the door, and Peter and Oleg took the windows while Ivan and Andrei dragged a struggling Roger into the room.

We wouldn't hurt him too bad.

He hadn't won yet, so all the power he had was nothing.

With my hand on my gun, I stood waiting.

"Mr. Volkov, I've been meaning to talk to you," he said.

"Really, because for the past two weeks, you've been able to avoid my calls and every single chance to talk to me." Ivan shoved him into a chair. With the doors closed, there wasn't much we could do.

"Well, if you phone my secretary, we can arrange a meeting, and I know I'm fully scheduled."

Ivan clucked his tongue. "Actually, I think right here and now. You see, the speeches you're giving, they're a little trying on my nerves. I wonder how the general public would feel to know the very man they're putting all their faith in has a … gambling problem. The people that feed you, you want to rub into the dirt."

I was bored as Ivan pulled out a blade. The security in this place was easily bought. It was how we got our guns through. Everyone here was on our payroll, which was why no security footage was being recorded.

After the standard five minutes of my presence, I made my excuses and headed in the direction of the security office.

As per my instructions, the guard on the door had

taken a stroll.

I sat, glancing over the footage as Ivan made his threat. Within ten minutes, Ivan was leading Roger out of the room as if he'd not just threatened him. I extracted the data, wiped the system, and was heading back to the dance floor when I noticed my wife walking into the bathroom.

Following her inside, I stopped her from locking me out of a stall. The door closed, and I pressed up against her.

"This is the woman's bathroom."

"Do I look like a man who follows the rules?"

She shook her head. "No. I guess you're a man who does exactly what he wants."

"You've got that right."

She nibbled on her lip. "Is there something you wanted to say to me?"

"Thank you," he said.

"Whatever for?"

"You know what for."

"Is this hard for you?" she asked.

This made me smile. Saying thank you didn't come easy. "Why did you help?"

She shrugged her shoulder. "I'm your wife. By marrying you, I pledged my loyalty to you, didn't I? I'm not longer a Fredo. I'm an Ivanov." She didn't look into my eyes.

What was going on here?

The door to the bathroom opened and Aurora tensed up.

For some reason, I didn't want to embarrass her. I stepped back and allowed her to leave the stall. She stepped out of the stall, and I heard the women giggle and say hi to her.

I didn't know what the hell had just happened or

why I was still stuck in a bathroom stall. I could have easily followed her out. I didn't care what people thought of me. Aurora continued to mess with my head. My wife shouldn't be a problem to me and yet, she'd proven to be more of a challenge than I realized, and it pissed me off.

"Oh, my God, do you know who that was?" one of the women asked.

"No. She looks familiar."

"She's Aurora Ivanov! Oh, my God, I saw the pictures of her wedding. You know there is a rumor that said her husband is part of the Russian mafia, right? There's this whole thing going on across the country. I don't know the general working. It's like the worst-kept secret."

I frowned as I listened. I had no time for female gossip. Personally, I wanted to correct her that I was Bratva, not fucking mafia.

"I heard Slavik, the hot guy, he had to put a bag over her head to fuck her." A round of giggles.

"Please, he couldn't even be bothered to kiss her. You had to have seen the pictures. He brushed his lips across her cheek. I'm betting he can't stand to touch her."

The insults went on, and they angered me.

I had this desire to draw my weapon and kill them all there and then. Or better yet, to pull them out of the bathroom and force them to apologize to her.

This wasn't the time or place.

Rage rushed through my body. I shoved it down.

All I wanted to do was kill. I held swift control even as I did want to kill. Who did they think they were? My wife was a fucking queen. Had Aurora dealt with this her whole life? I didn't get a chance to confront them.

They left the bathroom after throwing more insults at my wife.

I walked out of the stall, then the bathroom, entering the dining room. I saw my wife standing with Ivan.

My boss talked to her, and I saw her smile.

Was my kiss to her cheek an insult?

She'd looked terrified, and I hadn't wanted to cause her to panic on our wedding day. I'd also never kissed her.

Ignoring the strange looks, I advanced across the room. Everything seemed to fade all around me, and the only focus I had was on the woman.

I didn't care who saw.

Ivan pointed toward me, and Aurora turned.

She frowned as I reached out. I cupped her face, drew her close to me, and slammed my lips down on hers. The electric current that rushed through me shocked me to the core. Never had I kissed a woman and felt so fucking whole and complete.

Chapter Five
Aurora

Getting the meeting with Roger Hampton had been the right thing to do. There wasn't a lot I could do properly but any way I could help, I'd be willing to do it.

Women were supposed to stay out of men's business, but there was an opening, and I took full advantage of it. I doubted it would ever happen again. Now that Roger knew who I was married to, the chances of it ever happening again would be slim.

When Ivan approached me on the sidelines of the dance floor, it had been a welcome distraction. This guy still scared the crap out of me, but it was manageable. I knew why I was afraid of him, and what I should do to keep myself calm in his presence.

I wanted something to do with my hands. I kept opening and clenching them, trying to figure out what I was supposed to do.

This party was starting to get to me.

"Your husband is here," Ivan said.

I turned to see Slavik advancing toward me. The frown on his face startled me. Why did he look so mad? I hadn't done anything wrong.

All of a sudden, I felt the need to run. To get the hell out of his way. He looked ready to kill.

I stayed grounded, fear racing down my spine.

The moment his hands touched my face, the room seemed to freeze, and then, much to my surprise, my very first kiss. Slavik's lips slammed down on mine. At first, I stilled, unsure what to make of his lips on mine.

This was a kiss.

Our mouths melded together.

Almost like one, but it was so much more than that. The hands on my cheek moved. One sank into my hair, and the other went to my hip, drawing me in.

The world faded away, and my hands went to the front of his body, running up to curve around his neck, pulling him close to me.

I moaned as his tongue traced, and I opened up my lips for him to explore. My eyes closed as I basked in this feeling. It was so consuming.

The books and movies hadn't been wrong.

The moment the right man kissed you, the rest of the world didn't matter.

I felt connected to Slavik.

I didn't want it to end.

Of course, being part of the Volkov Bratva came with problems.

I jerked back as screams and the sounds of bullets rained down in the room.

Slavik pushed me to the floor at the same time as Ivan.

Glass shattered. The bullets wouldn't stop.

I reached to cover my ears.

Slavik yelled for me to stay down.

I closed my eyes, trying to stop the panic.

My very first kiss and it ended in gunfire. This was so not fair, and I wanted to scream at whoever was ruining it. I stayed perfectly still even as Slavik's weight eased off me. Even as I told myself to keep my eyes closed, to stay down, I couldn't. Curiosity got the better of me.

I opened my eyes and glanced around. Men and women were on the ground. One of the waiters had fallen close to me. His eyes were wide open, and I screamed, jerking back as I saw half of the back of his head had blown off.

Sickness swirled within my gut, and I scrambled to my feet. Just as I did, more bullets came tumbling down. I covered my head, whirling around, looking for a weapon.

All of a sudden, a large body slammed into me, and I was taken to the ground, landing on the broken glass, which impaled my skin.

I whimpered, struggling against the man who was on top of me. Fear worked its way down my spine. Whoever it was slammed their fist against my face.

Everything went numb for a second as I struggled to gain focus. Pain exploded at the back of my eyes.

"You're a traitorous bitch," he said.

The gun was cocked.

I was going to die. I always knew I'd have a short life.

Five months into my marriage and here was my death.

The blow came, but I was still alive.

The man fell onto me. A bullet hole in the center of his head. I scrambled out from underneath him, screaming.

Arms wrapped around me, and I started to flail against him, fighting him off.

"I've got you. I've got you."

Slavik's voice calmed me. Another surprise of the day. He shouldn't be the one to calm me.

What the hell was wrong with me?

My heart raced. I felt sick.

We'd been attacked at a party full of civilians, including politicians and wealthy businessmen. What was even scarier was I knew the man who had attacked me. He worked for my father. This attack came from my old family, and as I looked up into Slavik's eyes, he knew as well.

The sound of police sirens filled the air.

Neither of us spoke.

Slavik handed me over to Sergei. "Take her home. A doctor will be by to look at her."

I didn't have any wounds, just cuts from landing on the glass. I followed Sergei without argument. Slavik didn't follow. Within seconds, I was in the back of our car and Sergei drove us back to his penthouse suite. There was no time to waste.

As he got out of the car, he drew his weapon, helping me from the vehicle. We got into the elevator and still, Sergei held his gun.

"I don't think it's worth holding your gun out. If we pass any children, they'll be terrified."

"I'm not going to risk it. Your safety is more important."

I chose not to argue.

Tonight had been … crazy.

I touched my lips. My fingers were dirty and some of them were cut. I had a throbbing behind one eye, and it was becoming a struggle to see, but my lips still tingled.

Did this seem to matter more because it was my first kiss?

The elevator doors opened, and Sergei went inside the apartment first, only allowing me to follow once he was sure the house was secure.

I kicked off my heels, happy to feel the ground once again.

I went immediately to the freezer, taking out a bag of peas and pressing it up against my burning eye.

"We're all clear."

"They attacked the party. I doubt they'd follow us."

"We have many enemies."

"All of which are not after me." I couldn't help but think of the vile words the man had said to me. I wasn't a traitorous bitch. I'd been given to Slavik by my family. If there was a peace treaty, why were my father's men attacking the party? Were they planning to incite war? What was the point of this marriage if that was the end game?

"Are you okay?" Sergei asked.

"No." I winced. "I mean, yes, I'm fine. I just, ouch." I lifted the bag of peas for him to look.

"Ouch," he said.

I couldn't help but laugh. "You're trained in all elements of torture and hurting people and you call this *ouch.* I'm a wimp." I couldn't help but pout. I'd screamed and been terrified. I'd even stood up as if it was safe to do so. I was a fucking idiot. I hated my reactions and it pissed me off.

"You're a woman. It was a scary situation."

"I could have helped."

"Really? Do what?"

"I don't know. Shoot a gun." I hated that Slavik had to go and I had to stay. What if he'd gotten hurt? Why did I fucking care?

Ugh! I hated all these questions. I hated my husband.

There was a knock at the door, but it didn't exactly ease my troubled thoughts. Sergei left me, but I didn't like how his touch seemed to linger. I had to be going crazy if I thought Sergei was being … inappropriate.

Slavik would kill him if he even doubted for a second my feelings for Sergei. He was a friend. Not even that. We were companions. Even that didn't sound right.

An old man with a head full of white hair and wrinkled eyes around the corners stepped in to the room.

"Hello, Mrs. Ivanov. I'm Doctor Smith," he said.

There was no way Smith was his real name.

"Hi," I said, releasing the bag of peas.

We ended up in the dining room. Sergei stood guard as the doctor assessed the damage. I had several fragments of glass embedded underneath my flesh. It wasn't too bad. With the dress I wore, I had no choice but to place a bath towel in front of me as he released the back of the dress. There was support built into the bodice which meant I could forgo a bra.

I winced each time he released a piece of glass. I felt even more ashamed that I couldn't take the pain.

After years of being hit or whipped by my father, I figured I'd be used to it.

When he removed a piece of glass, his fingers paused on a spot at my back. "This is an old scar," he said.

I stayed perfectly still.

Whenever my father beat me, he'd rarely take me to the hospital. One day, he'd been so angry about something. I'd been skipping down the hall. He'd told me I was making too much noise and girls, especially ugly ones, needed to know when to stay quiet. He'd torn my dress, removed his belt, and whipped me until there had been blood.

It was the first time he'd used his belt.

The doctor had no choice but to use stitches to help heal the wound. The scar had remained. For several months, he never came near me. I did get more toys after that.

The memory of it was so strange and sudden. Along with many others, I'd pushed it to the back of my mind so I didn't think about it.

Life got easier that way.

I said nothing.

The sound of the door opening had Sergei tensing.

The doctor cleared his throat as Slavik came into the room.

"What is going on?" he asked.

I saw his shirt was covered in blood. There was some bruising on his face, and I saw a cut on his side that already had a white bandage covering it. Life was so unfair. Why did he have to look so good while I got to look like this?

"She had some superficial wounds. The glass wasn't too deep. She has a couple of cuts, but in a few days, they'll heal. I see no reason to apply stitches."

"Are you done?"

"Yes."

"Leave," Slavik said.

With the way he looked at me, fear raced down my spine. I don't know what was happening right now, but the doctor quickly packed away his stuff.

Sergei hesitated, but Slavik repeated the order.

Alone. I stared at my husband.

"You knew that man tonight," Slavik said.

"Not personally, but I recognized him. He worked for my father."

"Do you have any idea why he'd attack that party?"

"He's an idiot?"

"This is not a joke."

"I have no idea. I've been trying to figure out why they would attack the party. None of it makes any sense to me." I told the truth. I had nothing to hide.

****

Slavik

The attack had come from the Italian mafia. They were Fredo's men, but I also noticed they were not his close, most trusted men. They were a small group of soldiers, and several men had been outsourced with clear training. I already had my computer guy run a check on all of the men we'd killed. Their IDs had to be fakes.

I'd expected an attack at the party, but not from Fredo.

We had enemies far and wide. Some from within the Bratva.

Ivan had taken the brotherhood into a new era, and some preferred the old ways of dealing dirty and hiding in the shadow. However, Ivan had an idea that expanded across all areas. It was why we were all wealthy and had several businesses across all industries. It gave us ties across the entire world and not just in one city.

Where the old generation was happy to be on the streets, taking on the weak, Ivan went after the strong to make his force even stronger. We all worked together.

Staring down at my wife, I had to ask the questions now. Ivan wanted her for questioning. With how she looked, she wouldn't survive it. She'd been petrified. "What is going to happen?"

"Volkov wants to talk to you."

Her lip wobbled. "Of course he does." She nibbled on her lip. "I had nothing to do this with. I swear. I saw an opportunity with Roger Hampton, it's not a ploy."

"I know."

She gasped. "You do?"

"I saw the way the man attacked you. I was getting to you. If you'd been part of this, you'd have seen it coming." I had no doubt she was innocent of this attack, but now, I was curious. Her father sent in those men, knowing we'd turn to her.

I rounded the table and looked down at her back. There were several cuts, and the doctor had put some Band-Aids on the worst ones. The others already had dried blood on them.

"Change quickly. Ivan doesn't like to be kept waiting."

She stood up, holding the towel to her chest. "If … if I have to die tonight, will you be the one asked to kill me?"

I gritted my teeth. She knew our world so well. From the look in her eyes, she seemed devastated. I'd never taken the time to read people for these kinds of emotions. I wasn't sure if I liked what I saw in her eyes.

"Get dressed," I said. Without another word, I turned my back and left the bedroom.

I folded my arms and waited. Sergei stood, ready and waiting. Over the past few weeks, I'd started to notice the way he looked at my wife. I didn't like it.

"Sergei, you know your job is to protect my wife," I said.

"Of course, sir." He bowed his head, performing all the necessary respectful moves, but I didn't see it, and he knew it.

"Keep your eyes off my woman or I'm going to have to remove you from this position and find someone else who can follow my rules."

Sergei didn't get a chance to respond as Aurora chose that moment to appear in a pair of jeans and a crisp white shirt. Not exactly the choice of clothing I'd have recommended.

I took the lead, not complaining, grabbing Aurora's hand and leading her out of our apartment.

The elevator ride was awkward. I kept my gaze on the doors, which allowed me to look at my wife.

She was nervous.

Who wouldn't be? They were about to see the leader of the Volkov Bratva. It was an honor and also a death sentence.

Sergei stood in the corner, and it gave me the perfect opportunity to watch him. I'd picked him because of how loyal he was, but now I was starting to realize my mistake, and I didn't like it.

His gaze was on my wife's ass. Did he not realize I could see him? I had a feeling I was going to have to drill in some more respect.

The doors opened, and reaching out, I rested my hand at the base of Aurora's back, leading her toward the car. I couldn't resist the tips of my fingers grazing her ass, allowing the man behind me to see that he was looking at my woman, and I would kill him for it.

Aurora tensed up in my arms, but I didn't care.

Our marriage had survived five months, it would last longer. I was sure of it. I helped her into the car, and Sergei took the wheel. To drive home who Aurora was, I made sure to take my place by her side, resting my palm on her knee.

She shook a little.

I stroked her inner thigh, trying to calm her.

Ivan didn't like scenes of any kind. If Aurora broke down and started to blubber, it would reflect badly on me.

"Why does Mr. Volkov want to see me?" she asked.

"You know why."

"I had nothing to do with that."

"Either way, he's going to want to talk to you."

She nibbled on her lip, and I had the urge to reach over and suck it out before plunging her mouth with my tongue. She tugged her knee away from me and turned her entire body toward the window.

Her lack of respect didn't amuse me.

She wanted to play this way, then fine, we could play.

I grabbed her body, and even though we were seated at the back of the car, I pulled her against me, securing her against my body.

She didn't fight me, even as her body tensed up. Nor did she argue. Sergei was in the car, and she knew the rules.

"What are you doing?" she whispered the words so low I could only just hear them.

Tilting her head back, I stared into her eyes. Her plump lips called to me. Of all the women I'd been with, I'd never felt this overwhelming need to kiss one before. In fact, I often made it my mission not to put my lips on any of the women. All I cared about was getting my dick sucked.

Aurora was my wife.

A few hours ago, I'd kissed her.

I wanted to do it again.

Cupping her face, I traced my thumb across the plumpness of her lip. It looked slightly sore from where she'd been nibbling it, but I wanted to taste her again. Enemy or not, I felt like I was drowning in the very essence of who she was, and I couldn't stop.

Before I got a chance to worship her mouth, the car came to an abrupt stop.

We were here.

I hadn't even noticed we'd arrived at Ivan's secure location. He liked to live outside of the city. He moved around a lot. It was one part of keeping himself alive and confusing his enemies. He was never in the same place long enough, which meant if there was ever an attack, they never had time to prepare and were always so fucking sloppy with it.

I opened my door as Sergei did the same. I offered a hand and I watched as Sergei struggled with opening Aurora's door.

She took my hand, sliding out of my side of the car.

I was going to have to have a talk with my wife. For a woman who didn't have many prospects, she seemed to be taking one of my most loyal men and turning him into her little pet.

The very thought of Sergei touching my wife. Loving her. It awakened the beast within me that needed to lay his claim. To show the world who Aurora belonged to.

Holding her hand, I walked up the steps, nodding to the guards. No one stopped us as we passed.

Aurora kept up with my pace, and when I entered the dining hall, I saw Ivan was waiting.

It was rare for him to want to talk to someone like my wife. I imagined it was down to the peace treaty that he broke protocol. Then again, Ivan never followed the traditional brotherhood of the Bratva. He paved his own way. Fulfilled his own path.

With my wife before him, he stood, and I had no choice but to press Aurora into the chair that had been left in the center of the room.

"Leave us," Ivan said.

The soldiers each left, one by one, filtering out. Sergei had followed us in, and I made him aware he was to leave too.

His gaze landed on Aurora one last time, but he didn't save her.

Instead, he left.

"Aurora, you're looking good."

"Thank you." Her hands rested on her thighs. I saw the slight shake in her body.

I couldn't resist reaching out to her. I placed my hand on her shoulder, not that it gave her any comfort. If anything, it appeared to make her more nervous, which only served to piss me off.

"I had nothing to do with this, I swear."

"The man you saw, he was in employment with your father, correct?" Ivan asked.

He dragged a chair over, and I felt Aurora try to jerk back.

"Yes," she said.

"Aurora, when you married Slavik Ivanov, you swore your loyalty to him, and in doing so, you gave your life to me."

She nodded her head. "Yes."

"Anything you know, anything you believe your father has done, you will have to tell me."

"And I would," she said. "I only recognize him. I don't know if my father removed him, or if … I don't know. I swear."

I believed her.

"But your loyalty, it is to me and your husband?" he asked.

"Yes."

"Then it's time you graced the mark," Ivan said, standing.

He snapped his fingers, and that was where I saw Mark, the tattoo artist. There were times Ivan would punch his brand into the flesh of his subjects with a hot branded iron. This was far more subtle.

"Hold out your arm."

Aurora cradled her arm against her chest. "I don't like needles."

"It will hurt, but this will guarantee your safety. You're pledging your life to mine."

"You're removing me from my family," she said.

Ivan sighed. "Aurora, we both know they're not your family. I'm very much aware of what your father thinks of me and my organization. He's willing to put your life on the line. Now, if what you say is true, if you bind yourself to me, to us, to your husband, you will never have to be questioned after an attack like that, again."

He was talking total bullshit and yet, I had a feeling he meant what he said.

"Now, I can either make this as painless as possible for you or you're going to hurt for several days, if not weeks." He moved over to the small firepit he had burning and held up the branding iron. In response, my wife held her arm up as if offering to the gods.

I stifled a smile.

I had no choice but to stand perfectly still as Mark touched my wife. The design was wrapped around her wrist. The wives were always given the ink around their wrist. It was an easy part of the body that was seen. People would know who they belonged to.

The world would now see that Aurora Fredo, now Aurora Ivanov, was my property, but also the subject of Ivan Volkov. Even as he marked her flesh for loyalty, in doing so, he'd also sworn to protect her.

This I found interesting.

I didn't know why he was doing this.

Mark kept on working, and Aurora winced. He'd stop, and she'd signal him to continue.

I left her side and walked toward Ivan.

"You wanted to question her," I said. "Why the branding? You could have done this on our wedding night, but you chose not to. Why?"

"I don't have to answer to you."

"As one of your brigadiers, I have no choice but to ask why. You can keep the information from me, but to protect you, I need to know the truth."

Ivan smiled at me.

"Did her father send those men?"

"No," Ivan said. "Before you got here, I ran the information. The men had been let go before the wedding with Aurora. It would appear your wife had a little … following."

"Excuse me?"

"The moment her father gave her to you, it set a ripple running through his soldiers. First, they were suddenly going to have to follow the peace treaty, but it would also seem your wife has a reputation for being … liked and respected."

I glanced back at Aurora.

She was different from the women in our world.

All I'd seen were people who couldn't seem to stand her.

"We all know her father gave me her because he didn't want to waste his beloved daughter on a piece of shit like me."

Ivan smiled. "Yes, I know. We got the waste of space. The insult. It would seem to a lot of people, she is second best. She's not as beautiful or as charming. But those who clearly got to know her, they become … besotted."

I thought of Sergei.

"I can see that," I said.

A whimper escaped Aurora.

"Do you think she's behind the attack?" If my wife had done this, then why did she put herself in the line of fire? "Wait a minute." I turned to Ivan. "Your sources are wrong."

"Excuse me?"

"Aurora was not … she was attacked tonight. They called her a traitorous bitch. Aurora doesn't have her own following."

The only sign that Ivan had heard my words was the clenching of his jaw. He looked ready to commit murder.

Mark finished up the ink, and as he did, Aurora whimpered. I took a step toward her. Mark applied a Band-Aid to keep it covered. The tattoo was in an easily infected area. He gave her the rundown of care.

The moment he finished, she stood up, and I went to her side, tucking her against me.

"Aurora, can I ask you a question?" Ivan asked.

She nodded her head.

"Were you liked at home?"

She jerked within my gaze, and I saw the tears in her eyes. "Why? Is this to punish me for what my father did?"

"Were you respected? Loved? Liked?"

"Mr. Volkov, people didn't even know I existed, and if they did, they made me very much aware of just how unimportant I was."

Chapter Six

Aurora

My wrist hurt.

My head hurt.

My back hurt.

Everything fucking hurt. Yet, nothing seemed to be quite as painful as the knowledge that my family and everyone around them didn't like me.

"Were you respected? Loved? Liked?"

Ivan's questions played in my head on a mocking repeat. No one liked me. No one even cared about me.

I was given to Slavik and the Volkov Bratva because my father didn't want to give away the daughter he actually loved.

Tears filled my eyes, and I hated how I felt, the way I was reacting. Tilting my head back, I stared up at the pool room. Sergei had cleared the pool so I could use it. Every other time, I always felt a little embarrassed at the power he used for my comfort. Today, a week after getting the tattoo that aligned me with the Bratva, I needed to do something other than sit in the apartment. Even reading wouldn't rid my mind of these thoughts. I tried so hard not to let them consume me, but it was next to impossible.

Rubbing at my temple, I took a deep breath, aware of Sergei watching me. He'd been really sweet and kind to me. I didn't know if that was part of his job description, but I didn't know how to handle it.

I wasn't one for a pity party. At least not every single day.

Today, a week after the attack and the questioning from Ivan Volkov himself, the pain of my past just wouldn't go away. All the memories surrounded me, refusing to leave me be. The way people ignored me, even as a child. When I wanted to play. I was never good enough. Often left to read as the other kids couldn't stand me.

My mother would tell me to leave the kids alone. If they didn't want to play with me, then maybe there was something wrong with me.

No matter how kind I was, I wasn't liked. At parties, I was ignored. No one asked me to dance. I spent most of my time standing in the corner, watching all the fun happening, knowing I was never going to be part of it. The shopping trips. I watched Isabella so often get invited.

I'd be close by, but no one would extend the invitation in my direction. If I asked if I could come, some excuse would be made.

In the end, I stopped trying to be involved.

No one wanted me. No one liked me.

I'd spend hours, staring out of a window, trying to figure out what people hated about me. Why I was so disliked, and even now, I couldn't figure out a reason.

"Are you okay?" Sergei asked.

"I'm fine." I wasn't swimming. The pool wasn't helping to alleviate my troubles. I'd stopped trying to figure out long ago why people couldn't stand me and yet here I was, still attempting to find a reason.

I climbed out of the pool, wrapped a towel around my waist, and walked toward the doors.

Sergei was there, and no one else waited to enter the room.

I took a deep breath as we headed toward the elevators, but today, I didn't want to stand with the doors showing my reflection.

"I'm going to take the stairs."

"Aurora," he said.

I stopped at the door and turned toward him.

"You know you can trust me, don't you?"

"I don't know you, Sergei."

"I know you."

This made me laugh. "No, you don't. You know what you're told to know."

"You can trust me."

Staring at him, I truly believed he thought that. "I have to go."

My hand was bound up so no water got to the ink that now stayed on my skin. Removing the plastic cover, I released my hand and took the stairs, heading toward the penthouse suite.

I couldn't stand heights.

Sergei stayed at my back and knowing he was right behind me didn't fill me with comfort. I'd noticed the lingering looks he'd been giving me over the past few weeks. They weren't good. He was a bodyguard.

If Slavik saw him and jumped to the wrong conclusions, we'd both be dead. I didn't want to be the one responsible for getting a man killed, and Sergei seemed nice.

Entering the apartment, I was stopped as Sergei reached out and grabbed my arm. I froze. He tugged me close and he further surprised me as he pulled me into his arms.

"Sergei, stop," I said.

"I'm not going to hurt you. I can see that you're hurting, and I can't stand to see you in pain, Aurora. Please, let me be your rock."

He stroked my hair.

This was so wrong.

He shouldn't be touching me. I needed to get him to stop, but as he held me, at that moment, a wave of emotion struck me hard. Against my better judgment, I held on to him and sobbed.

I didn't find Sergei attractive.

He was a very good-looking man, but he was a guard. I never made it a habit to fall for a man I could never have. Sergei worked for my husband. This put me in a place I didn't want to be in.

There was no way I could allow my husband to think anything was going on between us. Sergei was … a friend? I didn't even know if I could call him that. I never had friends. People didn't like me.

Was this a ploy to get rid of me? Had Slavik put him up to this so he'd have a reason to kill me?

Fear raced down my spine, and I jerked back. "You shouldn't have done that. Slavik, if he ever finds out—"

"He won't," Sergei said.

"He's your boss. You can't hug me or treat me as anything other than work." I was dressed in a bathing suit and a towel. "You're a guard."

"And you think I don't notice you? You think I haven't guarded other women and I don't see the difference?"

My throat felt like it was on fire. "Has … Slavik used you to protect his other … women?"

"I'm not going to say it," he said.

"Let me guess, they had more of a social life. If you're bored, I can talk to him. Ask him to arrange for someone else to keep an eye on me."

"For fuck's sake, no, that's not what I'm getting at. What I'm saying, Aurora, is I can see you. I know you're hurting. You're right, you're not like other women. I'm offering to be your friend. The shoulder you cry on."

"If Slavik heard you, he'd get rid of you. I don't need friends."

"Then what do you need?" he asked. "The way I

see it, you're fucking lonely. You have no friends, and your husband comes around to what? To fuck you so you can have his child."

I physically flinched. "Stay away from me."

"Damn it, I didn't mean it like that."

I'd turned on my heel, intent on putting some distance between us, and now, I whirled around. "You didn't mean it like that? Then how did you mean it? You were spot on, remember? I have no friends. Slavik is probably out there now with other women, enjoying himself. I'm nothing. I'm no one, but tell me this, Sergei, if you're such a good friend and you want to be there for me. Tell me what the fuck is wrong with me."

I didn't like to curse.

I was normally in control of my emotions, but today, I was all over the place. The ink around my wrist, the attack, the accurate words thrown my way, it was all too much, and there was only so much I could take.

This time, rather than create more distance between us, I advanced toward him. "Tell me, Sergei. Tell me all the great advice about why all my life, people hated me. How I've never matched up. How I've always been second best in everything. Tell me."

"Because you're beautiful," he said.

Now this made me laugh.

"Wrong."

With that, I spun on my heel and I left him alone.

A friend would be so fucking welcome, but Sergei wasn't my friend.

I went straight to the bathroom, stripping naked, and stepped beneath the spray of the water.

Men in our world had mistresses all the time. I had no doubt some of the women enjoyed a lover or two.

I didn't know where I stood with Slavik.

In the week since the attack, he hadn't been

around. I didn't know where he was. Some nights he didn't even come home.

I turned off the shower, wrapping a towel around me, I stepped out of the bathroom, into the bedroom, and gasped.

Slavik stood in the bedroom.

"Wear this. We're going out to dinner."

"You scared me."

"I don't have all day. Reservations are in thirty minutes."

"I didn't know we were going out," I said.

"Now you do."

I hadn't even heard him come home. For several seconds, I just stood there in the bedroom, dressed in a towel. The last place I wanted to go was with him or out in the world. The cuts on my back had mostly healed. Some of the larger wounds had scabbed over, and the pain was no more. I didn't want to go out, but there was no room for argument.

Drying my body, then my hair, I set about styling it, adding in a few curls, allowing it to fall naturally.

The dress was beautiful, modest. Black with a low front bodice, which would show off my chest, and it fell to the floor, but had slits up either side, giving a hint of thigh.

The arms were also exposed.

I was surprised by how snug the dress fit. I left the bedroom and found Slavik waiting. He held a pair of heels in one hand as he typed on his phone with his other. He didn't even look up. Not that I should expect him to.

Sergei took the heels and knelt at my feet. After the conversation we'd had, this felt so wrong.

I kept glancing at Slavik, expecting him to explode and kill us both. Sergei wasn't attracted to me, but I didn't even know if I was allowed friends. With the heels on, I was ready to face whatever I had to.

Slavik put his cell phone away and stared at me.

No compliments.

He held out his hand, which I had no choice but to take. After Sergei's confrontation, I felt acutely aware of everything I did with Slavik. This was … wrong. I had no interest in Sergei. He was my guard. A friend would have been nice. Seeing as I spent all day with him, I started to wonder if it would be at all possible to see him as a friend. To enjoy lunches together. To go out shopping.

It was a lame idea.

Neither me nor Slavik talked as we rode the elevator down to the underground parking.

He sat beside me in the car, and Sergei drove us to whatever restaurant we were scheduled to appear. Normally, I could go through these motions, but today, everything felt too tender, too tight. I felt the spiraling sickness in my gut.

Did Slavik know?

"How are you?" Slavik asked, causing me to jump.

"I'm fine. You?" Did I answer too quickly?

"Good."

The tension in the car mounted.

I wanted to ask about the attack, but I knew it wasn't my place. A woman's place in this world was to be seen when he wanted you to be seen. Or in my place, to stay hidden for as long as possible.

I felt … sick.

"Er, how was your day?" I asked.

"Productive."

This time, I chanced a glance at him. His gaze was on me, and I quickly averted mine. This man was my husband, and the truth was he was a stranger to me.

"That's good," I said.

"You?"

"I … went to the pool." I didn't dare look toward Sergei.

Nothing happened. I had to get that through my thick skull. All Sergei did was offer me friendship. There was no crime in that, even if it did feel wrong. Why did it make me nervous? Was I so used to not having friends, I pushed people away?

The car came to a stop outside a very nice-looking restaurant. I didn't recognize the name. Slavik opened the door, giving Sergei instructions.

I followed my husband out, taking the hand that was offered, but he let me go, wrapping an arm around my waist. I wasn't entirely sure if I wanted him to hold me like this. Like the good woman I'd been trained to be, I didn't pull away, even though I was tempted with every fiber of my being.

We entered the restaurant and after one look at my husband, the maître d' escorted us to our table.

Slavik held out my chair and I sat down.

A quick glance around the room and I saw people were looking our way. Slavik had a way about him that commanded attention the instant he entered a room.

With my hands in my lap, tightly clenched together, I waited for him to order the wine, and he did. Then he asked for the menus to be brought to us at once.

All this time, I didn't say a word. These *dates*, if they could even be called that, were always trying. The truth was I had no idea what to say to him.

We were so different. In age. In our likes. He was a stone-cold killer and I had no place.

Silence fell between us.

Slavik like always, held his cell phone, typing away.

Other couples were looking at each other, swooning. Or at the very least with lust. What did I get? Sat at a table, pretty much ignored. Slavik refused to give me the time for strained conversation.

Time ticked by, and along with it, my patience.

All my life, I'd been told to be quiet, to not make waves. I was nearly killed a week ago, and I'd followed all the rules. Not once had it helped me.

Sitting up, I put my arms on the table and looked at my husband. "Did you talk to my father?" I asked.

I must have taken Slavik by surprise because he finally looked up.

Silence.

I would not look away. This time, in a restaurant, we would at the very least pretend to want to be around each other.

Not that I should care. I was already a mockery wherever I went. For some reason, I felt rebellious tonight. Like I wanted him to notice me. Sergei had terrified me, to be frank. The only person offering to be my friend was the one person who could get killed for being so.

"I don't talk business," he said.

"Then what would you like to talk about?" I asked.

"What is this?"

"You drag me out of your home. Dress me up. Sit me here, for appearances' sake. Am I right?"

He didn't say anything.

"Then we sit here and you make me a complete laughing stock because you cannot even give your wife the time of day. You're always attached to your phone. Are you, like, addicted to social media? You do the endless scrolling?" I needed to shut up. Clearly when I was attacked, something went wrong inside my brain because my lips kept on working when they should stay shut.

"Are you on social media?"

"No," I said. I wasn't allowed an account. My sister had been until she did the stupid thing of taking a selfie at a private party. Guess who got the punishment for that, little old me. Daddy didn't like to punish his sweet girl. "Just because I don't have an account doesn't mean I don't understand it. I don't know you or what you do, but I can guess. If you don't want to talk shop, fine. Just don't ignore me. I'd rather eat at home if that's what you want. I'm sure you have a lot more to do other than this."

"Women like being taken out to dinner."

"This woman likes to be acknowledged as actually existing. You've ignored me all week."

"I've been busy."

"With work you won't talk about." I shrugged. "We're running around in circles right now."

The waiter came, and I stopped, taking a deep breath. What the hell was wrong with me?

"Excuse me."

I got to my feet, ignoring my husband, and walked to the ladies' room. Entering, I saw there was no one there. I had no need for the toilet, so I went straight to the sink.

"What the hell is wrong with me?" I kept my head down. The last thing I wanted to do was look in a mirror. What I'd see looking back at me scared me.

I was going to get myself killed if I kept this up.

My face felt incredibly hot, but with the small amount of makeup I'd put on, there was no way I could splash my face.

After running my wrists beneath the cold tap, I reached out for a towel when my arm was grabbed and I spun around. Slavik was in the ladies' room. He pressed me up against the bathroom counter.

I nibbled on my lip and tried to get as far as I could with the counter stopping me. There was nowhere for me to go.

"What is your problem?" he asked.

"I don't have one. I don't see a point in being here wasting our time if we're not even going to have a civil conversation." Why would I even want to have Slavik talking to me? The man was scary.

He made grown men afraid.

Here I was offering up a conversation with a man whose expertise was death.

"You've never seemed to mind before."

"I always minded. Once or twice was fine, but we've been doing this same dance for far too long and I'm bored of it."

In the back of my mind, I literally screamed for myself to shut the fuck up. Whatever I was doing, or thought I was doing, was going to get me killed.

"You're bored."

"You can't tell me you're excited about eating dinner with me when you're checking your cell phone every two minutes."

He didn't say anything.

His body pressed against mine, and not for the first time, I became very aware of him as a man.

****

Slavik

I caught the flash.

Aurora didn't understand it, but I did.

My wife felt a spark of attraction. The way she moved her body, like she wanted to get away from me, but only made me aware of her as a woman.

In fact, I'd been made aware of it several times.

I'd never allowed myself to get attached to anyone. Not even Ivan or Cara. I cared for them, and they were like a family, but the truth was I had no real emotion when it came to them. It was business. We'd survived by banding together and creating the world we now lived in where we were on top.

Aurora was different. I'd sensed it the first time I met her.

Now, she proved it. Even as she was afraid, her mouth couldn't seem to stop, and I, for one, fucking loved it.

Don't get me wrong, the women in my life had all known the score. I was good for a quick fuck, nothing else. I never got close. Always kept them at arm's length. They always knew I was there for a release and I didn't always care if they felt it too. In fact, I'd even used lubrication when I hadn't been in the mood to make them wet enough to take me.

Aurora shouldn't have been any different.

I didn't love her. I didn't have a crush on her. She wasn't strikingly beautiful, and yet for me, I picked her out of a crowd with ease.

Staring at her now, with her soft body so close, I hated that we were in the restaurant. Along with the spark of attraction, she also held fear.

Even with her emotions all over the place, I liked her mouth. The way she talked back. Some men would have backhanded her. Not me. I didn't want a puppet or a submissive that couldn't think for herself.

This was the most refreshing moment of our marriage so far.

Tilting my head to the side, I looked at her, really looked at her. She possessed brown eyes. At first, I had thought they were dull, but they were anything but. They sparkled. There was a lot going on inside Aurora's head, and I didn't have the first clue what half of it was about. I had no doubt she was afraid I'd kill her. Tonight, she was safe.

She'd curled her long brown hair, and it fell around her like a frame. I happened to love the length. How long it looked, and there were times I wanted to run my fingers down it. I hadn't taken nearly enough time to appreciate my wife.

She had a small nose, full lips, and nice cheekbones. Nothing was too sharp. She had curves on her as well.

Some people might think she needed to drop a few pounds, not me. The few times I'd fucked her, I'd loved there was more than a handful. I wasn't afraid of pounding inside her. She wouldn't break beneath me and could take all of me. That alone held an attraction.

Her tits. The dress I'd given her accentuated the size of her breasts, and again, I wanted them naked beneath me, swinging above me.

There were moments like these where I wanted the time to explore Aurora. Where our marriage, the treaty, the Bratva, or her mafia family didn't get in the way.

Years of training were hard to let go. We both had our past.

"You want to sit and talk while we eat dinner?" This was new to me.

In the past, women had been more than happy for me to ignore them, just so long as I paid the bill. The same went with all areas. If I paid, they were happy to give me what I wanted.

Again, Aurora was different. She'd yet to use my money on anything. The clothes she'd gotten were the ones I brought for her.

"Yes," she said, cutting through my thoughts.

"Then let's go and talk."

She nodded her head, but I hadn't moved. "You need to step back."

"I will, but it's going to cost you," I said.

"What?"

"Kiss me."

"Excuse me?"

"You heard me," I said. I could have taken the kiss. Aurora wouldn't fight me. The training her family had thrust into her was hard for her to ignore. She'd let me do anything to her. This was our world. Women, unfortunately, were nothing more than a commodity. A price someone was willing to pay. For Aurora, the Bratva paid in peace as did her family.

"You want me to kiss you?" she asked.

"Yes. Like you mean it."

"I don't know how."

"Simple. Kiss me like your life depends on it."

"That's not a good reason to have a kiss."

"It's the only reason you need. We're not leaving until you kiss me."

"You'd keep the restaurant open all night just so I'd kiss you?" she asked.

"Yes."

"You're bluffing."

"I own the restaurant. They'd do as they're told."

She licked her lips, and I saw her struggling, but I'd won. She just needed to realize I had and there was no point in fighting it.

I wanted that tongue on mine.

For a few seconds, nothing happened. She stayed perfectly still, and I kept her trapped. I had no problem holding her here. This worked for me because I had her close to my body. The soft curves of her breasts calling to me.

Slowly, almost too slowly for me to appreciate, she put her hands on my chest. Her touch light, soft. She slid her hands up to cup my face. Aurora touched my face and let me go.

I saw the fight in her gaze and I stayed perfectly still, giving her the time to make all the moves.

She cupped my face and waited.

Did she think I'd kill her for touching me?

I'd done so in the past, but this was different. I'd asked her to kiss me. I wanted her touch, but she was treating me like a bomb about to go off.

Even with the heels I'd given her, I was still much taller than her. She had no choice but to go on her tiptoes, which brought her body flush against mine, and fuck me if that didn't feel good.

The soft press of her tits.

I wanted to grab her.

Instead, I held myself perfectly still as her lips brushed across mine. The touch was fleeting, and she pulled back.

"Not good enough."

"It was a kiss."

I was done playing games. Grabbing her ass, I sank my fingers into her hair and tugged her close. I slammed my lips down on hers and ravished her mouth, taking control, giving her the kiss I truly wanted.

She released a moan, her fingers sinking against my shoulders as she held on to me. It wasn't enough. I traced the fullness of her lip, and she opened up, deepening the kiss. Then I lifted her up on the counter, spreading her thighs so my cock was close to her.

As much as I wanted to continue, fucking her in the bathroom of a restaurant wasn't what I had in mind for today.

I jerked away.

The dress had ridden up. The slits were open, exposing her thighs. She touched her lips and shook her head, getting to her feet.

She nearly fell to the floor, but I captured her, not letting her go until I was sure she was balanced.

"I'm fine."

"I ordered dinner for you. Let's go and eat." I held my hand out. She took it.

Sergei was outside of the bathroom. Again, I hated the way he looked at my wife. I made a note to look into a replacement bodyguard for my wife. I wouldn't kill Sergei for having a little crush, if that was even what he had. I wasn't a fool. I was very much aware of the bonds that formed between wives and bodyguards. They were always around each other. They became friends and for some, it turned into a relationship.

Not all husbands liked their women fucking the help, though. For me, it wasn't Sergei's social standing that was the problem. I simply didn't want him or any man touching my wife.

She belonged to me.

I'd taken her virginity. All of her firsts, and every encounter after that all belonged to me.

I wasn't going to give her up.

Back at our table, I nodded for the waiter to bring out our dinner. Staring at Aurora now, her lips swollen, her hair a little disheveled, she looked everywhere but at me. The fire no longer in her eyes, but now, I wanted to talk.

"Your father had nothing to do with the attack. He didn't send those men."

Her gaze landed back on me, exactly where I wanted them. "Oh."

"Yes. It would seem the men who attacked the party had formed what they felt was an elite group of soldiers."

"I don't understand." Her frown was cute.

"To put it simply, the soldiers that worked for your father, and the other Capos, decided they didn't like taking orders. They formed their own group, considering themselves the best of the soldiers. They weren't, which is why they were let go with ease. We don't make it a habit of driving out our best soldiers."

"Why attack the party?"

"They didn't like the Bratva connection. They attacked the party as it contained the two of us."

"They were intentionally going to kill us?" she asked. "They attacked and hurt people. Killed people because of us."

"Our marriage is a peace treaty. It is what stops the streets from running red with blood. They hoped to kill us to void the peace treaty, or to make us believe they'd attacked, voiding the treaty and starting up a street war."

"Why are you telling me all this?"

"You wanted conversation. You asked what I'd been doing this week. This is what I'd been doing."

I'd never talked work with anyone outside of who I dealt with.

Aurora sat back. "Does that mean there are more soldiers out there? No one would attack and leave themselves vulnerable, would they?"

"You're right. They recruited more soldiers who were not happy with the alliance, as well as people, mostly ex-military men, who are not good at taking orders. They created a small army within a matter of weeks, if not months."

"So we're in danger right now as we're having our meal?"

I nodded. The truth was, even without the small

army, I was in danger every single second of my life. She didn't need to know that. So far, the dinner was going well.

"I don't know how you can be so calm."

"Easy. They're not the first people who've wanted to kill me and I have no doubt they won't be the last." I sipped at my wine.

Our dinner arrived.

The waiter left.

"You're … amazing," she said.

I smiled. "Why?"

"I'm freaking out and I don't have the first clue what is going on or even why, and yet, this just seems all a little surreal. You're a strong man, Slavik."

I didn't pay attention to the compliment.

All my life, I'd lived with the threat of being killed. It was not new to me and fighting to survive was second nature.

"How was your week?" I asked.

"Boring. I didn't do anything quite as exciting as you. I used the pool. Cooked myself some food. Read. That's about it."

Just as I was about to say something, a couple stopped by our table.

I recognized Andrei Belov. He controlled section two of cities under Ivan's control. He was a brigadier like me and answered to the Volkov Bratva. With the attack, Ivan had organized a meeting with all of us to take place in my territory, seeing as this was where we were attacked.

The woman on Andrei's arms was his intended. Her name escaped me.

"I thought it was you, and you were not wrong. This place is amazing," he said.

"I only have the best."

"Bethany, I'd like you to meet Slavik Ivanov and his wife, Aurora."

"It is so nice to meet you both." Bethany shook my hand and turned to Aurora. "We need to organize a lunch or a shopping trip. I would love to do both." She put her hand on Andrei's chest. "I know we're going to be leaving soon, and it's so hard to make friends here. What do you say?"

Aurora smiled but didn't say anything.

"My wife is available tomorrow. I'll make the arrangements with you, Andrei."

"Call it a date."

Andrei shook my hand and they made their excuses to leave.

I wasn't like Andrei. To look and to listen to him, men believed his position of power was unfounded. What they didn't know was he had a mean streak and in fact, I wouldn't wish my worst enemy to be alone with him when he was on the warpath.

Ivan Volkov did not pick soft men to run his cities. It was why he'd gotten six of the best, divided up his cities into sections, and we ruled them all.

"Do I have to go to lunch?" Aurora asked.

"Yes. It would be rude not to and he's a friend. You'll be safe."

"It's easy for you to say."

"What is the problem?"

"She doesn't really want to have lunch with me."

"Did I see her talking to someone else?" I asked.

"You don't understand. It's fine." She waved her hand in the air, dismissing me. Whatever had happened in the bathroom was gone, and I was pissed off Andrei had interrupted my dinner.

Chapter Seven

Aurora

Maybe I had prejudged Bethany because I actually had an enjoyable lunch with her. She was a nice woman. Came from a media background. Her parents were more than thrilled with her marrying Andrei Belov. The arrangements had already been made and the wedding set for December. Not too far away, and she was excited.

During all of her talk of her wedding, not once did she invite me, but I figured it had something to do with Slavik and the whole Bratva thing.

We had lunch several times a week. I invited her to dinner. We talked about everything and nothing. In fact, I'd been that heavily involved with Bethany, I had nearly forgotten about the uncomfortable conversation with Sergei.

He was there all the time, watching and waiting.

Each day, I had a new date with Bethany.

She'd be returning with Andrei to wherever he lived. I couldn't recall where, but it was in one of the cities. I was never good with locations.

"You and Bethany seem to be hitting it off," Sergei said.

"Slavik wanted me to be nice and have dinner. She's only here for a couple more days and then she's leaving."

Sergei nodded.

What also played on my mind was the kiss I'd shared with Slavik in the bathroom. There was no one to talk to about it. I wanted to know what a kiss like that meant. Was it normal to share one so intense? Every time I thought about it, my lips tingled, and like now, I touched them.

Would it be so wrong to give in to him?

We hadn't had sex.

My period had started a few days ago, so that meant no baby. To have a baby you did have to do it regularly, right?

Talking to my mother was useless. She never came to the phone. Isabella was always talking about a party she'd been to and what fun she had. Me, I'd been left with Slavik, confused.

The only place to go would be the internet, and trying to figure out the truth was way too complicated. Also, my searching had sent me to a porn site. If Slavik had a way of checking through what I looked at, there would be questions.

Even our sex didn't match up to the porn videos.

Sergei parked the car outside a cute Italian place. I'd read the reviews, and they were amazing. I called Bethany up immediately.

I arrived at the table and took a seat. Bethany was ten minutes late, but she arrived. She wore a low-cut dress that stopped above the knee. She was so beautiful.

I got to my feet, kissing her cheek as we'd started to do. This was the first time I'd ever had a girlfriend, and it was glorious.

"Sorry I was late, Andrei, well, he didn't want me to leave."

"Oh, are you living with Andrei?"

"Yes."

This was another part of how different we both were. Her family was happy with her traveling with her husband. The engagement ring was on her finger, and to the rest of the world, they were going to be married. Bethany had confided in me that Andrei wasn't her first boyfriend. She'd gone to an all-girls school and had met a guy there. She wasn't a virgin.

A lot of details to take in, but I hadn't shared a single secret with anyone. Part of me was scared for her.

My virginity for my wedding to Slavik had been a necessity.

I didn't know if she loved Andrei, not that love played a part in my own marriage. Once again, Slavik kept his distance. He came home and slept beside me, but the only reason I knew that was the dent on his pillow the next morning.

Thinking about my marriage, I felt cold.

There was no love, nor was there any passion. Little by little, I felt like I was dying inside.

Bethany distracted me, telling me about a movie she'd watched. I liked how she talked a lot. It filled the silence. Our meal came, and I noticed she always pushed her salad around the plate.

Her cell phone went off, and she glanced down at the screen and groaned. "I've just got to take this. I'll be right back."

Again, I was used to her taking calls through our lunches.

I wasn't hungry.

The waiter came to the table, and I saw Sergei watching me.

"I'll be back in a moment." I needed to use the bathroom and with Sergei close, he'd watch the table to make sure none of our stuff was stolen.

I went to the bathroom, washed my hands, and when I chanced a look in the mirror, I saw … sadness.

After pinching my cheeks to add a little pink to my complexion, I left the bathroom, coming to a stop when I saw Bethany just down the hall near the kitchen.

I approached.

"No, please keep talking to me. Anything to stop this from dragging."

I stopped.

What was dragging?

"Andrei made me ask her to go to lunch, and the last few weeks, that is all we've done. She eats all the time, and I've never known anyone so dull in all my life. Honestly, I can't wait to get home. We can go and have some fun. Aurora wouldn't know fun if it bit her in the ass, and let me tell you, she's so ugly. Slavik is hot. He's dangerously hot, he deserves someone so much better than Aurora."

Biting my lip, I stepped away, leaving her as she continued talking about me.

I headed back to the table, feeling kind of numb. The waiter came and asked about dessert. I told him no and asked for the check.

Looking over at Sergei, I wanted to burst into tears. I'd been so desperate for a friend I hadn't read the signs.

I was empty. I'd eaten lunch and yet my stomach cramped.

My throat started to burn.

Bethany arrived, and as I looked at her now, I realized the signs I'd been ignoring over the past few weeks. She always arrived late. There was no invitation to her wedding.

"What did I miss?" she asked.

She smiled at me, and part of me thought about playing along, but the truth was, I was so tired of this dance.

The waiter arrived.

I saw the cost and paid it with the cash in my wallet. "I've had a call. I've got to go. Sorry to cut this short."

She looked shocked, but I got to my feet, already leaving. She wasn't used to me being the one to end our time together. Always the damn same.

"I'll call you," she said.

I didn't say anything.

Sergei took the lead, heading out of the restaurant ahead of me. The car was already waiting, so I guessed he'd called ahead. He opened the backseat passenger door, and I climbed in. Sitting back, I took a breath, wiping at my cheeks to make sure the tears wouldn't fall.

"Take me home," I said.

I rarely thought of Slavik's apartment as home.

He didn't question me.

I stared out the window.

Boring. Ugly. These were words I was used to. They shouldn't hurt me anymore, and yet, I thought Bethany had started to become a friend.

There was no friendship there. At least I heard the truth before I got too attached.

No friends.

This was how I was just going to have to live my life. People didn't like me. Simple as that. No matter what I did.

Fine. I wouldn't make friends.

The drive was a blur.

When he parked the car, I shot out of it, going straight to the elevator. I didn't give Sergei a chance to catch up. The doors closed and the elevator took me up. No one stopped the elevator in its tracks, and for that, I was relieved.

I had a key to the door and I let myself in, tempted to lock the door, but I refused to cause more of a scene.

Gently, I put my bag down and went straight to the kitchen. I opened the fridge and saw the bottle of water.

I'd been starving myself these past few weeks.

Working out at the gym. The gym.

I rushed to the bedroom, changed out of the skirt, sandals, and crop top into a pair of gym shorts and a shirt. When I was changed and ready, Sergei came into the apartment. He was panting.

"You didn't wait for the elevator?"

"I'm to keep you protected at all times."

"Yeah, well, this is not one of those times."

I made to go around him. He stepped in my way. He was out of air, but he still thought he could take me on.

"I'm going to work out. I need to go to the gym."

"What happened?" he asked.

"None of your business. Your job is to take care of me. Consider your job well done." I reached out, patted him on the shoulder. "Congratulations. I'm still alive."

"Aurora, you're hurting."

"I'm not. I'm completely fine. I've got no reason to be upset or hurt. I'm alive. I've told you that."

"You're going to cry."

Tears had already flooded my eyes. "Get out of my way."

"No."

"This is not doing your job."

"Like you said. You're alive. You're safe." He reached out and touched my face.

I jerked back. "No."

"Aurora, come on, I know you feel it too."

I frowned. This was so very different. "I have no idea what you're talking about."

I continued to take a step back, and he followed. I kept on walking until the wall stopped me from moving. I tensed up as his hands came out and were placed on either side of my head.

"You think I don't see the way you look at me? Slavik doesn't deserve you. No one does. I see it. I notice your pain."

"Sergei, you've got to stop." I didn't have any feelings for him. He was my guard and it mattered to me that my actions didn't get him hurt or killed, but that was all.

"No, I don't think I need to stop. I see how they all treat you. They all ignore you. I can't stand that." He pressed his body against mine and the hurt I'd been feeling morphed into something else. Fear.

Before I knew what was happening, Sergei had grabbed my face and started to kiss me. His tongue traced across my mouth, and I instantly tried to push him away. This was not a kiss I wanted.

I'd only ever kissed Slavik, and right now, this made me feel like I betrayed him. I didn't ask for Sergei's kiss, but because I hadn't reported his inappropriate behavior to Slavik, did he think this gave him a right to me?

I tried to cry out, but Sergei was strong. I was no match for him.

I kept trying to hit him, to force him to get away.

All of a sudden, he was off me, and I panted for breath until I saw what was going on. Slavik had come home and now he pounded his fist against Sergei's face.

Within the few seconds it had taken me to gain my composure, the sheer violence Slavik displayed shocked me.

Over and over, he slammed his fist against his face.

Blood spilled, splattering on the floor and the wall.

"Slavik, stop it."

I couldn't get through. Over and over, the

pounding went. I reacted, grabbing Slavik's arms, trying to get him to stop, but he shoved me away and I fell hard, my ass hitting the floor.

There was nothing else for me to do.

Right there, in front of me, Slavik drew his gun and shot Sergei in the head.

My mouth fell open. No sounds came out.

Sergei, my bodyguard, was dead.

Slavik spat on him and got to his feet. His hands were covered in blood, Sergei's blood.

He turned toward me, and as he advanced, with all the blood, I scrambled away. I was no match for Slavik either. He grabbed my arm and dragged me up, slamming my back against the wall.

I cried out. Tears ran down my cheeks as he pressed the gun against my temple. I whimpered as the heat seemed to burn right through my head.

"How long?" he asked.

"What?"

"How long have you been fucking him?"

"I would never do that. Never."

"You expect me to believe that after what I just saw?"

"If you saw correctly, you'd have seen that I was fighting him off." My entire body shook.

I'd seen people killed before. Dead bodies were not new to me, but right now, I was in shock. I had to be.

The sheer violence, that was new to me.

He didn't stop to ask Sergei any questions. He just killed him. Now he had the same gun pointed at me and thought I would betray him. Seconds passed as Slavik looked into my eyes.

"I saw," he said. "Now tell me what the fuck happened."

I nodded my head. The action felt jerky to me,

but I stood there and told him everything. About coming home and Sergei pressing me against the wall. The kiss. I even told him about him wanting to be friends and getting close. I didn't have any secrets.

All the while, Slavik looked at me.

What did he see?

Was he debating how to get rid of me?

"Go to your room," he said. "Stay there until I come to you."

"Slavik?"

"Now!" He yelled the word, and I didn't stick around. I ran as fast as I could, tripping over my feet. Once inside the bedroom, I flicked the lock closed and ran toward the bathroom. Staring at my reflection, I saw the blood. Sergei's blood.

This was all my fault. I tore my clothes off my body, scrambling to get myself clean.

I stepped beneath the water and cried out as the cold hit my skin. I didn't move for a short time, trying to process everything that had happened. Grabbing the soap, I started to scrub my hands and my body.

Sergei had died because of me.

I should have told him no. Told Slavik.

I felt sick.

Getting someone killed had never been my intention.

I felt so cold. So alone. This wasn't fair.

Tilting my head up to the shower, I couldn't believe what had happened today. I'd lost a friend, and another who had wanted to be mine had been killed. What the hell was wrong with me?

****

Slavik

The cleaning crew knew not to ask any questions.

Sergei's body would be removed. His apartment

was already being cleared out along with any personal effects. There was no family for me to call. No one to shame with his behavior.

I waited as they cleaned my apartment. All that was left was my blood-soaked clothing. I stripped out of it, handing them the clothes, and they left my apartment. Everything had a price, even covering your tracks.

Seeing Sergei on my wife, I'd snapped. I'd never been possessive about any woman in my life and yet, seeing him kissing her was more than I could stand.

Deep down, I knew she'd been trying to fight him. Aurora hadn't asked for the kiss, and still, I'd been hyped up on rage and the need to kill.

Sergei got an easy death, and for me, that didn't sit well. I hated it.

With my hands on my hips, I stared around my now pristine apartment. The last five, no, nearly six months, Aurora had lived in my place and still, she hadn't done a single thing to make her mark.

There was nothing here that stood out.

No trinket to tell anyone who visited—not that anyone did—that she lived here. This apartment wasn't even mine in the true sense. I owned the building and I'd taken residence here, but there weren't any personal effects of mine either.

Laying down roots was hard for me to do. It wasn't something I could just do with the snap of my fingers.

"What the fuck am I doing?" I ran a hand down my face and headed toward the bedroom. The door was locked. I tried the handle, realizing she'd tried to keep me out. Not happening.

Aurora needed to learn there was no easy way to keep me away. With a simple snap of the handle and my body weight shoved against it, the door came open.

I expected to see her on the bed.

At least hear a scream.

Nothing.

The bathroom door was also closed.

Like the main bedroom door, this one was also locked.

"Aurora, open the fucking door," I said.

My patience was at an all-time low. If I had any sanity left, I'd try to talk to her, but right now, I needed a shower.

"Go away," she said.

Gritting my teeth, I clenched my hands into tight fists. "You think this door is going to keep me out?"

"No, but you need to calm down. I didn't do anything wrong."

"I'm not angry."

"You just killed Sergei."

"And I'll kill any fucking man who thinks they can put their hands on you and get away with it. You're mine, Aurora."

"I'm what you had to have. I'm not yours."

I slammed my fist against the door. Her anger actually aroused me. She wasn't simpering in a corner. I liked the fact she talked back to me.

This felt good. Really good.

"Stop banging!" She screamed the last part, and I put my palm against the door, gritting my teeth once again.

I had two choices. Wait for her to open the door, or break it down.

I chose the latter.

The moment I broke the lock and entered the room, Aurora let out a little cry.

She stood with a towel wrapped around her, and I smelled bleach. I saw her clothes were in the sink and she'd poured bleach all over them.

Her hair was still damp from the shower.

My hands were covered in dried blood.

Aurora nibbled on her lip. "I … I didn't know what to do with these."

"I'll handle it," I said. I turned on the shower, waiting for the water to warm up.

I stepped into the stall, and Aurora tried to make her escape, only I wouldn't let her. I grabbed her arm and dragged her into the stall right along with me. Pinning her up against the wall, I flicked the towel, allowing it to fall on the floor, and I simply looked my fill.

"You're not going anywhere."

"You're angry."

I grabbed the soap and rinsed my hands. The blood fell away down the drain as if nothing happened. "I'm not angry."

"You didn't have to kill him."

"You think he was only going to be satisfied with kissing you? He didn't even have the sense to listen to you tell him no. Sergei would have raped you to get what he wanted."

She released a gasp. "You believe me."

"Yes. I saw it."

"But why did you blame me?"

"I was angry, Aurora. No man wants to come home to find his wife kissing another man. At first, it didn't register that you were fighting against him. Sergei's dead now and I've handled everything."

"Oh. Will his death cause you trouble?"

"No. Sergei was alone in this world. No one will care that he's dead."

I watched her swallow a lump in her throat. "You care?" I asked.

"Yes. He … for the past few months, he'd been

really nice to me."

"He wanted to fuck you. Any man would be nice to you."

She snorted. "Yeah, right. Can I go now?"

"No." I handed her the soap. "Wash me."

"Are you kidding me?"

"No." I took hold of her wrist and forced her to touch my chest. Staring at her, I waited. What Aurora didn't seem to know was how patient I'd been with her. It never happened for a man in my position to give their wife time to adapt. I hadn't forced my will onto her. Demanded she spread her legs for me so I can put a baby inside her. I'd given her time.

What was my reward? To find another man kissing her and have blue balls for the pleasure of it—not happening.

Staring at her now, I noticed her movements were kind of jerky, but I wasn't going to give her an out she clearly sought.

The soap ran over my skin, but that wasn't the touch I wanted.

"Lather your hands up."

She followed the instruction, and I took the soap from her. "Now, clean me."

She shook a little as her hands went from my neck down to my chest. I was sure she hesitated at my neck as she'd been tempted to throttle me. I smiled. It wouldn't be the first time a woman wanted to kill me.

Aurora was a good woman, though. She'd been trained well and so she worked her hands down, being careful not to touch my cock, which had swelled the moment she started to touch me.

When Ivan first told me I'd be marrying the Fredo daughter, there had been no attraction. No desire to marry this woman. I'd known her family had tried to insult us by giving us what he considered his second best, but something was happening to me.

I wasn't entirely sure what.

I craved her touch on me, but more than that, I wanted Aurora to want me, to beg for my touch. Our wedding night had been a disaster.

The whole tradition of bloody sheets had fucking infuriated me. The way the men looked at the evidence of her broken virginity, that was mine. All mine. I should have put a stop to it, but I played along, as was the rules.

I was a powerful man.

I'd been with a lot of women in my time. Fucked them and forgot them. I'd never known what it was like to have a virgin. Not just any virgin, my wife. Untouched by all other men. No one else would know how tight her cunt was, how sweet her mouth tasted, and how soft her body was next to mine. So very addictive. I couldn't wait to feel her once again.

She continued to ignore my arousal until I finally snapped and placed her fingers around my dick. She froze, and I paused, staring into her eyes.

"You know what I want."

Aurora shook her head.

With my hand covering hers, I made her work up and down my length. She nibbled on her lip as if this was the strangest thing she'd ever encountered but she didn't stop and I liked that. I liked that she kept on going. The tip already leaked pre-cum, and I groaned. I closed my eyes for a split second, basking in the pleasure she evoked within me.

My balls were so fucking tight.

Letting go of her hand, I pressed mine against the wall, caging her in.

"Faster," I said.

I was so close.

She worked my dick faster, and I stared into her eyes.

Her brown ones stared back at me with wonder as well as hunger. *That's right, baby. This is what you're doing to me.*

I couldn't hold back my release, and as she continued to stroke me, my release spilled out, coating her stomach.

Even before my orgasm ebbed away, I gripped the back of her neck, slamming my lips down on hers as I finished my orgasm.

I wanted to be inside her, but this was second best.

Any anger I had slowly fell away.

I wouldn't hurt Aurora.

She was my wife, and regardless of what she thought, I was going to protect her.

Chapter Eight
Aurora

In a matter of days, I'd gone from spending my time being bored, reading one book after another, to being escorted around by Slavik.

He'd killed my guard, and rather than hire another one, he kept me to himself.

I had no choice in the matter.

He had so many businesses. When we arrived at some, he kept me in the car. The doors locked. He even kept the windows down when it was really warm as if I was some kind of dog.

Each day, the anger kept on simmering inside me, waiting to explode.

The work never stopped. He was everywhere and nowhere. We ended up taking a private jet to travel to different cities. All of them under his rule. He kept watch over it all. He worked during the day and at night; there was no space.

After three weeks, taking our marriage over the seven-month mark, I stood in one of his nightclubs. This time, he'd allowed me to change. The first time I came to this nightclub, which was simply called The Club, so very cute, I'd been in sweatpants and a shirt. This time, I wore a tight dress.

It was the only one he'd allow me to wear. It was tight against my body, and I couldn't stop wriggling in it. I was worried I looked fat and frumpy.

The women on the dance floor were goddesses.

Each one looked so happy and free. Like they held all the power within their lives and I had nothing. My husband controlled me. I wasn't given a single reprieve.

Even when some men, business associates, dared

to comment on my presence, Slavik told them to mind their own business or they'd see his very bad side.

How many other men like Slavik escorted their wives around to everything?

With my palm on the private window overlooking the dance floor, envy flooded me. It was an emotion I didn't like.

The music vibrated the room, but I couldn't hear it.

Slavik spoke on the phone. He spoke in Russian, which was so hard to think about as his accent rarely came through.

I kept on glancing back at him, and each time I did, I found his gaze was already on me.

We hadn't done anything else since he made me work his penis in the shower. Who am I kidding? I knew it was a cock. Thinking about it, I got aroused. He'd been so hard and as I played with him, I'd worked him into a fever where he had no choice but to come. I'd never felt that kind of power over a man, and the truth was I wanted it again.

Slavik put the phone down. "I've got to go and handle something downstairs. Stay here."

I wanted to argue with him, but he was already out the door.

We were back to him treating me like I didn't exist. Actually, scrap that, he treated me like a dog. I was surprised he hadn't put a little bed in the corner and didn't have treats in his pocket.

I hated him.

Folding my arms beneath my breasts, I spun back to the window and glared out at the dance floor. Anger rushed through me with no place to go.

I'd seen how violent he'd gotten with Sergei.

I pushed some hair back from my face, breathing

in and out, hoping to calm my nerves, but nothing seemed to want to stick.

I felt angry at him.

Thinking back to that day, I recalled Bethany's words. She'd tried to call, to set up another dinner date, but I declined. Slavik even tried to arrange for me to go and see her, but I refused.

There was no way I was going to force my company on others.

With my arms wrapped around myself, I stared onto the dance floor, finding Slavik.

He spoke to a couple of men who nodded and fanned out.

Slavik headed toward the bar, and I hated that he was so handsome. He wasn't the boy next door. He was far more dangerous and with it, potent.

Women turned to look at him. Yearning swirled within their gaze. He showed no sign of noticing them as he talked to the man working behind the bar.

I smiled at how he acted. I knew he saw their gazes. Did he know I watched?

Licking my lips, the happiness died instantly as a cute redhead launched herself at him. She wore a shorter dress than the one I wore and as I stood in his office, I watched this other woman rub herself all over Slavik.

He didn't push her away.

Anger, pain, and hurt, it all melded in my gut.

I spun on my heel and stormed out of the office. No guards to keep me locked up in this room. Wow. I wasn't even worth the extra security. He clearly was used to me being the good girl who didn't do anything wrong.

I'd fucking show him.

With each step I took, the two sides of my personality conflicted. I kept telling myself to show him I was not to be ignored. Another side told me I was being a complete and total bitch. I needed to go back to the room.

The rebel inside me kept on walking.

Being the good girl had gotten me trapped in a loveless marriage, where I spent most of my days attached to his side.

He still had all the women in the world around him. For all I knew, he had a dozen mistresses. He may take me everywhere, but that didn't stop him from being with anyone.

Stepping into the nightclub, I pressed my back against the nearest wall.

The rebellious side of me was suddenly a little afraid.

I'd never been to a nightclub as a customer, or participated in the dancing. The air was hot. The energy in the room pulsed around me, startling me.

The music was loud. There were no songs, just a constant thumping noise. The people in the nightclub were going a little crazy. The drinks flowed.

I stayed by the door, knowing I needed to escape.

Out of the corner of my eye, I saw Slavik. He held the woman's shoulders, and I didn't give myself time to analyze what I was doing. Rather than go onto the dance floor and make a fool of myself, which would have been a lot of fun.

No, I decided, in these murderous heels, to cross my path all the way to the bar where Slavik stood.

I made sure I was at his side so he saw it was me as I ran my hands up his body. "Hey, baby, I was getting so lost without you. There are so many men here who want me to dance, but I told them my card is full." What the fuck was I saying? I hated the words spilling from my lips, but they were the first ones that came to me.

He's going to kill you. This is a mistake. You should just turn away and leave.

This was all good advice, but I didn't take any of it.

"Who is this?" I asked.

"She's leaving."

With that, I stepped forward, gripping the back of his neck, pulling him down toward my lips. I expected him to fight me. To make me look like an idiot, but his lips brushed against mine and I couldn't help but moan.

One of his hands went to the curves of my ass, and I gasped as he pulled me close. His cock was still soft, but the moment he had my body flush against his, I felt him start to harden.

Breaking the kiss, I had to keep in control. I was so bored. Holding his hand, I led him out to the dance floor, ignoring the redhead completely as I asked him to dance with me.

Here was the problem. I couldn't dance.

I noticed the crowd parted for him.

No one got in his way. Did the world around him know who he was, or were the rumors enough to keep him safe?

With the music causing a heavy beat in the air, I paused on the dance floor, but I shouldn't have panicked.

Slavik wrapped his arm around my waist, pulling me close.

I released a gasp as he kept one hand on my ass, and the other lay loose at his side, but I knew better. Slavik was ready for any kind of attack.

Neither of us spoke.

The music filled the silence as he took control. We danced together, and it was more like I humped him, but he didn't let me go, and I liked being in his arms.

I wanted to know who the woman was. Why she felt she could touch my husband. I was pissed off. Slightly humiliated.

Had he come down to speak to one of his whores? Had I kept him from getting his release?

"Who was she?" I asked.

"No one."

"She didn't look like no one."

We were having to scream.

He grabbed my hand, and even as I fought him, he won. Of course, he did.

We moved toward the door I came out of. He didn't take me to his office, instead, he pressed me up against the wall.

"I told you to stay upstairs in your office."

"You're welcome. Or did I interrupt your foreplay with your whore?" I asked.

Jealousy was an ugly word. One I couldn't stand.

I stared at him and he tutted.

"You didn't interrupt anything."

"Then who was she?" I asked.

"I don't owe you anything."

"No, of course not. I'm the wife you've been saddled with. Let's face it, you don't want me. You've never wanted me. You're probably getting your fix with all of the other women, right?" I needed to keep better control of my temper, but once I started, I couldn't seem to stop. "I'm supposed to live with you having a lover, a mistress, but the one guy who showed any interest in me at all, he had to die!"

Slavik slammed his palm over my mouth, silencing me. "Be careful what you speak of."

He pulled out his cell phone, and within a matter of seconds, I was bundled into the back of a car, and the driver was ordered to take me to the penthouse suite.

I'd guess our argument was over.

I was never going to think of his apartment as home again.

****

Slavik

I should have known she wouldn't just go to sleep and be the nice, sweet wife I once had.

Aurora stood in her pajamas, pacing the hallway when I entered. I'd instructed the driver to remain outside, stopping her from trying to escape. Before he left, he told me she didn't try to leave.

I'd hoped she'd be asleep.

I couldn't be done with dramatics.

They were tiring, but as I looked at my wife, it would seem the last three hours I'd left her alone, she'd been more than prepared.

Damn.

She stormed toward me and as her hand came up to slap me, I captured it, not allowing her to even connect with my face. She growled at me and tried to jerk away, but I grabbed both of her arms and pressed her up against the wall, stopping her from going anywhere else.

"Let me go."

"No."

"You're an asshole."

"Look at you, using all these big words. I didn't even know your father let you know the insults you could throw at a man. You're supposed to be trained to be obedient."

"Fuck you."

This woman was making me hard. I liked that she fought back.

I wouldn't hurt her.

There was no desire to cause her pain, but she had started to piss me off by trying to hit me. I'd killed more men for less of an insult.

She wriggled against me, and I made her aware of how aroused I was. She stopped.

"Did you sleep with her?" she asked.

"No."

She growled. "Did you have sex with her?"

"Not tonight," I said.

She jerked within my hands. "So you have … slept with her."

"There was no sleeping involved with us. Dawn is a woman who likes to fuck. She was easy, and I don't like it to be too difficult. She was an easy woman to pay off."

"Let go of me."

"No."

"Can I take a lover?" she asked, startling me.

"No!" I growled the word out.

She snorted. "So you can have all the women in the world but I have to what? Deal with you? Other women have lovers. I can be discreet."

I liked my wife being only mine and the fact she stood there willing to be with another man, well, now that really pissed me off.

Glaring at her, I wrapped my fingers around her throat. I didn't squeeze, I merely held her. "If you ever look or allow another man to touch you, their death will be your fault."

Tears filled her eyes. "I hate you."

"Join the club."

"You get to have your fun. To enjoy other women, and I've got to stay here and what? Wait for you?"

"Yes." What my wife failed to see was that I hadn't slept with another woman since I'd made her my wife.

I let go of her neck. "This conversation is over."

"Why? Because you said so?"

"Yes. Do as you're told!"

"No!" She shoved me in the chest. "I'm tired of being told what to do. I won't allow it anymore. I will find a man and when I do, I will sleep with him."

I snapped.

Grabbing the back of her neck, I walked her into the sitting room and bent her over the sofa.

She cried out.

I pressed my cock against her ass.

"Let me go."

"You want to know what it's like to take a man? Do you think you're going to have any control over them? They want one thing." With my other hand, I cupped her pussy. She cried, trying to get away from me.

I rubbed her through the soft fabric of her pajamas, but I knew she wasn't aroused. I was scaring my wife.

"The only cock you will ever know will be mine." I spun her around, and I saw the tears glistening in her eyes, the fear. Any arousal I had faded.

I pulled her up against me, slammed my lips down on hers, and kissed her hard. There was no gentleness. This was rough, hard, and I had to have it.

She didn't fight me, and at the end, I thrust her away from me, storming toward the bathroom.

I slammed the door closed—it had been fixed, along with the bedroom door.

I removed my jacket and shirt, pressing my palms flat to the counter, and I stared at my reflection.

Why did I care if she took a lover?

Aurora was all mine and I liked it that way. The thought of another man touching her… I couldn't; a cold rage seeped into my core. The need to mark her, to make sure every single man stayed the fuck away from her was strong.

I'd never known this rage. This was new.

I'd dealt with my anger so many times in the past, but this was unlike anything I'd ever experienced. This was a whole new level of anger, and I didn't like it.

My reflection didn't help.

I removed the last of my clothes and stepped beneath the spray of the cold shower. I stayed under the water for a good thirty minutes. When I closed my eyes, all I saw were the tears and the fear.

Aurora shouldn't look at me like that.

I was aware a lot of men got off on hurting women in our world. How their tears turned them on and the harder they fought, the easier it was for them to take. Rape never appealed to me. Forcing a woman sickened me. There was no power there.

I turned the shower off, wrapped a towel around my waist, and glanced over to see the bed was empty.

Leaving the bedroom, I found her curled up on the sofa, crying.

"I … I'm sorry," she said.

She looked so fucking fragile. My wife was not supposed to be doing this to me.

Annoyed with myself, I pulled the coffee table closer. "I'm not fucking any other woman. I haven't been with anyone else since you."

"How can I believe you?"

"I haven't lied."

She sniffled.

There was more I wanted to say, but the words didn't come. Instead, I picked her up in my arms.

"I'm too heavy."

I ignored her. She was heavy, but I liked the weight of her in my arms, and I carried her to our room. The covers were already pulled back, and I slid her beneath.

I tossed the towel into the laundry basket and

climbed into bed beside her. Rather than wait for her to go to sleep, I pulled her against me. She snuggled in close, wrapping her arm around me.

It wasn't much, but it was a start.

Chapter Nine

Aurora

Two more weeks, and I had enough of being trapped in a car, or in an office, waiting for him.

Slavik still refused to provide a bodyguard for me, so I went wherever he went. I couldn't do anything. He didn't even allow me to bring a book.

Boredom had become my new best friend.

Until one morning, I had enough. Rather than wait for him to drag me out, I'd made my escape. There hadn't been a guard on the door, and I'd noticed this a few times when Slavik marched me out of his apartment.

Rather than take the elevator, I took the stairs, making my way out of a fire escape.

Alone in the big city, I'd had a taste of freedom.

It was wonderful.

No guards.

No Slavik.

No commitments.

I had his credit card, and so I did something I never did, I went shopping.

It was early, so a lot of the shops weren't open, but I walked around, watching people while I waited for stores to open.

The moment they did, I went in and shopped.

Maybe what I did was so childish, but I didn't care. The moment some of the women who were helping me enjoy my husband's money saw the name on the card, they had a mini freak-out.

Of course, by the time they made the necessary calls, I was out of the shop. The clothes and shoes were all being sent back to the apartment.

Still not calling it home.

Childish or not, that place was not my home.

I didn't know what had gotten into me. Slavik still hadn't touched me since that night where I'd pushed him too far. When he'd pushed me over the sofa and cupped me between the thighs, I truly thought he was going to rape me.

He hadn't.

The way he held me in bed that night, though. I loved that so much. Since then, he hadn't touched me.

The space on the bed mocked me.

One night of feeling afraid one second, and then comforted the next. I wanted it again. Not the fear, but certainly the comfort. I liked it when he held me. The simple things, especially when he held my hand. Damn it. I sounded like a sulky teenager. I was going to be twenty soon. I shouldn't be having these feelings, wanting my *husband* to hold my hand.

I left the tenth shop I'd spent a fortune in and came to a stop.

Slavik stood, sunglasses on, arms at his sides.

I folded my arms. "Yes?"

"Are you done?" he asked.

"No. You told me I could shop any time."

"Get the car," he said to his driver.

I stayed perfectly still, refusing to make a scene out in public. People kept looking toward us. Where I blended in, Slavik stood out like a sore thumb. A very handsome and dangerous sore thumb, but still sore.

"Do you have any idea how many of my enemies would have loved to have captured you?" he asked.

He gripped the back of my neck, pulling me in close. His lips brushed across my forehead. To any onlooker, we were enjoying an intimate moment. They didn't know the threat he was warning me about.

This morning, I didn't go out thinking about his enemies. I just wanted freedom and the harsh reality was that, for me, there would never be any freedom.

I was Slavik Ivanov's wife. I would be worth so much to his enemies.

"Slavik?"

"They would've raped you, torn you apart, and delivered me each piece of you. I'd have failed you, Aurora." He pressed a kiss to my forehead.

"I only went shopping."

"And you were a fucking fool to not have a guard with you."

"Nothing happened."

"Today."

"Next time, I won't—"

"There won't be a next time." He grabbed my hand, ending our conversation.

He led me to the car, and like that, my rebellious shopping trip was over. I hadn't even made it to lunch. He must have run a trace on his credit card. I didn't know how he could have found me so fast. It wasn't like I held a neon sign.

Sitting back, I stared out the window.

We came to a stop at a fast-food place. He handed me a brown paper bag and ordered me to eat. I hated how he treated me like a child. Still, I ate my food without a single complaint. The milkshake was nice. I wasn't a big fan of the chocolate as I preferred strawberry, but I didn't tell him that.

He didn't eat.

With the food finished, he took the bag, and the next thing I knew, we were entering a private gate, driving down toward a private residence.

The house was huge. Reminded me of my parents' house. They had a huge country estate and often had many soldiers patrolling the grounds.

Slavik got out of the car and held out his hand.

I took it, again being the good girl I was, without complaint.

We walked into the house, and I knew it wasn't any ordinary house.

This was … different.

No words were spoken as Slavik put me at the bar. "Sit and stay."

With my hands pressed to the counter, I had the childish urge to get up, but I stayed seated.

He left me alone.

There wasn't a guard left to wait with me.

I just sat here.

Bored.

Again.

He would rather kill me with boredom than hire another bodyguard. What the hell was wrong with that?

I quickly came to the conclusion I didn't like to be told to wait. Sitting at the bar in this … I wasn't exactly sure what this place was, but I was annoyed. Slavik had interrupted my shopping spree, which I'd taken out of anger and desperate need to get away from him. Now he'd brought me along for his business again, and this time, rather than leave me in the car, he'd dumped me at the bar.

This wasn't fair.

I knew many would argue life wasn't fair, well, so what. I'd played the part of a doting wife. I'd done everything he asked of me, and it still wasn't enough. Today, I'd attempted for the day to all be about me, and instead, it ended up with Slavik invading my time. I didn't even get to have lunch by myself.

The man infuriated me.

Why couldn't he just leave me alone to deal with these feelings I had about him? I still didn't like him.

He was so bossy, and it was proven today with

the way he dragged me off the street. Not that I'd had a whole lot of fun. Maybe I had when it came to handing over his credit card, but the clothes were pointless, as were the lingerie and the shoes. I wasn't the kind of woman to need a new outfit every day. Today was a waste of my time. There were going to be many packages to send back.

I needed to find something to do.

Now I sat in this house, I think it was a house, waiting for him to come back to me.

The scent of cigar smoke and alcohol was heady in the air.

No one was around.

No guard to keep an eye on me.

I'd been playing the good girl role for too long now. Look where it had gotten me. A loveless marriage and a boring life. Still with no friends, but that wasn't a surprise. No matter what I did, no one seemed to like me.

I spun around on the chair and glanced at the furniture. It was all expensive and classy. Getting to my feet, I moved toward the door and opened it. Rebel in the house. There was no guard on the door, and I smiled. Slavik clearly expected me to be good, or he simply didn't care to have another guard wanting to kiss me.

I had no idea where I was.

Nibbling on my lip, I explored, checking out a couple of the rooms, but they were all vacant. Soft music played through the walls. Seductive. Somewhat alluring. I liked it. Still, no one stopped me.

Slavik wasn't there to yell at me.

I set about my newfound freedom and rebellion with relish. Putting my hand on the staircase, I made my way up. Each step gave me a thrill that I was finally fighting back against the chains of my life.

Death had always been a threat.

Life always seemed like a gift and a curse.

Tucking my hair behind my ear, I walked past a couple of doors. I heard moaning. The kind that I imagined couples made. I paused. On instinct, I spun away as if to hide. This was a world I wasn't allowed to be a part of. My only sense was that of duty. I had no other role to play.

I got to the top of the stairs and paused. No. I refused to run and hide. I wanted to know what those noises meant.

Quickly, I made my way back. The doors were all shut until I got to the end of the hall. It was open wide enough for me to see.

The feminine sound echoed around the room, and I felt an answering pulse between my thighs. I couldn't help but press them together. This was arousal. Licking my suddenly dry lips, I focused on the occupants in the room. I saw a woman. With long red hair, she was completely naked, and between her thighs, she was bare. She wasn't alone. A man stood behind her. His hand in her hair. He was naked, like her. I saw his naked body. Not a single mark of ink, but he had chest hair.

I didn't recognize the man or the woman.

"Yes, fuck, just like that, baby," she said.

"Yeah, I can feel how tight you are." He growled and sped up.

All of a sudden, she tugged out of his hold, and she sank down beside him. I saw everything.

His cock was huge, and it was covered in a condom that she pulled off. Then she covered him with her mouth.

He groaned. His hands went into her hair and used it as leverage, forcing her to take his cock.

I heard his moan and hers.

When he pulled her in close and he rocked his

hips fast, she gagged on his length but didn't stop. The woman on the floor grabbed his ass as if she wanted him to go deeper. Tears fell down her eyes, and the man groaned. I watched his neck tense up and then he released her.

The woman sat back, opening her mouth, and then I watched her swallow.

I'd read enough books to know what she'd done. The man looked hypnotized, but he wasn't done yet. He grabbed her, pulling her back up to the bed. Within seconds, his mouth was between her thighs, and the woman in question cried out, begging for more, and then arched up, looking like she was in a state of bliss.

I couldn't move.

The man, once he was done, dropped a kiss to the woman's lips, stood, and gathered his clothes.

"Next week?"

"Yes, next week, and I can't wait."

"Love you, Cara."

I stepped back, but the man stopped when he saw me.

"It's okay, Drake. I'll deal with it."

The woman, Cara, came to the door with a smile on her face. I didn't know what to do. I'd been caught watching them.

My cheeks felt hot to the touch. I was aroused. I'd watched this couple have sex, and I was so wet, it was crazy.

"Hello, Aurora," Cara said. "Come in."

"You know my name?"

"I think I should. I was at your wedding."

"You were?"

Cara laughed. "Of course. It's not every single day I get to see Slavik married. I had to be there."

"You know Slavik?"

"I do. We go way back." Cara began to strip the bed. "Damn, fucking is so much fun, but it does sure get messy."

I looked at the bed. Cara seemed happy.

I was being rebellious today, so I might as well go all in.

"You enjoy … what he did to you?"

Cara turned to me with a smile. "Fucking? Hell, yeah. There is no better feeling in the world than having a man rock-hard inside you." She groaned. "Sorry, I've always been in touch with my inner sex goddess."

I frowned, looking at the bed then at Cara. I'd read about a lot of sex. The times I'd done it with Slavik, well, it wasn't like I was lining up for a repeat performance.

"You have no idea what I'm talking about, do you?"

I wanted to bluff but at the same time, what I'd just seen, was it wrong to want that?

"No."

"Wait, you are Slavik's wife, right?"

"Yes."

Cara snorted. "Wow, leave it to him to leave his woman hanging." She shook her head. "Look, sex can be horrible. I'm not going to lie. With the wrong guy or girl, it can be crap. There's no other word for it, but with the right person, it can be, well, you saw. I personally love it when Drake visits me. He knows what I like, and he's not afraid to give it to me."

I felt like she was talking in riddles.

Her gaze looked me up and down. "The life you've lived, I doubt many men have given you the time of day, have they? You were a virgin, if my memory serves me right."

"Er, yes, I was."

Cara sighed. "I will never understand why women don't help each other out." She tutted. "You know you can take care of yourself, don't you?"

"What do you mean?"

Cara smiled. "Slavik brought this on himself. When you're alone, and you have these same feelings you're experiencing now, touch yourself. We know what we like. Put your hands on your pussy, and stroke, explore. See if you like it hard or soft. You're the only person who is going to give you that kind of pleasure." She moved toward a drawer and retrieved a card. "If you have any kind of questions. Call me."

I took the card she offered. It had a couple of phone numbers.

I went to open my mouth to ask her more questions, but suddenly, my name was being yelled, and I tensed.

"Oh, I'm guessing someone is learning to be naughty. I like it." She winked at me.

I spun on my heel, about to find Slavik, seeing as he seemed intent on waking everyone to find me.

He was at the doorway. His gaze landed on me then on Cara. She'd put a robe on, but she still looked like she'd been having lots of sex.

"Slavik," she said. "Did you take care of your problem?"

"Yes."

He grabbed my arm, and without another word, he pulled me out of the room.

"Ouch!" I tried to tug away from him, but he wouldn't let me. In the end, he pulled me over his shoulder and I was being marched out of the house.

My curiosity hadn't been sated though. I wanted to know more about what I'd just seen. Cara had all the answers to my questions.

It was like I'd been awakened, and now I couldn't just accept living a half-life.

"I want to go and talk to Cara."

"Not happening," he said, growling.

I slammed my fist against his ass. I only got the one shot in as he dumped me into the back of his car.

****

Slavik

My wife would be the death of me. I needed to hire a guard for her and stop bringing her on these trips. One day, they were going to get violent and she'd end up hurt. The truth was … I liked her company.

We didn't talk and I bossed her around, but seeing the way she acted, it was refreshing. The more I annoyed her, the easier it was to read her. She started to let her guard down, and as she did, I liked to play with the woman before me.

I shouldn't be enjoying my woman, but the truth was I did.

This marriage had been a trap. I hadn't wanted to be part of it, but it happened. As the months ticked by, I found myself more enamored by her.

Right now, she was at the bar while I handled the final details of Cara's in-house money trouble.

Ivan had found a pattern, and along with it, the culprit. Brandy—fake name—had come to work for Cara as she had a drug problem. The addiction had been hidden, but the issue came to a tipping point when her dealer wanted more money. We weren't paying her enough, and she'd started to work her way into the system to take the necessary money, stealing from all the men and women working here to pay for her addiction.

It was sad, and she'd been dealt with accordingly.

A knock on the door had me looking up to find Cara scantily dressed as she often was here. She made the additional effort when we arranged business meetings outside of her exclusive club.

"I heard what happened," Cara said. "I had no idea about Brandy."

I looked at Cara. I hadn't told her who the culprit was. I was assuming Ivan told her, but that didn't make much sense since he never came to this establishment.

Being the boss, the leader of us all, he had to hold a certain distance. I often spoke to Ivan on behalf of Cara.

"Prior to hiring any more employees, a full screening will be needed. Drugs, alcohol, anything that raises a flag, they will not be permitted to work here."

"And what if they're hooked on the coke Ivan sells?" Cara asked. "We let them go?"

"Yes."

"Why?" Cara asked.

"I'm not going to talk inner house politics with you. You know the rules. He doesn't want addicts working for him, and to be frank, neither do I. You shouldn't either."

Cara sighed. "You're right. I'm normally a good judge of character. Brandy's threw me."

"Was she a nice girl?"

"The best," Cara said. "She was … a strong person. She had a kid at home, I think." I sat back and watched Cara swipe at her nose and sigh. "Oh, well, you can't help them all, no matter how hard we try."

I raised my brow and she laughed.

"Tell me, Vik, how long have we known each other? Twenty-five years? Nearly thirty?"

"Your point?" I hadn't counted how long I knew this woman. I'd known Ivan longer. Cara had come into our life a little later.

"I don't know, I guess I always imagined that

you'd be the kind of guy who would know how to satisfy their woman."

I tensed up. "What's your fucking point?"

Cara closed the door, flicking the lock into place, then came toward me. She leaned over the desk, grabbing a single remote.

A television screen in the far corner flickered on.

It was a recording.

I recognized my wife instantly.

Next, the volume went up.

"Did you touch your pussy?" Cara asked.

"Er, I don't feel comfortable with this." Aurora glanced around the room.

I turned to look at Cara. "When was this?"

"About twenty minutes ago. Keep watching."

On the screen, Cara approached my wife. She was a good foot taller, but she always preferred to wear heels while Aurora wore pumps.

"I know you touched yourself, and I know you didn't allow yourself to come." Cara touched Aurora's arms, and she tensed up. "Relax. Have you ever thought about going to Vik, asking him to touch you?"

"He wouldn't want to."

Cara tutted. "You're so very wrong about that."

She lifted the remote and hit *pause*. "You've been married nearly ten months now, right?"

"Eight."

"Either way, that girl hasn't had an orgasm by you. Not a single one. Are you like brain dead? Do you want to be in a loveless marriage? The whole peace-treaty thing is real. No war. No shit going on in the streets and yet, you're not giving the woman who will one day have your children an orgasm?"

Before I argued with her, she pressed *play*.

Pissed off, I turned to the screen. If Cara had been

anyone else, I'd have already killed her.

"Slavik can't stand me. I think he's trying to figure out a way to kill me."

Cara paused, and her gaze actually focused on the camera. *"Come with me."*

I watched as Cara led Aurora to the bed. She slipped off her pumps and sat down. She'd been wearing a wraparound skirt, and as she sat, the skirt fell open.

Cara moved on the bed. *"Close your eyes."*

"What are you going to do?"

"Trust me."

Aurora hesitated and slowly closed her eyes.

Cara cupped Aurora between the thighs, and my wife jolted in her touch.

"I know this is going to seem a little strange. I'm only trying to help you."

"I'm not sure about this."

Cara flicked her tongue across Aurora's neck, nibbling on the delicate flesh.

"Trust me. I want to know if you're ... healthy. Make sure there is nothing wrong with you."

"Do you think there could be something wrong with me?"

Anger ran up through my body. There was nothing wrong with my wife, and as I sat there, I watched as Cara moved the skirt out of the way, sliding her panties to one side, and began to finger my wife's pussy. All the while, she whispered words to her. Words I didn't hear because I was infuriated.

She'd touched my beautiful wife, and I had no choice but to watch as she brought Aurora to orgasm.

The sight alone was enough to turn me on. My cock pulsed to life. She let go completely, rubbing herself against Cara's fingers.

"Slavik will kill me," Aurora said, coming down

from the high.

"No, he won't."

Cara turned off the television. "I'm all for taking a woman's cherry, but I took your wife's first orgasm. A job you should be doing. Are you trying to make this harder than it is?"

"Cara, I suggest you shut the fuck up because right now, I really want to fucking kill you."

"For making your wife see that she can have an orgasm. I saw her the other week when you were here, and she watched me, you know. Watched me get fucked, and I'd never seen a woman with so much yearning. What the fuck are you doing? Just bending her over and taking your pleasure?"

I wasn't about to tell her I'd been taking care of my own needs in the shower.

Women were around me all the time, every single day. None of them appealed. Nor did forcing my wife to fuck.

I stood up. "She's not like us."

"No, she's not, but that doesn't mean she doesn't want to feel passion. There's something about Aurora. I don't know if it's because she wears her heart on her sleeve, or if she's been hurt. But she's different. I get that, and if you actually gave it a chance with her, I truly believe you could love her. Really love her."

I get to my feet, slamming the ledger closed. "We're done here."

"You know there's no shame in finding her attractive or wanting her," Cara said. "She's not the enemy. I see the ink on her wrist. She is bound to the Ivan Volkov Bratva. She is yours. Why don't you enjoy it while it lasts? One day when she realizes the monster you are, you won't get a second chance."

What Cara didn't know was that Aurora already

knew the monster I was. She'd seen it. I hadn't tried to hide it from her either.

I found Aurora downstairs. She sat at the bar as I'd hoped she would be the first time we came here.

The moment I cleared my voice, she stood, and I saw the pinkness in her cheeks. She quickly averted her gaze. Rather than put her at ease, I took her hand, leading her out to the car. The driver was already waiting.

I told him to take us home, and I sat back. I still held her hand.

"Slavik, I need to tell you something."

"No."

"Please."

"No. Not until we get home."

I pulled out my cell phone, ending the conversation. I sent an email to Ivan with an update, checked through my mail to make sure I hadn't missed anything, and pocketed my cell.

The city was busy today, and the journey to our apartment took longer than I expected.

By the time we stood in the elevator, Aurora shook.

I held her hand still, refusing to let her go.

Once on our floor, I told the guard to leave. I didn't want him hanging around while I *talked* to my wife.

I closed the door, finally releasing Aurora's hand, and she spun toward me.

"Slavik, I need to tell you something. I don't want you to be angry."

"I want you to go to our bedroom, strip completely naked, lie down on the bed, and spread your legs."

"What?"

"I don't make a habit of repeating myself. Do it."

Aurora paled, but she turned on her heel and left.

I removed my jacket, hanging it up on the peg. I kicked off my shoes.

Walking into my bedroom, I placed the gun and the holster on the chair. I had weapons all over the apartment in the event of a break-in. In the past forty years, I'd only been caught once without a weapon, and I held the scars to prove it.

I kept my back to Aurora, opening the button at my cuff, rolling each sleeve up, and then I turned.

The first thing I noticed was her hands. They were clenched into fists.

"I know Cara touched you. She touched what belonged to me. She showed me the video."

"I'm so sorry," Aurora said. "I didn't want to."

"I know what I saw, and Cara has a way of making people do what she wants." I moved toward the bed. "However, she had a very valid point." I reached out and grabbed her ankles, dragging her down the bed until she was close to the edge.

I saw the flash of fear in her eyes, but she didn't beg me to stop.

I stared at her, seeing the nerves and knowing I'd caused this.

With my fingers on her ankles, I kept my gaze on hers, not rushing.

Her body was a dream. Large tits, full thighs and hips. She made me ache. I hadn't been with anyone else but her, and we hadn't been having sex regularly, and the truth was, my balls were blue. I wanted to fuck her more than anything else in the world.

"Slavik?"

"Watching you with Cara, I realized I hadn't been giving you the attention you deserved."

"Don't hurt me."

"I'm not going to." I stroked from her ankle up to her knee and back down again. Sinking to my knees, I pulled her so she spread open, and her pussy was so close to my mouth.

Running my hands up her thighs, I squeezed the flesh.

"If you don't like this, ask me to stop."

I placed my hands near her pussy and spread the lips open. On our wedding night, she'd been bare, but as the days had gone, some hair had returned. I didn't mind.

Her cunt looked dry.

Fear captured her at this time.

This was all my fault, but I'd rectify that.

Holding her open, I slid my tongue across her clit. The first touch had her jolting upright.

"What was that?"

I looked up at her and smiled. "I'm going to lick this pussy until you come all over my face."

"You don't have to do that."

"I want to. Lie back."

"Slavik?"

"Have a little trust. I haven't hurt you, have I?"

I knew she replayed that night when I could have taken her against her will, but I didn't.

Slowly, she leaned back on the bed, and this time, I slid my tongue across and I didn't pull back. I worked back and forth, circling her clit before taking her into my mouth. She cried out, but it wasn't in pain.

I kept my touches light.

She'd never felt this touch from a man, and I did everything I could to make it as easy on her as possible.

Her moans echoed around the room, and my cock tightened to an unbearable length. I hadn't sucked a woman's cunt in a really long time. I'd avoided it because I didn't know where else they'd been, and to be honest, no woman interested me enough to even want to do it.

Sliding my tongue all over her pussy, I teased back and forth, going down to her entrance and plunging inside.

I'd been the only cock in her pussy.

My cum.

All me.

And that sent a fucking thrill of possession rushing through me. I couldn't get enough, and I tasted her sweetness. Moaning as she flooded my mouth.

Her cream building.

Finally, my wife was fucking aroused. Not only that, but she'd stopped lying still and her pelvis thrust against me. Offering up her pretty pussy as I licked her.

Grabbing her ass, I pressed my face against her and licked and sucked at her cunt, driving my tongue in deep, fucking her, drawing up to tongue her clit, then back down again.

I felt how close she was by the pulsing of her pussy.

Focusing back on her nub, I tongued her clit, and with each stroke, her body rocked against me.

The moment she came, I held her down even as her screams of release filled the air. I tongued her pussy until she shuddered and pleaded for me to stop.

I pressed a kiss to her swollen clit and sat back.

My face was covered in her cream.

"From now on, there is no more hiding."

Chapter Ten

Aurora

"From now on, there is no more hiding."

Slavik's words echoed in my head as I stared down at him.

Two orgasms in one day, but this one with Slavik had been … the best. Cara's touch had made me nervous.

She was a nice woman and very attractive, but I'd felt strange with her touch. Slavik was right.

It wasn't because she was a woman. It was because she wasn't mine.

"You're not angry?" I asked.

"Why would I be angry?"

"I … you said…" I truly didn't know how to finish my sentence.

One moment I'd been talking to Cara, the next I was on the bed, her hand between my thighs, showing me. Telling me how to please myself and how every woman had the right to know the key to her own pleasure.

I'd been so overwhelmed. I hadn't been sure if this was cheating.

"Cara is not allowed to touch you. I'll let today slide, but no more. She touches you again, I won't be held responsible for my actions."

"I'm not sure what to do right now," Aurora said. She nibbled on her lip. "I've read all about … everything. But what about you?"

Slavik and I were married, but our relationship wasn't anything like in the books I read.

He stroked my thighs and I had to wonder if they were large compared to the other women he was with. Did he hate my size?

Why did I even care?

I hadn't stopped my mission to lose weight. Being out with Slavik every day had really put a wrench in my plans of weight loss.

He stood up, and I looked at him, a little unsure as he tugged his shirt off, displaying the large expanse of his heavily inked chest. I couldn't resist licking my lips, and I felt an answering pull between my thighs. I was soaking wet. I'd never felt like this. Some of the books I read aroused me, but never like this. This was all new to me.

He grabbed his belt, loosening the buckle. The sound of clinking metal, followed by the zipper, turned me on.

His pants hit the floor, along with his boxers, and he stood before me naked. The hard length of his cock jutted out, long and thick.

I wanted to touch him. I kept my hands to myself.

He wrapped his fingers around his dick and began to work from the base up to the tip, then back down again.

"Lie back down," he said.

I lay on the bed and spread my legs. This was what I did on our wedding night.

The bed dipped down, and I couldn't help but tense up.

"On our wedding night, I was an asshole. I didn't like that I had to give them the sheets after I had you." He kissed my thigh and I jolted.

Opening my eyes—I hadn't even realized I'd closed them—I stared up at him, waiting.

He moved between my thighs, and I held myself perfectly still.

"I didn't get you to enjoy it and that's my fault. The next time, you were completely dry and I used lubrication." He reached down between us and I felt the hard tip of his cock as it brushed between my slit.

He nudged my clit, and I couldn't contain my gasp as he touched just the right spot, causing me to arch up.

"Today, there is going to be no need for lube. No dirty bastards waiting to see the evidence of your virginity." He placed the tip at my entrance, and I paused. "And no pain either."

He slammed to the hilt inside me. I'd been expecting the pain, but nothing came.

No tear.

No hurt.

Just the hard tip of him sliding inside me, and it felt amazing.

Slavik smiled down at me. "And this is how it's going to be."

He pulled out of me until only the tip of him remained before plunging back inside, fucking me hard and fast. After a few thrusts, he stopped, holding himself deep within me.

Neither of us said a word. I couldn't look away from him nor did I want to. This was so different from anything else I'd ever experienced. Slavik surrounded me and filled me in ways I didn't think were possible.

Consumed.

Delighted.

I felt his hands on my hips, holding me still as he pulled out of me. "Watch me."

There was nothing dirty within those words and yet, I felt hot all over.

I stared down at where he held himself deep within me. The length of him was naked, covered with my arousal.

Biting my lip, I try to contain my pleasured cries as he pounded within me.

One. Two. Three. Four. He fucked me hard. The bed hitting the wall with the force of the thrusts.

He put his hands on my shoulders, pinning me to the bed.

"Wrap your legs around me."

I circled his waist and the depth took my breath away. He was big, but I hadn't realized how much. Each time we'd had sex, I wished it would end. Not today.

The way he rode my body, driving in deep, I couldn't think.

"Fuck, baby. That's it."

I didn't know what he expected from me, but I couldn't look away. The way he stared at me. The sheer power of his body as he drove inside me. He plunged inside one final time, and I felt each pulse as he came inside me.

This time, he stayed within me. His touch lightened and he stayed over me. He opened his eyes. There was no desire to look away. No hatred.

This was sex.

I … had no idea it could be this way.

We were both panting.

He leaned to the side, but his cock was still deep within me. "You want to be fucked?"

It wasn't the most romantic way to end a sexual encounter.

"Don't you want to leave?" I frowned.

"No."

His cock had gotten soft, but even flaccid, I felt him. This was … strange.

"I, I don't know what I want."

"You wanted sex. I saw the way you were with Cara. You're not afraid."

"She was a woman, and to be honest, I didn't know what she was doing until afterward. I enjoyed it too much to make it stop." I covered my face with my hands. Was this a normal conversation to be had?

"I thought you were afraid and didn't want sex."

"What?"

"Our wedding night and the time after."

"We've been married for eight months. You didn't think to, I don't know, tell me it could be better between us? It's not like I've got some kind of roadmap for this. I don't know what I'm doing. Everything I know is from the books I read and the classes I took at school." Even then there hadn't been a whole lot of information. My mom had always been vague about what went on between a man and woman.

The books made me yearn for something more. Not an abusive relationship. I witnessed that between my parents. I wished for something better.

Slavik cupped my cheek, turning me to face him. "Talk to me."

"How?"

"Use your words."

I burst out laughing. "Isn't that what they say to kids?"

"You're behaving like one."

"We just had sex. You don't want to be thinking of me as a kid," I said. This was bizarre. Was this a normal conversation between a man and wife?

"What are you thinking about right now?"

"My thoughts are private."

"Not from me." His thumb grazing across my cheek.

"You're not mad at me?"

"No."

"Cara did say you were best friends. Have you ever been … together?"

"God, no. Ugh. So fucking disgusting. I get that

she loves sex and she runs one of the best damn brothels in the city, but no. She's a friend and a colleague. Nothing more."

"Wait? A brothel?"

He laughed. "You didn't figure that out."

"No!" I drew out the *o*. "How?"

"There are men and women, and if you've got the right price, you can have anything you want within reason. People are addicted to what they can't have and others find a way of putting a price on what they want. Sex is one of those products. Kind of like drugs. You get a taste and you can't stop."

"I can't believe I was in a brothel. Does that mean I owe her money?"

"It was free of charge."

"That's not funny."

"If you're me, it's hilarious."

"I don't think you're funny at all."

He winked at me and I couldn't help but smile.

"This is nice," I said.

"What?"

"Talking. Not being afraid to say the wrong thing."

"I scare you that much?"

"No. I think this life scares me that much." I shrugged. "People die. Men, women, children, it's all part of this world. There are times I sit and wonder what it would be like to be a normal person. How they can go out and live their lives. Be free."

"You are free."

I averted my gaze.

"Why don't you feel free?"

"I couldn't even go on a shopping trip. You're always around," I said. "You're waiting to find me a guard." I blew out a breath. "College was a big no as well."

"You wanted to go to college?"

I nodded. "My dad said no."

"What would you have studied?"

"Business, I think. I like numbers. English as well. I love to read."

"You've done a lot of reading while you've been here."

"True, but then I haven't done anything else."

He stroked a curl back from my face. Slavik didn't look as dangerous or as scary as he stroked my cheek. I started to feel his cock swell inside me.

As she touched me, Cara had told me to be honest with Slavik. He needed to know what I wanted in order for him to be able to give it to me.

Staring at him now, he no longer seemed scary.

"I don't want to hate this marriage," I said. "I … I don't want you to hate coming home or to regret marrying me."

"I don't regret it."

"I know it's the peace treaty, but I know I'm not your first choice. Do you think it would be possible to make this work?"

He stayed silent.

Had I made a mistake?

Had Cara given me really bad advice?

I felt sick.

Panic flooded me.

"Touch me," he said.

"What?"

"I don't like to repeat myself."

I rolled my eyes and put my hand flat on his chest. I felt the scars beneath the ink and I waited.

"I don't want to hate this marriage either," he said. "How do you suggest we change this path that we're on?"

"We … on our dates, you don't look at your cell phone. You talk to me. We communicate through words."

"I can do that."

"I…" I held up my wrist. "I'm loyal to you. To Volkov. Is there any way you can trust me?"

Slavik stared at my wrist and said nothing.

I knew it was a long shot.

Why would he trust the woman he married? I wasn't a choice for him. He didn't care about me. I was just another job to him. One he needed to keep alive because his boss told him to.

This was never going to work, and I was a fool for believing it would.

He took my hand and pressed a kiss to my inner wrist. "Trust is earned."

"You expect me to trust you? You haven't earned it."

"Yes, I have."

"How?"

"I never once hurt you. Sex does not count. I could have hurt you, but I didn't."

"You took me to your boss in order to torture me at the attack on the benefit," I said.

"You were there to be questioned, not tortured."

"I have to earn everything with you?" I asked.

"Yes."

"This isn't fair."

He shrugged.

Silence rang between us.

The orgasm he'd given me, the sex, it all seemed empty, hollow. "You want to have a crap marriage?"

"No," he said. "You didn't marry a fool, Aurora. I don't give an inch for anyone. You want my trust, you earn it. You want me to believe a single word you say, don't lie to me. I'm willing to work to make this marriage between us bearable, but don't for a second think you will get a submissive man. It will never happen."

With that, he pulled out of me.

I felt his release leak out of me as I watched him walk away.

Tears spilled from my eyes and I hated myself for caring. Cara had been wrong.

Slavik and I couldn't make this work. Neither of us had anything in common. He'd gotten what he wanted, and now, I was back to being the irritating wife.

****

Slavik

I stared around at the carnage before me, pissed off. While I'd been fucking my wife, one of my most prestigious nightclubs, Shiver, had been attacked. There were three dead bodies, several injured, and now I was enraged.

Shiver was a civilian club to the outside world. No link to us, dealt with through a company of a company until you got to me, the owner.

This was where we handled some of the coke we distributed, but it was never within the walls of the club. We kept out illegal businesses running side by side and within the restrictions of the law.

No one thought to attack this place. This was private business. Only those closest to me knew about this, unless someone had talked and gotten sloppy.

With my hands on my hips, I knew the cop on my payroll wanted to talk to me. I nodded my head toward the back of my office. Daniel was a good guy. His kid got diagnosed with cancer five years ago. I saw an opportunity and took it. His salary didn't pay for the extensive treatment his son needed, and well, we came to an arrangement.

Arms folded, I waited as he closed the door.

"What do we have?"

"All the witness reports are unclear. Several men enter the establishment at approximately ten o'clock, and they start firing. Your barman is the first victim."

I made a mental note to deal with the family.

Ricky was a good guy. A family man and loyal. He'd been manning this bar ever since it opened ten years ago. He'd always been the first one to call when anything fishy was happening, which told me this attack was designed to look random but with the missing coke, it wasn't.

"The next two victims?"

"Women in their early twenties. They were out looking for a good time. Neither of them are related to your work."

I rubbed at my chin. "So we've got three dead people, many injured, and a busted-up nightclub."

"Is there anything else you need to report?" Daniel asked.

"Nothing you need to know."

"Look, Mr. Ivanov, this is pretty serious. I know you have your … company problems, but this might be completely random. This place isn't even associated with you."

He chuckled, but I felt no humor. "You know when you're a kid growing up and there's something you want? A cookie, a video game, some shit like that."

"Your point?"

"When you try to get mommy's and daddy's attention to buy you that, you talk about anything but that, right. Until they finally turn around and say, what do you want, sweetie?" I kept my voice low.

"What do you want me to do?"

I folded my arms. "I want the security footage for outside on the street."

"Mr. Ivanov, you know I don't have that authority."

"Then find someone who does, but I want a copy. I need to see what I'm dealing with here."

Daniel didn't look happy about it, and the truth was, neither did I. The little elitist group of soldiers hadn't attacked in a while, but why here, why now? None of it made any sense.

"Are you sure there's nothing I can do for you now?" he asked.

"No." I needed those security tapes.

"I don't like this, Mr. Ivanov."

"I don't pay you to like it. How is your son?" It was the fastest way to get him to leave. Daniel left the room to join the rest of his men working through my nightclub.

My cell phone rang, and I pulled it out to see Cara was calling me. I stared at the call for several seconds before finally picking it up.

"Hello," I said.

"Hey, you. I wanted to check in. See how you were," Cara said.

"Why?"

"I don't know. I'm a curious woman, you know."

"Cara, you haven't called to check up on me in nearly fifteen years. Is there a problem?"

"No, no problem. I wanted to see how my best friend was doing."

I looked around my office, suspicion rising up inside me.

"I don't want you touching my woman ever again, do you hear me?"

"Ah, we're back to that. Did you at least heed my advice? Did you make her yours? Showed her what a real man could do?"

"I'm busy right now, Cara." I hung up my cell phone and sent a quick email off to the private alerts for Ivan Volkov and the rest of the brigadiers to alert them of a possible impending attack.

With nothing in my office to keep my attention, I made my way out to the main floor where most of the damage seemed to have taken place.

I moved to the bar and looked around. Moving up and down the length, I checked out the entrance point, but from the bar, there was no direct shot of everyone coming in or out.

Then I realized the men coming in to attack didn't get through the front. My men were on the doors, and I hadn't gotten the chance to talk to them yet as the cops were taking their sweet time asking all the questions.

On the way past a forensic person, I stole a glove, sliding it on my hand. No one bothered me. I was merely the owner walking around. I checked the door and ran my hand across the lock.

The door had been pried open, and when I glanced down, I saw the crowbar. The people who attacked my club were sloppy. Why attack and not take their weapon of choice? Rather than give it to the police, I placed the crowbar out of sight with the intention of giving it to my own personal analyst.

I had more faith in the men I paid for than the cops assigned to help me out.

The room they came into was the storage room.

I followed the path and came to another door, which was even more interesting. This one wasn't pried open. This one appeared to have been opened with a single flick of the wrist, which I did, and stepped out.

The scent of cigarette smoke assailed my senses. I never smoked, and as I looked at the shaking woman who immediately stood, my nerves went to an all-time high.

"You shouldn't be out here. The cops are going to want to interview you."

"Have they talked to you?"

"No. I didn't see anything. I was dealing with inventory, you know."

I stepped a little closer, and this time, the woman whose name badge labeled her as Casey, tried to run. She dropped her cigarette as I wrapped my fingers around her throat and pressed her up against the wall.

"Please, don't kill me. I don't want to die. Please. Please."

Her sobbing filled the air, irritating me. She wasn't sorry for what she'd done.

"Why don't you tell me what is going on right now?" I asked. I was calm.

"I don't know anything. I swear, I don't."

I shoved her up against the wall, squeezing her throat tightly. She tried to claw at my wrists, but her nails had been so chewed down, she couldn't even leave a scratch. It would be so easy to watch her die. I didn't need her. She was the cause of three deaths.

But I needed information.

Releasing her neck long enough to let her breathe, I continued to stare at her as she whimpered and moaned.

"Please. Please," she said. "I don't want to die."

"Then why don't you start talking? Give me enough information, you'll live. You don't, well, we know what is going to happen to you."

She whimpered. "I … they didn't say what they were going to do. All I was supposed to do was open the door, that was all. I opened the door and I got my daughter back. I'm trying to be clean, but it was so easy."

"What's so easy?" I asked.

"All I have to do is fuck who they say and I get the money and the coke, and I … I did really well, I promise. I said no. I wanted my daughter back but, but, they found me, and they fed me and I remembered how good it was." She covered her face with her hands.

This woman was an addict and someone had gotten her hooked back on the dope.

"Is it mine?" I asked.

"The kid?"

I frowned. I'd never sleep with a woman like this. So helpless, mainly useless. "No, the dope."

"I don't know. I just know it's so good and after I've done what I've done, it makes everything so easy." She smiled as if she was in some fairytale land. "My kid is better off without me. She doesn't need me. I'm a failure. I want my own life. I never wanted to get pregnant. You can hurt me all you want, but I only have a couple of text messages that told me what to do. I didn't break any law." Her sobbing turned into aggression.

"Give me your cell phone," I said.

She scrambled on her person, handing me the phone. With my hand over her mouth and nose, I didn't hesitate or stop. I cut off her air and watched this woman slowly die, feeling nothing.

She crumpled to the ground, and I pulled out my cell phone, making a call. With the cops so close, I should have waited, but I wasn't a patient man when it came to getting rid of a problem, and this woman was a problem.

With her cell phone in my pocket, I checked the time and saw it was now a little after midnight.

My thoughts drifted to Aurora. When I got the

call to come down to Shiver, we hadn't spoken since I told her I wouldn't be a submissive man. There was no way I was going to trust her so easily.

"You expect me to trust you? You haven't earned it."

How have I not earned her trust? She wasn't dead, and it pissed me off for her to even think to doubt me. I'd been good to her, more than good.

Anger flooded me.

This was why I didn't want to get close to the woman. She got under my skin and pissed me off. This wasn't the time and place to be analyzing the shit we'd said to each other, and yet, here I was, thinking about it.

By the time my guy arrived, he was on his own, in the smallest van we owned. I helped him to pick up the body, throwing it into the back.

"Run dental records, or whatever shit you need. She mentioned something about a kid. I want to know everything about this woman as soon as you can."

The man nodded and left the scene.

With that, rather than go through the storage room, I made my way out of the back alley, onto the street. My car was parked around the other side. Standing on the pavement near my bar, I looked around.

There were so many avenues the men could have come from. I knew for certain they hadn't come through the front.

Who would take this much time to find the right opportunity to attack this club? The woman I'd just killed had been purposefully chosen because of her working here, preyed upon, and hooked back on the drugs.

It never took long to get an addict back on what they considered a lifeline.

The question was why?

Why go to so much effort?

I understood it, but if you wanted to attack a

nightclub, why not go from the front? This was personal, and I just didn't see the connection.

Chapter Eleven

Aurora

Two days later

I was in the library of the apartment building when I heard the front door open and close. I held a book I'd been trying to read for a few months, but each time I did, the words blurred together.

I put the book down on the small table that held my empty coffee cup, and got to my feet.

Slavik hadn't been back home ever since he got that call. We'd shared one incredible night together, and it felt like he'd been avoiding me. I knew he wasn't. There was no reason for him to.

I grabbed the cup, heading out to find Slavik hanging up the cell phone. He was covered in blood, and I saw a lot of it coming from his side.

"What happened?" I asked.

He looked at me. "Most of it isn't mine."

"That doesn't make it right."

I rushed to the kitchen, looking through the cupboards, trying to find the emergency first-aid kit.

"What are you doing?" he asked, stood in the doorway.

"I'm looking for the first-aid kit. Where is it? Surely you keep one around."

He chuckled. "It's in the bathroom."

I grabbed his arm as I brushed past him, not allowing him to leave my sight until I got him clean.

If I had to, I'd call a doctor. Not that I knew a good one. Since I'd been his wife, he hadn't given me the chance to have all the necessary contact details I needed. Who to call in the event of an emergency and where to go.

"Sit." I pushed him onto the toilet seat and looked

through the cupboards, finding what I needed. "Remove your shirt."

"If you wanted me naked, Aurora, all you've got to do is ask. This show of caring is sweet."

"You think this is a show?"

"What else could it be?"

The urge to slap him was strong, but I felt I should be getting some extra good points for not hurting him. He'd deserve it.

With his jacket off, he worked at the buttons, and I quickly slapped his hands out of the way. Even though he was the one shot, my hands shook as I released each button. The moment I started, Slavik didn't stop me.

He was calm. I was not.

There was so much blood.

"Let me guess, I should see the other guy?" I asked.

"A joke, funny," he said.

"You didn't laugh. It couldn't be that funny."

"The other guy isn't laughing. The other five men are not laughing."

"Five? You were attacked by five men?"

He shrugged.

"Please tell me no one else was hurt."

"You care more about people you don't know than your husband, Aurora?"

"I care … about you." I wasn't sure why. It wasn't like we'd talked or anything.

He had given me one night, and in the past few days, I'd thought nonstop about it. About him. About us.

Sex wasn't everything, and it had somehow dragged me into its mystical web of need. This shouldn't even bother me.

"You do?" he asked.

"Yes, you know I do." I filled the sink with warm

water, grabbing a cloth to wipe away the dried blood. "You got shot."

"How far does this caring go? I'm curious."

I glanced into his eyes to find him watching me. "It's nothing too serious. A lot of people care about each other. It's not important."

"I have a feeling you caring about me, Aurora, is important."

"You're my husband. I'm supposed to care about you."

"No, you don't. We both know your father gave you to me because he didn't care what happened to you."

I flinched. I couldn't help it.

I was very much aware of what my father had done. "What does that make you?" I asked. "Willing to take a daughter who is only second best? He didn't think you were good enough for his favorite daughter?"

Slavik reached up and touched the scar above my right eyebrow. It was a faint line and had happened so long ago.

"Your family strives on perfection. What happened to cause this little scar on a perfect face?"

"I'm not perfect."

"Your face is flawless, Aurora. Smooth. Soft. You're a beautiful woman."

"I'm not beautiful."

"Tell me about the scar."

I'd never told anyone about my scar. No one had cared.

"It's nothing."

"I'm your husband."

"And you're demanding to know the truth?"

"Yes."

I sighed. The excess blood had been cleaned off his body, and now I had to deal with the wound caused by the bullet. "Don't you want to go to the hospital?"

"It's a graze. I've got everything here I need."

I slapped his hand away and started to rummage through the first aid kit, finding the sterile wipes.

"Tell me," he said.

I got to work on cleaning his wound. The sight of it alone made me feel sick. If it was me, I'd be screaming and crying out in agony. Even as I cleaned it with the sterile wipe, Slavik didn't seem to notice the pain.

It was kind of scary how he was able to take so much.

With the area clean, I looked through the kit and he took over, pulling out a packet with a needle, as well as something that looked like thread.

"You need to sew it together. I'll instruct you."

"I'm not a doctor or a nurse."

"I don't need either. I'll tell you how to do it."

He took the needle and thread, which it wasn't, but I had no idea what the medical term was for it. For all I knew, it was needle and thread.

When he went to insert it into his flesh, I cried out. "Don't you need to take anything?"

"I can handle it. I'm just getting you started."

I winced as he pierced his flesh. He released a grunt and once he finished securing the first stitch, he waited for me.

"You're not going to hurt me."

I highly doubted that.

On my knees between his spread thighs, I worked slowly, trying not to hurt him, but each time I touched the skin, I wanted to vomit. I'd put on a pair of gloves to try to keep the wound clean. He should have called a doctor.

"It hurts, Aurora. Tell me how you got the scar."

"You're saying that to manipulate me."

"Is it working?"

"I got the scar when I was six or seven. I'm not sure exactly what age. Isabella had been out playing in the yard. She liked to play outside. I think she had a thing for the guards watching her. I'm not sure. She was always around them." I shrugged.

"Where were you?"

"In the library. My father has a giant room. He never reads them. Just seeks out the most expensive titles so no one else can have them. He stores them and I spent most of my childhood reading them."

"If you weren't playing, how did you get the scar?"

"Isabelle decided to start throwing stones at the house. I don't know why. I think she was angry because she'd been told no. One of the stones went through my father's window. He got me and Isabella into the same room and because he didn't want to punish his precious daughter, he slammed me around the back of the head, hard. I fell and I hit the corner of a cupboard. That's how I got the scar." I remember the pain from the blow. He'd always hit me. My father believed in physical punishments. I'd been belted, slapped, even kicked during my time at home.

Slavik's hands clenched.

"Is it hurting?"

"Did Isabella get you punished a lot?"

"Not always. She struggled to be … good. She had a wild side, and each time he hit me or took it out on me, she'd come and sit with me after, read. Marrying you is the first time she hasn't come to console me." I offered him a smile.

"Being married to me shouldn't be a punishment," he said.

"It's not." There was freedom with being with

him. Not a whole lot but at least I didn't have to worry about my sister's punishments anymore.

"You'll never get hit here," he said.

"You don't have to worry about it. You asked and I told you."

"And now I want to go and beat the shit out of your father."

I frowned. "Why?"

"For hurting you and treating you like shit."

A chuckle escaped my lips. "I've been treated like shit my whole life. There's nothing you can do about it."

"You've gotten so used to it, you're expecting it?" he asked.

I shrugged. "Let's just say I've gotten used to certain treatment. How do I finish this off?"

Slavik told me as I still reeled from our very normal conversation. I think it was the first time we spoke to each other without sex or anger being involved.

After finishing off the stitching, I covered his wound with a large bandage, using some tape to secure it in place. Pleased with my handiwork, I stood, gathering the used pieces of equipment.

Slavik grabbed his shirt.

"Do you want me to cook you something?" I asked. I didn't even know why I did. Every other meal I'd cooked for him had gone uneaten or in the trash. The day after, I'd seen the plate full of food in a pile as if it had just been slid right in without a single taste.

It had cut me.

"You can cook?" he asked.

"Yes. I've … I left you food out before. I gave you a note or something."

"I never saw it," Slavik said.

"What?"

"I never saw any meal waiting for me. It's why I started eating out or I made myself a sandwich."

"But all the food was dumped into the trash. I'd make myself and Sergei food, and I'd leave your plate in the oven. There was always a note." I paused and then looked away.

"Sergei," Slavik said. "He dumped my food in the trash. I had no idea you'd cooked for me, Aurora. I didn't even know you could cook."

"I can. I mean, I do cook. I don't know if I'm any good." I offered him a smile. He chuckled. "I'm sorry. I had no idea Sergei would do that."

"Sergei would do anything to win your heart. I can see that."

My mind replayed the moment he killed him. It was odd as I'd always felt sad about that moment. Knowing Sergei had done that, I was so annoyed. My marriage had been difficult from the start, and each time I attempted to make it easier, someone else came in and made it even harder.

Anger filled me as I turned to walk out of the bathroom.

Slavik grabbed my arm and tugged me close to him. I didn't have time to question what he was doing as his lips brushed across mine. I knew he was in pain and didn't touch his side as I kissed him back.

I liked his lips on mine, slowly growing addicted to his kisses. They always started out slow, tender, only to build to an inferno that consumed me. As he traced his tongue across my lips, everything faded into the background. There was no care in the world other than his lips on mine. I needed him, and I pressed my body against his, trying to get as close to him as possible.

Fire flooded my body.

Need pulsed between my thighs.

Everything was heightened.

I was hungry for more.

Desperate.

Just as suddenly as it all started, he pulled away, leaving me empty.

It was time to go and make food. Without a word, I left the bathroom, needing the space. I touched my swollen lips as I entered the kitchen.

It was just a kiss. To me, it felt like so much more, and I knew I wasn't going to be able to stop thinking about it.

****

Slavik

I cleaned up without getting the bandage wet.

Aurora's stitching had fucking hurt. I'd forgotten how painful it could be, but there was no reason to phone the fucking doctor or go to the hospital. They were a persona and place I tried to avoid. Besides, I had a very high pain threshold. It took a lot to get to me.

I left the bathroom, drying my body and changing into a pair of sweatpants and a shirt. I followed the scents coming from the kitchen, and I didn't alert Aurora to my presence as she worked. She chopped onions and garlic, putting them in a pan, sprinkling in some herbs and spices as she did.

Mesmerized by the way she moved in the kitchen, I thought about what she said earlier, about feeding me. When I'd asked Sergei what she had to eat, he told me she cooked for herself, but no one else.

My anger at the asshole I'd killed was renewed. I wished he was alive so I could have killed him again. Not only that, I'd have made him see who Aurora belonged to. She was mine. No one else's, and I was frustrated to know he died without me driving that point home.

I'd never considered myself a possessive person, not when it came to a woman. My turf I defended violently, keeping it belonging to me and in turn, part of Volkov's terrain. Women came and went. As a young man, I'd fucked my way through so much pussy. None of them had any faces. It had all been about getting myself off, and for them, it was about taking on the Volkov's meanest fucking brigadier. I was a badge to them, a title.

When Ivan told me I needed to get married for an alliance, I'd been happy to do it. I'd never intended to be faithful to my wife, or think about her.

Aurora had come as a huge surprise to me in so many ways. First, my desire for other women had faded. Even while we hadn't been having sex but had been married, I hadn't looked at anyone else. I hadn't cared to. Women had tried to capture my attention, but I'd ignored them. Each time they did, Aurora's face would flash in my head, and any desire for anyone or anything else faded.

It meant nothing to me.

Aurora opened a can of tomatoes, adding them to the pan, stirring, followed by some water from the kettle. She went to the cupboard, and I liked seeing her at home in the kitchen. The way she turned and worked. This was her home.

She had another pot boiling and I saw the packet of pasta on the counter.

I entered the room, alerting her to my presence, and she spun around with a smile. "You know I was just thinking, I don't have a clue what you like or don't like. I'm assuming you love pasta. I love it."

"I like pasta," I said, taking a seat, being careful not to pull the stitches. Tonight would hurt like a motherfucker, but tomorrow, I'd have no choice but to go back out there.

Aurora winced as she watched me. “Do you need to talk about it?”

“No.”

“Oh, well, Cara called a couple of hours ago,” she said.

I tensed up. “She did?”

“Yeah, she wanted to go out to lunch. At first, she said you wouldn’t mind, but then I recalled what you said about me going out or being alone with her again.” Aurora turned toward me. “Lunch would be safe, right?”

“Why do you want to go to lunch with her?”

She shrugged but her face went bright red. That was not the sign of a woman who didn’t know why she didn’t want to go.

“I just, I like her, and I think she’s nice.”

“Cara’s not nice,” I said. I didn’t want my wife going to lunch with Cara.

“Oh, fine.”

“Why didn’t it work out with that other woman?” I clicked my fingers, trying to figure out who she was.

“Bethany?”

“That’s her. I can talk to her. Andrei is visiting. I’m sure Bethany would love to have lunch with you.”

“No thank you.”

The smile on her lips faded. “Why not? Weren’t you constantly going out with each other? Having dinner dates?”

“It didn’t work out, and I don’t want to talk about it. I’ll let Cara know I can’t go.”

I didn’t like how she instantly closed off from me. There was something going on and I wasn’t sure what.

Glaring at her back, I locked my fingers together and waited.

She drained the pasta and served me some food

before finally showing me attention.

"Where do you want to eat?" she asked.

"Dinner table, and you will join me."

I got to my feet, spun on my heel, and went to the table, taking my seat at the head.

Aurora put my food in front of me and I ordered her to sit.

"Is there anything you want? Wine? Beer? Vodka?"

She'd never offered me vodka, and it made me smile.

"Sit."

She lowered her ass into the seat and her gaze was averted from mine.

I picked up my fork, speared a piece of pasta, and put it in my mouth. An explosion of flavor hit my tongue. There was tomato and a hint of spice that made my mouth water for more. I took a couple more mouthfuls. "This is really good."

She relaxed a little.

"What happened between you and Bethany?" I didn't care. I kept on telling myself I didn't care about the petty squabbles of women, but something gnawed at me. Something I was clearly missing about what went down, and I didn't like not knowing.

"I'm really happy for Bethany and Andrei. I hope they have a happy marriage."

"I'm glad, because we have to attend the ceremony in two weeks."

"Wait? Two weeks?"

"Yes."

"How did that happen? She told me it was going to be a December wedding."

"I got the call from Andrei. It has been moved up for speed. I don't question why. So tell me why you're not interested in being around Bethany."

Aurora ran her fingers through her hair as she sat back. "She … and I … she didn't like me."

"What?"

"It's what I heard her say. She didn't like me. I'm not going to force my company on someone who hates me."

I frowned. "That's not what I heard. You cut your lunch date short."

"I did after I heard her talking to someone on the phone." She shrugged. "She hated me and found me boring." She chuckled. "Whoever she spoke to said you could do so much better than me."

"What?"

Aurora told me in great detail what Bethany said. I knew for a fact she didn't lie. There was no reason for her to, but hearing her say this shit, I wanted to hurt this Bethany.

"Look, I'm not after pity or anything. I'm kind of used to it."

"Used to what?"

"People not liking me. I don't know what it is about me. I guess I come on too strong for a friend. I don't know. I'm … when someone seems to want to be a friend, I'm happy. I want to be the kind of friend you can rely on. I just, everyone, I'm, I don't know. I guess I'm a bad friend."

"I find that hard to believe."

She chuckled.

"I think you'd be surprised."

She shrugged.

"How long has this been happening?"

"All my life. Back at my parents' place, we weren't allowed a lot of freedom, but my sister often went out on shopping dates. Trips to the movies. Stuff like that. I was never invited." She held her hands up in surrender. "After a while, you get used to it."

She may have gotten used to being ignored but that didn't make the pain go away.

Aurora laughed. "I was only ever good enough when Isabella was ill or they needed someone to make up the numbers. Bethany was never on time. She always had a reason to be elsewhere and after hearing what she said about me, I didn't want to sit through the remainder of lunch with a person who can't stand me."

"I'll talk to Andrei."

"No, please don't."

"He needs to know the kind of woman he's aligning himself with."

She groaned. "It doesn't matter. Honestly."

"Bethany is lying to him."

"Of course she is. Why would she tell him the truth that she can't stand to be around Slavik's wife because she finds her boring?"

"As his wife, she should be telling him the truth. No questions asked."

Aurora groaned. "Now that you put it like that, it makes so much sense. You're going to cause trouble. I don't want trouble."

I got up from the table, cupped her face, and tilted her head back to look at me. "Aurora, you're my wife. I will not stand by while someone makes your life miserable. You're worth causing trouble over."

"No, I'm not. You're going to make waves, and you can't even stand to be around me."

"Excuse me?"

She tried to pull away, but I wouldn't let her.

"Slavik, please."

"Tell me."

I didn't have the first clue what was going on in

this woman's head. She was all over the place.

"We have sex and you haven't been around for a couple of days. I don't know what that means, but to me, I guess I was awful." She winced and visibly recoiled.

I took a seat.

I'd already finished my food, and I pushed my plate to the side. "Come here," I said.

This time, she frowned. "Why?"

"I won't repeat myself."

She rolled her eyes but got to her feet and stepped in front of me. I lifted her up on the table. At the same time, I grabbed the waistband of her sweatpants and pulled them down her thighs, throwing them to the floor.

I didn't have my blade on me, so I tugged at the flimsy material of her panties and they tore easily. With her naked, I spread her legs wide open.

"You think you were a bad fuck?"

"Slavik?"

"Yes or no."

"Yes."

I cupped her pussy and she gasped.

She was already slightly wet.

I slid a finger between her slit, stroking over her nub. As I stared at Aurora, she closed her eyes. Her legs quivered from my touch, but I slowed my movements, taking my time, making her feel every caress as I played with her.

"I've had a busy couple of days. As you saw from the way I came in, we've been attacked in a couple of our nightclubs. It started at one place and has extended to five nightclubs all across the city. Three of them were owned by me. Tonight, I shut down a place, but my men were present to make it look like it was still open. The attack happened and I was able to capture one of the men, however, before I could question him, he impaled himself on a piece of metal, killing himself instantly."

I'd never seen a man so frightened, and I'd seen a lot of men who were on the verge of facing death. I'd been the one to take them to their maker. "All the while, I've been frustrated because I didn't want to be in a nightclub or talking to the police, handling business. No, for the first time in my life, I wanted to come home to explore the woman in my bed. At the time, her pussy was just a memory, and I craved it. No woman has ever made me lose focus like this. What are you doing to me, Aurora?"

"Don't tease me. It's not fair."

"I have no intention of teasing you, baby."

"Please don't lie to me."

"You think I'm lying to you about what I wanted tonight? How I've been trying to get home to you?"

I slid two fingers inside her slick heat, watching her come apart, and it was so beautiful. I couldn't look away and the truth was I didn't want to. She was a fucking dream.

There was nothing false about her reaction. How slick her cunt was, that was real. No lube to keep her wet. I slid my fingers across her pussy, driving her arousal even higher. She moaned my name, and touching her wasn't enough.

Replacing my fingers with my mouth, I licked across her slit, circling her nub. She tasted just as good as I remembered, if not even better. I sucked her clit into my mouth, hearing her pleasured cries fill the air as I teased her. So incredibly tasty.

Gliding down to her entrance, I fucked her as if it was my cock, hearing her gasps and moans, begging for more and telling me to not stop. I loved to hear those words.

She thrust up against me, riding my face, trying to

take her pleasure with each thrust and moan.

So beautiful.

Fucking stunning.

I craved more.

Aurora made me ache, and I wasn't used to this feeling. Not only did she make me ache, but I needed her. This wasn't an easy emotion for me to accept. For months, I'd tried to ignore her. Seeing Sergei kiss her then Cara play with her, I'd been pushed to my limit.

The only person I wanted for her was myself.

"Please," she said.

"Come for me."

She cried out, her orgasm instant as I stroked over her clit. I pushed two fingers inside her, driving in and out of her cunt. Then I turned my fingers to stroke over her G-spot, and she rewarded me. Her release flooded my fingers, soaking them.

I watched her, unable to look away. Her entire body shook with the force of her release. Such a heady sight. One I knew I wasn't going to want to stop.

I withdrew my fingers as the last aftershocks of her release ebbed away. Sitting back, I stared at her as I licked my fingers one by one, sucking them into my mouth. She tasted so fucking good.

I loosened the cord of my pants and eased out my cock for her to see. "Do you think this is lying to you?"

She licked her lips. "What do you want me to do?"

"To put your pretty pussy right over it."

"You're hurt."

"The only pain I feel is in my balls. I need them empty, and I want my cum inside of you."

Her cheeks were a beautiful pink.

She slid off the table and I sat back. The chair didn't have any sides, so as she stood with her legs spread, there was nothing to stop her. She placed her hands on my shoulders. I held my cock, and she lowered down. I gripped her ass with my free hand, guiding her to my dick.

Aurora sank down, gasping as I filled her. She was so wet, but I was big. I held on to her hips when she'd taken enough of me inside her so I wouldn't escape. I pulled her right down onto my dick, keeping her in place, not letting her move an inch.

"This is what I've been wanting," I said. "This is what I need."

I lifted her up and pulled her back down. Together, we fucked, and she took my cock so perfectly. We fit. There was no other word for it. The rest of the world could overlook this woman, but what Aurora didn't seem to get was that I saw her. I noticed her, and I liked what I saw.

Over and over, she rocked on my length, and I relished her tight cunt taking me in deep. I wasn't going to last.

The months without being inside her had caught up with me, and with a final tug, I slammed her down on my length. My cum flooded her pussy, making her mine once again.

Chapter Twelve

Aurora

"Do you enjoy going to those events?" I asked.

The dress Slavik picked out was a little tight. My breasts were thrust up, almost as an offering, and the slit at the side was a little too indecent.

I wasn't used to dressing like this, and for a banquet, it seemed out of place.

Slavik looked up from his cell phone. He'd offered to take me shopping. I'd sent back the clothes I purchased on my last and only rebellion. In the cold light of day, I didn't like a single item I picked, which sucked.

He looked at me, and I held my hands out and gave a turn.

I hated shopping for clothes. It was pointless. Having a body on the frumpy side compared to the slender women that surrounded me, I always felt like I didn't belong. My mom and my sister would always tell me my flaws. My chest was too big or too small. My fat arms were on display. They were an ordeal.

Slavik didn't look at me like I didn't measure up. There was a hunger in his gaze. One I wasn't used to experiencing.

"What do you think?" I asked.

"I want you to get that one but you're not wearing it to the banquet."

"Why not?"

"No other man is going to see my woman. Do I make myself clear?"

"Crystal. If I'm not going to wear it, why do I still need to buy it?"

"So I can tear it off your body and fuck you with what remains."

My mouth opened, but no sounds came out.

Slavik never sugar-coated anything. He got up from his seat and walked toward me.

The assistant was right outside, but he slid his hand through the slit and cupped my pussy. “See, this is tempting for you to wear, but if I can do this, I don’t want every man to be thinking the same thing.”

“They won’t be.”

“They will be.”

I wanted to argue with him, but I kept my mouth shut. Eyes closed, pleasure rushing through my body.

“You know what I’m starting to think?” he asked. His lips brushed against the sensitive column of my neck, and I shook my head. “You’re a very dirty woman, Aurora Ivanov. So dirty you’ve kept it hidden from me, but I better warn you, I will discover all of your secrets.”

“I don’t hide anything,” I said.

He plunged two fingers inside me. “Yeah, you did. A virgin you may be, in more ways than you realize, but your needs are far from innocent. I think it would be only fair for us to explore them.” He pinched my clit, causing me to cry out, then finally withdrawing his hand.

I watched him lick my cream off his finger and move to sit back down. “Try on the next one.”

He’d gotten me all hot and bothered and was on his cell phone as if nothing happened. I didn’t get this man.

In the last twenty-four hours, he’d touched me more than in the first seven months of marriage. Not that I was complaining. Even as I believed I hated the man, I still couldn’t stop myself from watching him, desperate for his touch.

I still wasn’t sure how to initiate sex. I pushed the thoughts to the back of my mind and instead focused on what appeared to be important to him. Picking out the perfect dress for this banquet.

"You didn't answer my question."

"No. I don't like going to these events. I find them pointless and unnecessary." He didn't look up from his cell.

"Why do you go then?"

"Image. To drive a point across."

I pulled on a pale-blue dress with a scooped neck that showcased my cleavage by pushing my tits together. Blowing out a breath, I spun toward him. The dress fell to my ankles. Very modest with a hint of reveal.

"This one?"

He looked up. "Yes."

"Will you need my help with anything this time?" I asked. I hated going to the banquets and special events. They were places I always felt the odd one out.

I licked my lips as my mouth had gone dry.

After changing out of the dress he'd picked and back into my jeans and a shirt, I held the two dresses he'd liked, and was ready to leave.

He looked up from his cell phone. "You're not going to try any others on?"

I wrinkled my nose. "No."

"And here I thought you liked shopping."

"Your credit card should show a full refund. I hate shopping."

He tilted his head to the side. "Why go shopping then?"

"It wasn't about the clothes or shoes. I just … I needed to get out. That's all. Call me childish. I'd been trapped after what happened with Sergei. It wasn't my fault and still, I was punished."

Slavik grabbed the back of my neck and pulled me in close. His lips so close to mine, but he didn't kiss me. "I know it wasn't your fault, but you could have told me the very instant he made any kind of hint he wanted more from you. Sergei shouldn't have gotten anything from you. His job was to protect you."

"Is that how you see me, as a job?" I asked.

"No. You're my wife. It's my duty to protect you."

I tried to pull away. I shouldn't feel anger or resentment and yet, that was exactly what I felt and I was so annoyed with the feeling. I put my hands on his chest. "I'm not your duty."

"But you are my wife."

"And … ugh, let me go."

"No. Tell me why you're upset."

I glared at him. "Tell me how you'd feel if I had to … have sex with you out of duty? Out of it being a job."

His lips brushed my ear. "You do have a duty to fuck me."

I jerked back and shoved him hard.

He didn't move.

This man was like a damn rock, and just knowing I couldn't get him to move upset me.

"No part of me being with you has been a duty. I don't sleep with you or fuck you because I have to. I've done it because I wanted to."

"You think I believe our wedding night and the time after was for fun?"

"Don't mess up my words. That was duty, but the times since, I liked it, and I didn't do it out of obligation. I happen to enjoy your hands on my body, but right now, I want you to let me go."

I tried to shove him away. He held me closer. His lips brushed against the curve of my neck, and I hated how weak I felt toward this man.

"You're not a duty to me, Aurora."

"After what you just said, you expect me to

believe you?"

"Have you ever considered the fact I say things to find out what you think?" he asked.

I looked up at him. "What?"

"You heard me."

He wouldn't repeat himself. It was why whenever he talked, I forced myself to listen to every single word.

There was a knock on the door before it opened. The woman who'd been assisting us stepped in.

Slavik released my neck but placed his hand on my hip.

I gritted my teeth. He never seemed to want to let me go and it both thrilled and annoyed me. Slavik had my emotions all over the place.

"I want those dresses wrapped up and ready to go." He took the dresses from my hand, gave them to the assistant, and within a matter of seconds, we were out of the shop.

His men surrounded him.

"How are we going to pay?"

"Everything has been taken care of."

"Oh," I said, feeling like an idiot for asking.

We walked through the city center. People avoided us, some crossing the street to get as far away from us as possible.

Slavik kept his head held high. He'd donned a pair of sunglasses, and I couldn't see his eyes.

I walked by his side. His hand on my hip. A brand of ownership.

We made our way to a restaurant. Two of his men entered and we followed. The maître d' was there to offer us a table, and we sat down.

Wine was poured into our glasses. Slavik spoke Russian to the waiter, and then we were left alone.

I stared across the table. Rather than drink the

wine, I went with water.

"Why are we here?"

"We're going to enjoy a meal."

"We have the banquet tonight," I said.

"Not for another six hours, and I'm not going to go that long without food. This is one of my favorite places to eat, and the Stroganoff is delicious."

I nodded.

The restaurant was bustling with activity. I sipped at my water. I expected Slavik to go back to his cell phone.

He'd put it away. His gaze was on me.

I locked my fingers together.

"Do you know how to make small talk?" he asked.

I shook my head. "No. We're in an open place."

"We're fine. My men are on guard."

"Doesn't that scare you?"

"I'm not afraid. What will happen, will happen. Nothing I can do to change that. I have to react. You know what it's like. I seem to recall reading three years ago there was a shooting right outside the school you and your sister attended, correct?"

"How did you know about that?"

Slavik smiled. "Who do you think arranged it?"

My mouth fell open. This couldn't be happening. "You're telling me that I'm married to a man who tried to kill me?"

He shrugged. "Your father had attacked one of my ports, killed six of my men. The ports were supposed to be safe territory. We hadn't attacked his, or anyone else's. I had to find a way to hit back. His wife and children were very easy targets as they were … never guarded quite as well."

"I don't know what to think about that."

He shrugged. “You can be pissed off with me or accept it is in the past. Neither your sister nor you were hurt in the end. If memory serves, no one was.”

“Weren’t you disappointed?” I asked.

“No. The end result wasn’t to actually kill you.”

“Then what?”

“It was to begin the talks that led us to this day.”

“Oh.” I looked down at my hands, which were clenched together. “Is that why you wanted marriage? You saw my sister.”

Slavik sighed. “They really are in your head, aren’t they?”

“I don’t know what you mean.”

“Yeah, you do, and I find it sad that they can so easily get under your skin.”

I hated how easily he read me. All my life, I’d been told I didn’t compare to my much prettier older sister.

“Everyone wants Isabella.”

“You’re right. She is a pretty girl, but that is where the attraction stops. You think when your father offered up you in place of Isabella I didn’t do my research?”

I didn’t want to ask, but I found myself doing so. “What kind of research?”

“To see how you and Isabella compared. Even in your secluded world, there were enough people who knew you. Everyone talked about how Isabella was a beauty. She’d make a fine wife and a trophy. Any man would be pleased to have her. No one said anything about her mean side. How she got good, loyal men killed because they wouldn’t do her bidding.”

I had no idea anyone knew about that.

Isabella was a flirt. She liked to drive men wild. I caught her once trying to feel up one of the soldiers. He called her an ugly soul, and that night, I heard the commotion and witnessed the death of said soldier. Isabella had told my father lies, and he'd believed her. That was the first time I realized my sister was not a nice person. Up until then, she had always been perfect. Everyone said so, so she must be.

"What did people say about me?"

"That was the mystery," Slavik said. "No one said anything. They had no idea what to say, other than she was the ugly sister."

Tears filled my eyes as I looked down at my hands.

"I'd seen you, Aurora. I knew there was more to you and they were wrong."

"About what?"

"You're not ugly."

"I'm not pretty," I said.

"Yes, you are, and that is the saddest part about all of this. You are so pretty, and you don't see it. Everyone around you has gotten you to see this person that, to me, doesn't exist."

"If you found this out, why did you marry me? Why did you wait all this time?"

He shrugged. "Duty was one. I'm loyal to the Volkov Bratva. He told me to marry you, I did my duty. I also wanted the time to get to know who you are."

"That's a lie, Slavik. We barely know each other."

"And yet we sit here, talking. There is plenty of time for us to get to know each other."

"If Mr. Volkov told you to, would you kill me? If the treaty became voided for whatever reason, you'd kill me dead. Even if I was the mother of your children?" I didn't know where the question came from.

My parents said my curiosity would get me

killed, and it would seem today was going to be that day.

"I will kill you, if I have to. Be loyal to us and our cause, and you live in peace at my side."

As a response, it wasn't very reassuring.

****

Slavik

I hated banquets.

Being surrounded by the rich, the powerful, all under the guise of helping those less fortunate. Even as I stood with my wife by my side, I looked at the sickening falseness surrounding me.

I was used to dealing with dirty people. The dregs of society, some would call it. I never stuck to the protocol of only dealing with my immediate Bratok. For my men and people who worked for me, I was everywhere. They never knew where I would turn up. Right now, as men and women donated money to several well-meaning charities to help the less fortunate from children to poverty-stricken families, I spotted one woman who owned a slave through human trafficking. This woman she beat on a regular basis. I had the footage of her beating this woman. She used anything from sticks to whips, to even clubs. Her anger was always taken out on this woman. She held a place in a senior role within the courthouse. The evidence I had was a good bargaining tool.

Most of the people here were under Ivan's thumb in one way or another. My presence, as well as two other brigadiers, helped to drive the point of our power.

No one could touch us.

"You're hurting me," Aurora said.

I loosened my hold on her hip with an apology.

"It's fine. I don't mind. You don't like these places. Why come?"

"Business."

"Do you ever donate to the causes?"

"Yes." The money donated did go to several foundations. I made sure of it.

"Excellent. Would you like me to go and make a donation?" she asked.

I pulled out my checkbook and gave her one I'd already written. I tore off a second for her to fill in. "Go crazy."

She chuckled and left my side. I nodded at one of my men to follow her. She was in a fish tank full of sharks. The people here would gladly try to take her from me, and the very knowledge of that pissed me off.

Andrei chose that moment to come my way. We shook hands and turned to look at the crowd.

"I can't stand half of the people here," he said.

"It's what business is all about. Our likes do not come into it."

"Will you be attending my wedding?" Andrei asked. "Bethany informed me no response had been sent."

I glanced at Bethany. She stood in the center of six businessmen. I hadn't liked the woman the instant I met her. Something seemed off about her.

"You know she's a whore?" I asked, turning to Andrei.

"Do you think it takes a rocket scientist to work that out? I'm aware she's not a princess. She uses her snatch to get what she wants. It pisses her off I have no use for it."

"Why marry her?"

"Business, and I need a wife to have a kid with. A slut she may be, but not all of us can have cute virgins to bed."

My gaze went to Aurora. She stood at the booths that displayed all the charities being showcased tonight.

My man was close and made sure no one approached her.

"How is it to bed a virgin?"

"I'm not going to tell you about my wife," I said.

"I have to say I'm impressed. Everyone thought you'd have killed her by now. Aurora must have a special pussy."

I reacted before anyone saw. Slamming the side of my hand against his throat, I immediately choked him.

His glass dropped to the floor, and I grabbed his shoulders, feigning concern to the onlooking crowd.

I made sure they were far away before I dragged Andrei away, slamming him against the wall, out of earshot and eyesight.

"Now you listen to me, my wife is not up for questioning. You talk about her, you insult me. You should tell your fiancée that the next time she thinks to insult my wife again, I will slit her fucking throat."

Andrei cleared his throat, taking a few minutes to get himself together. "What?"

I told Andrei all the details Aurora had given me. There wasn't a lot there, but enough to get his attention.

"I will deal with her."

"Is there a problem here?" Ivan asked, coming out of the main room to talk to us.

"No, no problem. A simple misunderstanding, but that is all," I said.

Andrei agreed and made his way into the room.

"Your wife is lonely," Ivan said.

I nodded and went to go into the room.

"What was that?" Ivan asked.

"Andrei believed he could talk about my wife disrespectfully, and I told him he couldn't. It was a misunderstanding."

"Your wife's not pregnant yet."

"I'm working on it."

"Knock her up. I don't want this treaty to blow up in our faces," Ivan said.

Movement from behind him had me cursing.

I saw Aurora's hair. "Duty calls," I said.

I walked into the dance floor and saw Aurora had moved as far away from the doorway as possible. She caught sight of me and went to the first man.

He clearly turned down a dance as she withdrew into herself and tried to shrink away from people being able to see her. I closed the distance between us, stepping into her space. I grabbed her arm.

"Dance with me," I said.

"No. I don't want to dance with you." She didn't make a scene, but she was no match for me either. I easily led her onto the dance floor.

With my hand at the base of her back and the other holding her hand, there was nowhere for her to go. I held her captive.

"You're not playing fair," she said.

"I never play fair." I glanced around the room, keeping an eye on any potential attackers. Andrei had a scared-looking Bethany in his arms. That bitch was going to know not to mess with my woman. "You asked that man to dance," I said.

She scoffed. "I don't know why. He told me no."

"That would be my fault."

"Why?"

"My presence scares the shit out of people. They all know you're my wife. No one will dance with you. Unless you're Ivan, of course."

"Great. You scare everyone. I should have known."

"Men would love to dance with you. I don't want anyone else to dance with you but me."

"Do you intend to control my life?" she asked.

"You're my wife. So yes."

Her cheeks clenched. "What about … getting me pregnant?"

"Do you want to talk about that or pretend you didn't hear?"

"You're only sleeping with me to get me pregnant?"

"No. I'm fucking you because I want to. Pregnant is a by-product of fucking you."

"You're still doing it because your boss is telling you to." She stopped dancing. Her eyes filled with tears, and she stared at me, almost accusing me.

I took a deep breath, grabbed her hand, and led her off the dance floor.

There was enough commotion going on that no one would miss us.

I opened the first door I came to and saw we'd entered a conference room. Pressing her up against the door, I pulled her skirt up and cupped her pussy.

"Stop it."

"You're soaking wet."

"And I don't want you to touch me."

"You're a liar, Aurora. This pussy is dripping." I teased beneath the band of her panty and fingered her pussy. Sliding in and out of her tight heat. She tensed in my arms, but there was no mistaking the heat of her need. She whimpered and I pressed my face against her neck, nibbling on her flesh.

She gasped. "Please."

"Do you want me to stop?"

She groaned and rocked against my hand. I knew how to make her melt. Drawing my fingers up to her clit, I rubbed her, and she rubbed herself against me.

"Take my cock out," I said.

She fumbled with my trousers, sliding down the

zipper and reaching inside to cup my dick. I lifted her up in my arms. She wasn't light, but I didn't fucking care. I needed to be inside her wet cunt.

"Put my dick inside you," I said.

Aurora reached between my thighs, holding my cock. I moved in closer, staring into her eyes as she put my cock to her entrance, and I sank her down on my length. Her tight pussy squeezed me, begging for my cum.

She wrapped her arms around my neck, her legs around my waist, and I rocked inside her, going deep.

"The table," she said.

"If you want someone to come in and see me fucking you, I can take the table."

"No. No. I … I'm too heavy."

I thrust against her, using the door as leverage to drive inside her, taking her as I wanted to.

"I want to knock you up, Aurora. I'm not fucking you out of duty. Feel my cock. Feel how hard I am for you. This is not duty. This is pure fucking need. I have to have you. This pussy, it's mine. You're all mine."

Screwing Aurora was a pleasure, and as I felt her come on my cock, I followed her over the edge, filling her with my cum.

"I don't know if I can go back out there," she said as I eased out of her pussy.

I helped put her panties back into place as I slid my cock into my pants, being careful not to get our releases on my clothes.

"You will. This is our duty. To be seen together." I held her hand, and hers shook a little as she placed it within my own.

I had to get her pregnant. Ivan had ordered me to. Any claim Aurora had over her family would go through to her children and as the firstborn son, it would belong to him.

The truth was I liked fucking my wife.

I also enjoyed spending time with her, and that was something I had to make sure no one else ever found out.

Chapter Thirteen

Aurora

"When are you going to find a new guard for me?" I asked.

It was three days since the banquet, and rather than be at home bored out of my mind, I sat in his office, staring out the large window overlooking the city. So many people were milling about, none of them realizing how lucky they had it. Three days Slavik kept me by his side, and it wasn't a problem being around him. I liked it, and that was the issue for me. I started to enjoy his company.

This morning, I woke up to him still in bed. Rather than try to escape, I watched him sleep. I was turning into a weird kind of stalker and that was what scared me. Slavik was my husband. A man I'd spent an equal time hating and fantasizing about.

"I haven't looked into another guard yet. There have been other things on my mind."

Spinning around from the window, I moved toward his desk. "Like what?"

"You think this world you live in comes for free?" he asked.

"No. I know it comes from the blood of the innocent."

"Does it bother you?"

I stared at him and nodded. "Yes. It always does, but other than being a good person, I can't do anything about it."

"And writing exceedingly large checks?"

I move away from his desk. At the banquet, I put a lot of money in a children's charity. "You saw that," I said.

"I got an alert from the bank when they tried to

cash it."

"Right," I said. "Did you allow it to go through?"

"It was a large amount and would be useful for a tax break. I didn't see the problem. It went through."

"Thank you."

"The real question, Aurora, is what you are going to do for that check."

I frowned. "What do you want from me?"

He reached out, clasping my wrist, and I followed his direction as he tugged me toward him. I stood between his chair and the desk. His thumb stroked my inner wrist. "You look pretty today."

I wore a pair of designer jeans and a crop top with one of his shirts over the top. Not a big deal. I'd seen his shirt in the closet and I hadn't expected it to fit. I didn't have the first clue why I even decided to reach for his clothing as it wasn't like I needed him to surround me. I'd started to realize Slavik wasn't an awful man, at least not all the time. He was downright dangerous and anyone who made an enemy out of him, I'd advise them to run for the hills, but in everything else, there was no danger, at least I couldn't see one. The rules were pretty simple. Stay on his good side or risk being killed. I opted to stay on his good side.

"Thank you."

It was a nice compliment. One I rarely got and rather than believe he lied, I smiled.

"You're not looking too bad yourself."

He let go of my wrist and began to finger the base of my shirt. "You took this."

"Borrowed. I'll get it washed and return it."

"I like it." He started to unbutton the shirt.

After overhearing the conversation with Ivan, I couldn't help but wonder if he did this out of desire or duty. The last thing I wanted to be was a duty.

The shirt fell to the floor as he stood, pushing it off my shoulders. He took the straps of the crop top and slid them down my arms until they were underneath my bra. The catch was around the back, and Slavik had to be an expert as with the flick of his fingers, the bra was on the floor.

My mouth went dry.

He cupped my tits, pressing them together as both his thumbs teased across my nipples. Each strike had an answering pulse between my thighs.

He closed the distance between us, taking one nipple into his mouth. I moaned, reaching back to grasp the edge of the desk as he used his teeth. I pressed my thighs together in an attempt to stop the pleasure, but it was no good.

Slavik let go and cupped me between the thighs. Even though I wore jeans, he knew the right moves to touch me, and I couldn't hold back my moan of pleasure.

He worked at the button and zipper of my jeans, the sounds filling the room as he pushed them down my thighs until they got to my knees. He stopped sucking at my tits to peel them off my body, and other than the shirt around my waist, I stood naked.

In quick easy moves, he had me sitting on the desk, legs wide, and his fingers teased my pussy. His expert fingers stroked from my entrance up to my clit.

"So wet. Exactly how I like you."

His words shouldn't affect me, but they did. In the back of my mind, all I could think about was pleasing him. I'd become a sucker, but I didn't care. I closed my eyes, enjoying his touch. Each stroke across my nub got me closer to that delicious peak.

"Look at me," he said, his voice gruff. The demand easy to detect.

I opened my eyes, staring at him as he brought

me closer to orgasm.

Slavik was the one in control. He wasn't in any rush. My release began to build, but he slowed the pace down, giving me chance to enjoy it. Each time I tried to close my eyes, he'd stop touching me.

He drove me crazy until I finally gave him all the attention he needed.

"Now, look between your legs," he said.

I wanted to disobey him, but I also didn't want him to stop what he was doing. I loved it. The pleasure was out of this world, amazing. He knew how to rile me up and get me so close.

This was what had been missing out of our marriage. I knew there was so much more we could experience together, but right now, all I could imagine was being with him in this way. This wasn't emotional, but physical.

Please," I said.

"You want to come?"

"Yes."

"Ask me."

"Please, let me come."

"Say my name."

"Slavik."

"Now ask me."

"Slavik, please, let me come." I didn't deny him. I was so close, and as my reward, he pushed me over the peak. I cried out, riding the wave of release as he gave it to me.

So good.

I expected that to be the end, but it wasn't. Slavik moved me off the desk and spun me around so my back was to him. I heard his zipper, and then I felt the hard press of his cock as he slid between my thighs.

He found my entrance, and I tensed up, crying out

as he slammed balls deep within me. He didn't give me chance to calm down or get accustomed to the length of his cock. He fucked me hard and fast. His hands a tight grip on my hips as he pounded inside me.

I wondered if I should hate this, but the truth was I loved it.

I didn't want him to stop.

The way he held me. The feel of his rock-hard cock deep inside me.

It all … made me hungry and desperate for more.

"I love how tight your pussy is. How you fucking feel. That's it, take my cock."

For several minutes, I stayed perfectly still, allowing him to take the lead, to take what he wanted. I didn't know what came over me. If this was a duty to him, then I wanted it to be hard for him to think of it that way.

I no longer wanted to be anyone's duty or burden.

As I pushed back against him, I started to ride his cock as he took me. For a few seconds, he paused, seeming to be a little shocked that I actually pushed back against him. Then, like his need took over, he started to take me deeper, fucking me harder, working my body, and what was more, I gave as good as I got.

I wanted this.

This wasn't a duty to me. The end result, pregnancy, might be the duty for me, but in getting to that point, I was determined for it to be nonstop pleasure.

Slavik slammed inside me one final time, and he was so long and thick, I felt each pulse of his arousal as it flooded me. Moments passed. Seconds turned into minutes before he reached over and picked up some tissues. He pulled out of me and I felt some of his cum spill down. The tissue helped to capture some of it. He cleaned me up even as my face grew hot from the attention. There was no stopping him. He helped me back into my panties, jeans, bra, crop top, and his shirt.

I had no idea what to do, so I stepped away from him, and he didn't stop me.

Not once had he kissed me.

My lips felt that loss.

The few times he'd taken the time to kiss me, I'd relished every single second. I enjoyed the sex, which was a huge relief as I knew many women in our world didn't. The sex I'd heard had often been violent and scary. Of course none of the women had known I'd been listening in on their conversations, slowly growing more terrified at the prospect of having my own husband.

The books became a source of comfort. While the ladies in our circles told scary sex tales, the books gave me hope that they simply didn't enjoy it.

"Cara called again," Slavik said, breaking through the silence.

Was he uncomfortable?

I turned from the window to look at him.

"She asked me permission to take you to lunch next week."

"And did you tell her no?"

"No, I didn't. I said you could go," he said.

So far, any attempt at friendship Cara had made, he'd squashed. They were supposed to be friends, and it hurt he didn't want me to be friends with his.

"You did?"

"Yes. I've already arranged a guard to be with you. It's important he stays with you at all times. You leave or don't follow my rules, you'll not be allowed to go anywhere else again."

I nodded. I was happy.

Cara seemed like a nice woman. She held a high position within the Volkov Bratva. She was the first woman I knew who didn't allow a man to talk to her like she was crap, or allow them to treat her like a piece of property.

My father had always been firm in the belief we belonged to him. We were nothing but pawns to meet his end goals. As much as I didn't have value, I became quite a useful cog in the peace treaty between our families.

Slavik checked the time. "We need to get going," he said. "I need you to change."

The sun had started to set, and I frowned. "Where are we going?"

"To a private event. Exclusive."

"You don't have any more details?"

"I'm not sure you're going to like it," he said.

"Oh."

****

Slavik

Noise greeted us the moment we entered the underground facility. The entire setup changed and moved between my cities, the invites going out via text or email. The location nothing more than a set of coordinates. The fights had been going for nearly five years now. In all that time, only two fights had been removed and the location changed because someone decided to cave and give the details to the police.

From my men on my payroll, they'd sent me the alert of the impending invasion, and I'd gotten plenty of time to move myself and the fight to another location. The police had found nothing more than empty space, even with some paperwork about the potential renovations for business purposes.

I was always one step ahead.

The very people who'd ratted the fight no longer had a very comfortable life. One of them was dead, the other lived on the streets, having lost their fortune. The warning was simple, don't rat us out, and we won't come after you.

These fights earned a great deal of money. Blood money. They weren't the standard, organized fist-slamming shown on television. This was a death match.

Many people liked to pay good money to see men fight for survival. The rich loved to be able to wave their cash to get anything they desired, even if they didn't know exactly what it was they wanted.

The more depraved, the more money.

Aurora's hand on my arm got even tighter as she saw the ring down below.

The basement of this fight was set out as if we were in a great opera. The space was decent, the crowd going wild.

Everything was safe. No risk of the building caving in on us.

"This is … oh, my God, gross," Aurora said. She released my arm to grip the railing. The man beside her looked at her, pissed as if she'd ruined it for him. I glared at him. Everyone knew who I was, and Aurora would be protected. "This is all real?" She glanced around the room, and as she took it all in, the frown across her brow deepened.

"Yes."

"Oh, God." She glanced back at the dance floor.

Some of the women were screaming for the kill. The fights always brought out the lust in some. I didn't need to look at anyone to see women getting off as the men fought. The blood covered the ground. The men looked exhausted, but no one called the fight to the end.

One final blow, and I heard the crack of knuckles. The man fell to the ground. This fight happened once a month. I never allowed it to go again. Once it played and people paid their money, I gave enough time and space to make them crave the fights. Their thirst for blood driving their need higher.

All of this was business.

The fighters all knew the risks entering the ring. They had to fight to the death. No exceptions unless someone screamed out for mercy for them. The crowd knew they could shout to save them.

The man was now on the floor, his body being dragged out, and no one had cared to give him the mercy shot.

Aurora didn't know the rules.

"Why did you bring me here?"

I hadn't attended the last two, and I always made sure to attend at least half of the fights. Men died. For all I knew, good men died for the pleasure of money. The least I could do was show up to some to bear witness.

I pulled Aurora in front of me. Her hair was held back with a small clip. The dress she wore drove me wild. The plunging neckline had me wondering how she kept her tits in place. The dress didn't cover half her body, and I knew because I'd picked it.

I pressed my lips against her neck. My hands grabbed the railing at either side of her, locking her against my body. No escape.

"No one saved him," I said.

This made her jerk. "Can they?"

"Yes." I nodded. I couldn't resist a lick across her pulse. I heard her gasp. It wasn't loud but subtle, and I heard it.

"They had a chance to save that guy and they chose to let him die?"

"Yes."

"And they all know they can save him?"

"Yes. It's why I'm telling you now." I kissed her

neck, and she moaned. “They would rather pay to see a man die than allow him to live.”

“I’m not like that.”

“You’re not?” I asked.

Another fighter was already making their way out. The previous winner looked exhausted. He had one chance. Double his chances of winning, or bow out, winning more than any job would give him.

I watched him, seeing the man who came out. Both were hard, muscular men. The one coming toward the ring had a certain walk to him. His confidence spoke volumes. The man in the ring held an air of desperation. He was here out of need to make quick cash, whereas the man who now entered the ring was in no rush, had no fear, no panic. It had been a long time since I saw such a man so calm.

This was going to be brutal.

I placed my hand on Aurora’s stomach. Her entire body shook as the first punch landed, and my assessment was clear.

The crowd started out silent, not sure which way to vote, or who to want to win. The previous winner had them all up his ass just moments ago, but now, they saw a different winner. Their cheering for the other ceased, the brutal newcomer earning their praise.

I was right, like always.

The new guy attacked, but he didn’t do it for the crowd. The moment the first punch came, they unlocked a beast.

Seconds passed, and the other guy bled from his nose, lip, eye, and some from his ear.

“Kill him. Kill him. Kill him.”

The chants came thick and fast.

Aurora continued to shake.

The new one shoved the guy down onto the

ground and punched him in the head. He didn't get up, but he was still alive, still breathing.

I watched as the one now looking like the victor stared around the room, building up the courage.

They all screamed for blood and death.

Aurora tensed up. "Mercy!"

Her shout was loud, clear, and the entire basement fell silent.

No one ever screamed for mercy.

I wasn't sure if Aurora would.

She was different, I knew that, and this was a test to see just how much she was.

"Mercy! Do not kill him. He was a champion. He doesn't deserve death."

By the rules of the game, the fight should end, and he would become champion. Disappointment rang out around the room, and I watched as he disobeyed the rules of my fucking game.

He stomped on the man's head, three times, and I heard the break, and the twitch, rendering him dead.

Anger rushed through me. I grabbed Aurora's hands as cheers rang out.

"You said they couldn't do that?" I heard the tears in her voice.

She'd seen death before, but this time, she'd tried to save the man.

The crowd parted for me as the men who worked for me cleaned up the mess of the man on the floor.

The brutal one held his fists up in the air as I stepped into the ring.

"Slavik!" Aurora cried out, and my two guards were on either side of her. I felt the hostility of the crowd as they looked at her.

I removed my jacket, throwing it out to my men, and the one who'd just violated my rules turned to me.

"Sorry, mate, no rich pricks in the ring."

This man clearly didn't know my name or who I was. "What's your name?"

"What's it to you? You need to teach your wife not to come to grown-up games. They're only going to get her hurt."

"I will not repeat myself."

The man scoffed and looked toward the men I allowed to run this event. The room had gone silent. Those who knew me were aware of what had just happened here. I had one simple rule. Once mercy was shouted by one person, the fight ended. No blood, no death, and they still had to pay up.

"I don't answer to any cunts like you. Get him and his ugly-as-fuck wife out of my ring. This is mine. No one can beat me."

"Ben," I said. "What is his name?"

"It's George, Mr. Ivanov."

The fighter, George, paled. "Ivanov?"

"Slavik Ivanov. You disrespected my rules. Insulted my wife. You had your chance to make a lot of money. Mercy allows you to have the payment of the kill without making it." I tutted. "You won't be leaving here tonight."

I saw the fear and panic in his eyes, and I felt no sympathy.

My reputation was well-known. Within the ring, I was a monster. I'd killed hundreds of men for the sport, drawing in the wealth we needed.

I hadn't fought in this ring in a long time, but I made sure I was always ready. This man would know pain.

I struck first, and George tried to defend himself, but he'd said bad shit about my wife and that, I couldn't allow to slide. Anger rushed through me, and I allowed it to feed my attack.

Silence rang out in the room.

By breaking my rules, no one could shout mercy. One of my guards would tell Aurora that. I was amazed she'd done what she did.

In a room full of bloodthirsty people, she'd tried to help save another. I hadn't expected it. It was rare for people to surprise me, even more so for a woman. My wife was nothing like I thought she'd be. She was kind, sweet, even when the world had shit on her. In our world, all her merits were nothing but weaknesses. To me, they were a strength. Even knowing what her father had done to her. What her sister caused, she still tried to help. I couldn't hate that.

I didn't hate my wife. There was nothing about her to hate. She was sweet, kind, caring, loving, terrified. She brought out the instinct in me to protect. I wanted to take care of her, to love her, to be everything she needed and more.

George tried. He got in a couple of blows, but they were not strong enough. No one was able to defeat me.

I took him down and staring into his eyes, I grabbed him just right. With the correct strength and the right angle, I snapped his neck, ending the fight.

Cheers erupted.

I ignored them. Without another word, I stepped off the floor, toward my wife, taking her hand. I led her away from the fight, out back to where the victory fighters could rest for a few moments when given the option.

"Are you okay?" she asked as I took a seat.

I nodded at my men to leave us alone. They'd guard the entrance into the room.

"Yes, I'm fine." I'd killed many men, but

snapping a neck sent adrenaline running through my body.

Tears filled her eyes and fell down her cheeks. “They told me I couldn’t help him.”

“He didn’t need your help.”

“This game is brutal. Does it happen every week?”

I shook my head. “Once a month.”

“And how many people die?”

“I don’t keep count.”

“Was I the first one willing to save someone?”

I nodded.

She sighed and swiped at her tears. “I don’t know how you can deal with that.”

“It’s not about dealing, Aurora. The men who fight here don’t have to.”

She laughed. “Do you think they have a choice?”

“Some do, yeah. The ones that don’t, I have no power to stop them.”

“I can’t believe he did that.”

“Clearly, he thought this was his castle.” I shrugged.

“You don’t care that you killed him?”

“Aurora, I’m not a saint. I’ve killed more men than that, believe me.”

Silence.

I grabbed her hand and pulled her close. The slits in the dress made it easy to drag her onto my lap. Her knees on either side of me. I grasped her hips, drawing her down to my erection. I wasn’t hard until I looked at her.

“You can’t be serious,” she said. “Even after what you just did? You want to?”

“I can’t get enough of you.”

“You’re bleeding,” she said. Her fingers hovered

over my eyebrow.

I tore a piece of her dress and handed it to her. "Wipe it for me?"

"Aren't you hurting?" she asked.

I thrust my aching cock against her. "What do you think?"

"I think you're crazy." She dabbed the cut above my eye, wincing. "I don't know how you do it. I'd be crying."

"It's pain."

"And pain hurts, Slavik. Do you think you need to go to a doctor?"

"No."

She wiped my cut. "It doesn't look so bad now that I cleaned it with a really expensive piece of fabric from this dress. There's no repairing it, you know."

"As if you'd wear it again. I don't even think you'd have the guts to donate a dress you wore that witnessed a death."

"You're right," she said. "I'm not like you."

"You're not like a lot of people."

"Is that a bad thing?"

"No." I was done talking though. I held the base of her back as I pushed the dress out of my way and stroked her pussy. She was dry. The fight hadn't done anything for her, but I needed this.

"Look at me, Aurora. I need you." I stroked her through the panties, staring into her eyes, making her see only me.

She sank her teeth into her bottom lip.

I didn't touch her naked pussy.

"Get your tits out," I said. "I want to suck them."

She peeled the plunging neck open, exposing her tits, and I saw the tape that had kept the pieces of fabric secure over those delicious mounds. Her nipples were big, and in the cool air they pointed at me, begging to be sucked, and I was more than happy to oblige. After sliding my tongue across each peak, I sucked the hard bud into my mouth. At the same time, I stroked her pussy, working her body into a frenzy.

I took my time, aware of the fights occurring in the other room. Once I'd taken my wife, I'd leave, and do the same again on our bed.

Aurora whimpered, pressing her chest against my mouth. Her fingers sank into my hair, and I worked the zipper of my pants down, easing my hardened cock out.

I tested her pussy to find her wet. She wasn't as soaked as I'd have liked her, but enough to make me find her entrance, and to sit her onto my dick.

She cried out, the sound echoing around the room.

Up and down, I moved her, getting her to work my dick. With my thumb, I stroked over her clit, feeling her pulse around my cock.

She didn't close her eyes.

Her gaze focused on me, and I was fucking hypnotized. There was nowhere else I wanted to be. I just wanted to hold her, to feel her wrapped around me.

My name spilled from her lips as she came. It wasn't strong, but I knew I'd have her begging for my cock by the time we got home. I grabbed her hips and thrust up to meet her, holding her in place as I took my pleasure.

She moaned and I growled, spilling my seed into her cunt.

Ivan Volkov may think I was doing this out of duty.

My wife might have also thought I was doing this out of duty.

I, Slavik Ivanov, knew I did this out of downright

desire for my wife.

Chapter Fourteen

Aurora

"I was surprised Slavik allowed you to have lunch with me," Cara said.

I smiled across the table. "Me too. It came out of the blue." I looked over at the beautiful redhead. She commanded attention. I'd been seated alone, my brand-new guard from Slavik's trusted men sat three tables down, watching us. Before I'd come, Slavik had given me strict instructions on what I could talk about. Anything relating to work was not allowed. I also had to agree to tell him everything I discussed, which was slightly more complicated.

I wasn't sure why he'd given me these boundaries.

Cara was supposed to be his friend. A colleague.

"Wow, what did you do to make him happy?"

I thought about it and the truth was, I had no idea. I shrugged. Slavik and I seemed complicated in my mind.

Cara placed her hand on top of mine. "Please tell me he's treating you good?"

I smiled. "Yes. We're getting along now."

She sighed. "That makes me so happy. Slavik can be a bit of a hardass. He has to be. Many are handed a position like his. He earned his."

I frowned. "What do you mean?"

She shrugged. "No. I couldn't tell you."

"Oh, I won't say anything if that is what you're worried about." The lie was hard for me to say, but I got through it.

Slavik had demanded I don't lie to him. That there were no secrets between us. It seemed reasonable. Deep down, I wanted to make this marriage work.

"Good. I want us to be the best of friends. The

moment I saw you, I knew you were different."

The waiter came over and Cara ordered us both a glass of wine. "Unless you can't have any?"

"I'm fine." I offered her a smile.

Slavik and I had been sleeping together often. Last night, he'd surprised me by climbing into bed only to wake me up to take what he wanted. He'd never done that before. The sex last night had led into this morning where we'd made love. I wasn't even sure if I could call it making love.

We had sex.

I couldn't think of Slavik on emotional terms. We were husband and wife through a peace treaty. To some, I was nothing more than his possession. We weren't a love match.

The waiter came back with our wine and Cara shooed him away.

"It has been a busy couple of weeks. Business is booming. Anyway, back to Slavik, I'm so pleased he's been able to find a good wife. For the longest time, I figured he'd spend it jumping from one woman to the next." She winced. "I'm so sorry. I hope I haven't upset you."

I forced a smile. "You haven't."

"Good. We all know men are dogs. They see a woman and just jump on them for the fun." She sighed. "Anyway, Slavik was … he wasn't the king you see now. The ruler of states and his section. Ivan and Slavik are bastards of men who ran the original Bratva within this area, in fact. It was many years ago, long before your time. They lived on the streets. I should know, it's where I joined them. There we were, three brats on the streets. No one wanted us. Slavik's father was a brigadier, like him. He knocked up a whore, and because she refused to pay for an abortion, she got killed and Slavik ended up on the streets. So sad. He'd fought for every single meal he had. He's a natural-born fighter. Ivan was a similar story, only … he had a stutter. Of course, his father, who was the boss back then, couldn't have a son who stuttered."

"Wow." This was all news to me. "Was the Bratva as big then as it is now?"

"No," Cara said. "You see, by kicking them out of the streets, their fathers thought they were so clever. Removing the problem. What they didn't realize is by doing what they did, they created enemies. Two men who wanted nothing but revenge. They took over the streets. Together, they became a unit. It started small. Fights. Taking on turf. Robbing. You name it, Slavik and Ivan have done it. It took many years for Ivan to get over his stutter. It was so cute at one point."

Cara smiled. "Anyway, word got back to their dads. Ivan and Slavik had built up this reputation in their late teens and decided to target Bratva territory. Slowly, they took it over until one day they had the meeting to end all meetings. Slavik and Ivan went in with their fathers, and the story goes they were the only two to come out. The others were removed in body bags. They took the Bratva and made it what it is today."

"I had no idea about that."

"There is so much going on around everyone. No one really knows the truth, but it's there if people are willing to see it. More often than not, they refuse."

"What about you?" I asked.

"Me? I was the one to help negotiate the meet. From a young age, I knew sex and women were the key to a man's downfall. Give them the right pussy and goals, and they're putty in your hands. They'll do whatever you want. I helped bring them both to power by using my many skills."

Cara smiled, but there was something off about it. I couldn't exactly put my finger on it, but alarm bells began to ring inside my head. The smile also didn't quite reach her lips.

"You must be very proud of them," I said.

"I am. It's great. They rule with an iron fist."

"How come you're not a brigadier?" I asked.

Cara's fingers tightened around the glass she held. "A woman is never a brigadier, Aurora. I was given the option, but the truth was no man would ever respect a whore."

"I'm so sorry." I grabbed her hand, and she smiled at me.

"It is so … hard to make friends."

I agreed.

"You must have a whole lot of friends."

"No, I don't." I sipped at the wine, not enjoying the taste.

Cara signaled to the waiter, and we ordered our lunch.

"I find that hard to believe," Cara said.

"What?"

"You not having any friends. There must be loads of people who adore you."

This time I forced a smile to my lips. "No. I've … for some reason, I don't know why, I'm not liked." I glanced down into my glass, insecurities rearing their ugly head. "I mean, I'm always there and I am a good friend. I keep secrets and I'm always on time, and I'm willing and able to make it work, but, no, for some reason, I'm … never liked."

"They're idiots," Cara said. "We don't need them in our life. Screw them." She held up her glass. "To new friends who don't suck."

I clinked my glass with hers.

She controlled the conversation, which I didn't mind. She talked about clients and stories with Slavik, which I enjoyed. Whenever she spoke of her customers, sex was always mentioned, and it would often have me thinking about Slavik.

Cara was the one to end our lunch. I moved my food around.

Gus, the guard, paid for my meal and escorted me out of the restaurant. We were waiting for the car to come when the first shot was fired.

Within seconds, I was on the ground as gunshots rained down on us.

"I've got you," Gus said. "Stay down."

I couldn't move. My heart pounded and fear crawled up my back.

There was a sudden break, and Gus was on his feet, firing back. "Call for backup." A phone was thrown at me. I turned it on and found Slavik's number. I dialed the number as pain exploded in my shoulder.

"Help!"

I screamed the one word, panic rushing through me.

Gus came to me, and with his help, we ran for cover. Sirens could be heard in the distance.

Everything seemed to fade around me, the noise becoming more like static.

My eyes felt heavy and the dull throb in my arm made it impossible for me to focus. Who would shoot at us? I never got to figure that out as the world went black.

****

Slavik

"We ran some blood tests," the doctor said.

I didn't look away from my wife. She was still out of it. I would never forget that cry. It had to be when the bullet hit her that she screamed for help. I heard the fear in her voice, the need.

When I got to the restaurant, Gus and Aurora had been on the ground. Gus had a stomach wound. Aurora had passed out from the bullet lodged inside her arm. They'd taken her to surgery, removed the bullet, and now she was bandaged up, recovering.

"What about them?" I asked.

"Congratulations, Mr. Ivanov, your wife is pregnant."

I turned to the doctor. "You're sure?"

"Yes. Blood work doesn't lie, and I know you like to be thorough. I double-checked it myself. Your wife is pregnant."

I looked at Aurora. This was good news.

"I would like to start making appointments for your wife's care—"

"No," I said. "You make that disappear."

"You want me to perform an abortion on your wife?"

"No. Those documents, change them. You didn't discover my wife was pregnant." I got up from my chair and walked toward him. "That information is between you and me."

The doctor looked at Aurora then at me. "Sir, with all due respect, pregnancies can be … difficult. We need to make sure she is healthy."

"I will personally keep an eye on her. When I believe the time is right, I'll let her know she is pregnant. Until then, you will be quiet about this, or do I have to make you realize who is the one with the power here?"

He bowed his head, submitting to me. Within seconds, he was gone.

I closed the door to the private room and stared at my wife. The men who'd been shooting at her were gone. All but one, who waited for me back at the warehouse. I should be there rather than here. I had men waiting to guard her. Gus was supposed to protect her. Not that I blamed him. He'd done his best.

I sat down. This wasn't what I was supposed to do. My wife would be taken care of.

So, the first lunch date my wife went on, she was attacked.

I ran fingers through my hair as I watched her.

Pregnant. Aurora was pregnant with my child.

I didn't know if she was ready to accept that news or if she'd scream at the unfairness of it. Now wasn't the time to be bringing a child into the world.

I tapped my fingers on my thigh, waiting. The doctor had said she'd wake up soon and she'd be a bit groggy. I shouldn't care about how she woke up, but I did.

Her hand lay by her side.

Flat.

Lifeless.

I never felt anything but anger in all my life. My rage had helped me to fuel my need to win, to fight. To be the best I could be. To be the monster who took lives and made others afraid.

Arriving at the restaurant and seeing Aurora passed out cold on the ground, I'd known real fear. My wife was becoming a problem because I refused to have feelings. They were a weakness, but my wife, she made me feel so many fucking things, and it wasn't good.

She was only a piece of property. My wife to cement Ivan's place. He wanted the treaty in the hope of one day taking over the Italian mafia. Their hold on their turf was sliding. We knew it, they knew it. Binding to us gave them the added power to scare off attacks, but it also meant in time, we'd own them. They would work for us.

This was always a careful balancing act of power, and Ivan was the master of it.

My wife wasn't supposed to mean anything to me. There was no way I should care if she was out cold or hurt, or injured, or even if someone had fucking upset her. Yet, here I was.

Andrei had changed the woman he was going to marry. Bethany was no longer by his side. The wedding was happening, but with her sister, Adelaide. No one was going to hurt my wife again.

She released a moan, and I leaned forward, taking her hand. "Aurora," I said.

Her eyes opened then closed. Opened again. I waited for her to get accustomed to the light, and she gasped, sitting up and wincing.

The doctor had given her enough painkillers to help manage whatever pain she experienced. I couldn't stand the thought of her hurting.

Sitting on the bed, she squeezed my hand. "Slavik," she said. "You came."

Even though she was hooked up to wires, she wrapped her arms around me only to gasp as pain likely shot through her system from the bullet wound.

"You were shot," I said.

"Ouch." She pouted. "How bad is it?"

"Not bad. They were able to remove the bullet and it didn't do any lasting damage. You've had a few stitches, and you'll hurt for a short time. Not too long."

She looked at her arm. "I remember."

"Do you have any idea who would have shot at you?"

She shook her head. "No. Cara had to leave. She went first. Gus paid the bill and was escorting me out. We waited for the car."

"Why wasn't the car there?" I asked.

"You'd have to ask Gus. Is he okay?"

"He's asleep. The doctors wanted to assess him for the damage." Gus had been shot in the abdomen, arm, and hand. Severe blood loss had him fighting for his life, but I wasn't about to tell Aurora.

"Why would anyone shoot at us? It makes no sense."

"A message." I stroked her hair back from her cheek. These feelings coursing through my body, I had no idea what they meant. They were coming thick and fast. She looked so beautiful. I knew she'd been pretty, regardless of what other people said. They always called her the ugly Fredo, but they clearly didn't see her, not really. Even I hadn't at the start.

Staring at her now, I was … enthralled. Even with the threat of death, she cared more about my men than her own welfare.

It was stupid of her, but after being around so many selfish people, this was refreshing.

"I'm so sorry for being a pain. It was only supposed to be a lunch, and now you've got all this to deal with."

"You have no reason to be sorry."

She wrinkled her nose. "I doubt that."

"How are you feeling?" I asked.

"I don't know. It hurts, but it's manageable." She held up her hand. "Is that because of this?"

"Yes. You'll feel it tomorrow when I take you home." Now that she was awake, I didn't want to leave her.

"You've got to go and take care of business?"

"Duty calls," I said.

She nodded, and I hated seeing her physically withdraw. I had no idea what was happening. I wasn't used to having feelings.

"I've got my men right outside the door. They're going to be here for you. Nothing will happen to you."

Nothing was meant to happen to her while she'd been eating lunch and yet, it still had.

I cupped her cheek, wishing to say more, but nothing would come to me. I wasn't a good man. I didn't do nice things. I'd never intended to take a wife. This was supposed to be all about duty and yet, I couldn't seem to turn it off.

I stood up and left the room without saying another word. My men knew what would happen to them if they allowed her to be hurt.

Within seconds, I was out of the hospital, in the back of my car, being driven to the warehouse where the only shooter I'd allowed to live waited.

Aurora could have died today. I didn't care about the treaty. Let the streets run red with blood. What I did care about was Aurora. The very thought of anything happening to her filled me with something I wasn't used to: despair.

The wrong bullet today, and she could have died. I shouldn't care. I wasn't the kind of man to fall for a woman. I used them. Aurora was different, though. I knew from the start she would be. I just didn't realize how much.

At the warehouse, my driver put the car into park, and I was out of the vehicle before he got a chance to open the door for me.

Buttoning up my jacket, I entered the warehouse to see the man hung upside down. His personal effects had been displayed on the table for me to see.

Six of my finest soldiers stood there, keeping guard. I also spotted the spy Ivan used to keep an eye on his brigadiers. He'd been on my land for several months, and so far, he hadn't caused me trouble, so I was more than happy for him to stay.

The wallet had been placed open and I saw his name was Ewan Smith. "Hello, Ewan," I said.

"Fuck you."

"You're very vocal for a dead man," I said.

I left the torture devices on the table. When it came to getting information out of people, I didn't go for elaborate or dramatic. Plain old kitchen and garden tools worked just fine for me. A hammer or sledgehammer to crush bones. Knives for obvious work. Pliers for the fiddlier work. Plain old twine used to repair fences were great and cut through flesh with enough pressure. I even enjoyed shears.

I dragged the chair over to stare at the man.

Spit was an issue for me, so I kept a distance.

"Fuck you, man. I'm not going to talk. You can't fucking make me. You're a piece of shit."

I'd turned the chair so I straddled the back. My chin rested on my hands as I watched him.

Patience.

When I didn't talk, he went a little crazy, trying to pull himself away from the binds. The bastard was hung upside down.

"Let me go! You're all going to be dead men. All of you."

"Do you know Aurora Ivanov?" I asked.

He looked like he wanted to argue but finally answered. "She's your wife."

"Do you know the woman you shot at today?"

"Yes."

"Who was she?"

"A problem," he said.

"So you were aiming for the woman today."

"I'm not the boss, mate. I was given orders. Today, after a redhead strolls out, the next person waiting for a car, we were to shoot. No questions asked. There was no other target. Aim to kill. That was all."

This was odd. I tapped a finger on my thigh. "You're a bounty hunter?"

"More like an assassin for hire. I was part of a team of men. You killed them all today."

"Any relation to the Fredo family?" I asked.

"Never heard of them."

I found this hard to believe. "You are part of a bunch of assassins for hire and yet you don't even know who the Fredo family are. They are my wife's family. The woman you were asked to kill today, she is my wife."

"Fuck, man, I know who you are, but I'm just a fucking minion. Okay? You killed the guy with all the details. I got nothing. Let me go. I will find out what you need me to find out."

His entire outfit was unprofessional.

I stood up and moved to the toys.

I should be getting a medal for all the restraint I'd shown today. I picked up the knife first. A plain old kitchen knife.

This man nearly took my wife from me. A woman I was convinced I didn't care about, but deep in the back of my mind, I knew that to be false.

Aurora … did something to me. I didn't have any answers, but my anger flooded my body and I reacted, plunging the knife into his stomach. I pulled it out and repeated the action five more times all around his body.

The blood dripped onto the cement floor. In my mind, all I saw was Aurora, heavily pregnant with my child, but with blood coming from a bullet wound in her chest. She could have died.

Dead.

The end.

Lifeless.

A corpse.

Ewan was dead long before I finished with him. His body nothing more than a mangled mess.

I stepped back, and the cleaning crew were already on standby to deal with it.

I was covered in blood. I stripped off my clothes and left the scene, going to the single shower which was last on the cleanup list.

Beneath the cold spray of water, I knew this wasn't Fredo's doing. Whoever hired these men to kill Aurora were novices. I needed to find out if they were related to the banquet attack, and also, who had hired them to take out my woman.

Aurora meant nothing in the Bratva world. She was under my protection as my wife. Her power came from me. Why take her out unless they were trying to get to me through my wife? And that only served to piss me off even more.

Chapter Fifteen

Aurora

"This is very unattractive," I said. "I look a mess."

"Because of your bandaged arm?"

"Look at it." I wrinkled my nose, indicating the clean bandage the doctor had applied. I'd pulled out my arm stitches by being in the kitchen. When the doctor said no heavy lifting, what he actually meant was to do nothing.

I couldn't sit around all day doing nothing.

"You're going to be fine."

"I'm going to stick out like a sore thumb. No, sore arm. It's my arm that's the injured party. Look at it."

Slavik laughed.

I glared at him.

He'd been so attentive the last few days. I hated how easy it was to enjoy his company. Nothing was ever a rush for him, and he'd been annoyed with me for hurting my arm. Sex hadn't happened.

He didn't even have to go out to work. He stayed at the penthouse, on a laptop and his cell phone, while I walked around him. Swimming was a no, as was working out.

My arm put a dent in my weight-loss plans. Slavik also didn't help. He ordered takeout from a nice Italian place. Their pastas were heavenly and well, I'd gained a couple of pounds. My clothes weren't tight, but my arm hindered me.

We were heading to Andrei and Adelaide's wedding. I hadn't seen a picture of the bride. She'd taken over from Bethany without a hitch. All I knew, the woman was a few years younger than Bethany.

The last place I wished to go was to a wedding.

My own wedding had been enough of an ordeal to get through, but Slavik insisted. All the Volkov brigadiers were going, and I was going as Slavik's wife.

"You know, this morning I woke up feeling a little sick. I told the doctor about it when he came to repair the stitches. He said it's a little bug going around. Nothing to alarm myself with. I don't think I should leave."

"If he thought you were contagious, he would've advised me to keep you home."

No matter what I seemed to say to this man, we were going to this wedding. We'd already taken the plane ride. I hated planes and being in the sky. Anything with heights terrified me.

Slavik offered me the window seat, which I declined. I didn't need to be reminded for an hour flight that I was above ground. Now firmly on the ground, we were traveling to our hotel. Two cars were in front, two at the back.

We would stay at the hotel tonight, and tomorrow was the wedding. I was supposed to be a bridesmaid. This was all news to me. Slavik had blurted out that news to me as we got in the car. The dress waited for me to try on at the hotel room.

The last thing I wanted was to be a bridesmaid to a woman I didn't know. This was Bethany's sister.

I leaned back, resting my hand on my stomach. I'd thrown up this morning. The sickness had struck me hard. After some dry toast, I felt a little better. The coffee I'd made for myself set it off again. I ended up drinking water.

"Are you okay?" Slavik asked.

It was on the tip of my tongue to lie. I went for the truth. "No. I feel sick. My arm hurts. I refuse to take pain medication. I'm going to a wedding I don't wish to attend. I'm now going to be a bridesmaid for a woman I've never met. Yeah, everything is great." The sarcasm dripped from my tone, and I froze.

I realized who I spoke to and I wished the ground would open up and swallow me.

I chanced a glance at Slavik to find him smiling. "It's cute to watch you panic."

"This isn't funny."

"It's hilarious. You're the first woman in my life to be honest with me."

"I find that hard to believe."

"Most people hate me, remember?"

"No, they don't hate you. They fear you. It's different." I'd been hated most of my life, or not liked. *Do not go down that morbid self-pitying hole, Aurora.* I forced a smile to my lips.

"Do you fear me?" he asked.

"Sometimes."

"You have no reason to fear me."

"You're my husband."

"And I will protect you."

"Unless you feel I'm trouble for Ivan Volkov. I know my value only exists while I play nice. If I cause you or the Volkov Bratva trouble, my days are numbered."

"Do you have any reason to risk your life?"

"No. I intend to live a long and happy prison sentence." I slapped my hand across my mouth.

"You find being with me a prison sentence."

I winced. "No. It's … I meant my family."

"Aurora, I'm not an idiot."

"It's not a prison sentence, okay? I didn't mean it like that and I know it sounded like that, but I promise, it wasn't."

I'd screwed up.

"You're a guy in this world. You wouldn't understand what I meant. It's different for men."

"Try me. I don't see much different. You were ordered to get married to me. I was instructed to marry you. We both serve the Volkov Bratva. Our roles are different, but we're the same."

"You can do what you want," I said.

"Elaborate."

My mouth went dry. "If you wanted a mistress or other women, you'd have them. I couldn't do anything about it. I could scream and get angry. You killed Sergei for kissing me. We weren't having an affair. You didn't see Cara as a threat. It's why she's still walking around. You get to do things. I … stay at your apartment. I have no purpose. I'm not allowed to go to college, or get a job."

"Do you want those things?" he asked.

I shrugged. "I think I'd like the option."

Slavik continued to stare at me, and I averted my gaze. The early part of our marriage was a nightmare, no doubt about it. There was no love, not even conversation. We'd cohabited the same space.

Now, nearly ten months together, we'd changed. We talked, made love, fucked, and spent time together. Not just for the cameras either, or the spies. I enjoyed his company. He didn't scare me. I never believed he'd hurt me, not really.

The threat was obviously always there, but it had nothing to do with him.

Our positions were thrust on us by our positions.

I wondered if he'd have tried harder with Isabella.

Don't go there. No pity party for Aurora.

When Isabella did visit the last time with the whole fish dinner, Slavik hadn't paid her the slightest bit of attention. He hadn't shown me any either.

I didn't know what would have been worse.

"Working is not an option, however, I have no issue with you studying. I'll arrange for a multitude of courses to be presented to you. You can take your pick."

We'd spoken about it before, but nothing had come from the conversation. This time, it was different. He already had his cell phone and was barking orders at someone to find the right college for me.

My mouth fell open in surprise.

The moment he finished the call, I hugged him, showing him my appreciation. "Thank you."

"We'll see if you'll be thanking me when we get back."

I didn't care. I was so happy we'd arrived at our hotel room.

It was a large building, fancy, private car parking. Slavik's men took the lead and were already booking us in as we were headed to the elevator.

I ignored the stares, refusing to let it bother me today. I was so happy. I was going to pick a college course and further my education.

I had no idea what I'd pick. Again, our conversation from before rushed through me but now with my choice of any course, I wondered what would hold my attention the most.

My smile dissipated when I saw the dress waiting for us on the sofa. Considering this was a hotel room, there was a small sitting room and even a table for us to take our meals.

"Can you cancel me being a bridesmaid?" I asked.

"It's good for public image."

"How?"

"Andrei is one of us. You're my wife. It shows a unity of power." Slavik picked up the dress. It was a pastel pink. "Come on. I'll help you get it on."

We went into the bedroom as the guards brought up our stuff. The last thing I wanted to do was wear the bridesmaid's dress.

Slavik helped me out of my current dress, sliding the zipper down. "Doesn't the bride want someone she knows to be at her wedding?"

"Aurora, shut up. You're not going to get out of this."

I rolled my eyes, stepping out of the dress and turning to Slavik. His gaze was on my ass and slowly traveled up my body. I was very much aware at that moment of how not perfect I was.

"You're beautiful," Slavik said.

"Would you please stop saying stuff like that?"

"You want me to stop paying you a compliment?"

"When it's not true, yes."

"And who says it's not true?" he asked.

I sighed. "Come on. You and I both know the truth. You don't have to pretend with me." I'd been told all my life how ugly I was. How I didn't measure up to my sister.

Slavik dropped the dress, and within seconds, I was trapped on the bed. My arms pinned above my head, his body flush against mine. In the process, my legs had spread open and he lay pressed against me.

Pleasure rushed through me. Instantaneous. A burning need only he could put out.

"I find you beautiful," he said. "I'm your husband. Your keeper. Your protector. My word, in your world, is fucking law. I'm getting tired of having to compete with all the bullshit going on inside your head. It doesn't have a right to fucking live there, Aurora. I don't say shit I don't mean. When I tell you I think you're beautiful, I mean it. Do you understand me?"

I nodded.

"Are you beautiful?" he asked.

I started to shake my head. He glared down at me.

"I can't."

"Wrong answer." He slammed his lips down on mine.

I kept my eyes open as he kissed me. Slavik didn't close his as he thrust his body against me. I gasped as he touched just the right spot. With most of my clothes off, I only had the lingerie to protect me. He knew this and used it to his advantage.

I gasped as he held my hands above my head, and with a single finger, he traced down my arm, going to the puckered bead of my nipple.

This man aroused me. Slavik was doing stuff to me that I wasn't sure I liked. I wanted to hate him, but the truth was he shattered my defenses. He took me by surprise and the guard I had up came down so easily around him.

He stroked my nipple gently through the fabric of my bra. I tried to keep my arousal in check. My body, the traitorous bitch that it was, had other ideas. She didn't want to play nice with me. No, she liked Slavik. The more he stroked, the hotter I got, my pussy heating with each touch. He pushed the cup of the bra back, and I nearly jolted off the bed as his mouth covered the hard peak.

He flicked his tongue back and forth and made no move to leave me alone. Then he slid his body to the other side, making sure not to hurt me. The pain in my shoulder was a dull ache. The pleasure far outweighed the hurt.

I didn't want him to stop. I liked the way he held me down as he played with me.

He did the same to my other nipple and released it with a plop, which seemed to echo in the large room.

"I fucking love your tits. They were designed for a man's pleasure." He cupped them both together and nibbled the edge of one. "You are beautiful to me, Aurora, and I'm the only one who should matter to you."

He thrust his cock against me, and I couldn't help but gasp. He was hard as rock for me. I sank my teeth into my lip in an attempt to get control of myself, but nothing worked.

Slavik let go of my tit to cup my face. His thumb held my chin, and he pulled down, releasing me. "I want to hear every single sound you make."

"Please."

"Do you want me to fuck you?"

"Can you?"

His gaze flickered to my arm and he smiled. "I can make it so it doesn't even hurt."

Was that a promise?

The moment he touched me, everything stopped hurting.

"Show me," I said.

Slavik eased off my body and reached for his pants. The sound of the zipper echoed in the air. I never knew this sound could be so erotic, but he worked it so damn well. He pressed the tip of his cock against my wet pussy. He slid up and down my slit, getting his cock nice and slick before lining it up with my entrance.

Slowly, inch by inch, he sank inside me so I felt it all.

It was amazing. So hard. I no longer cared about the pain in my arm. My only focus was the man inside me.

He cupped my hips and gave me a few firm strokes, each seeming deeper than the one before. The angle made me desperate for more.

Suddenly, he stopped. One of his hands released me but not for long as his fingers began to stroke over my clit while he was still inside me.

"I want to feel you come all over my cock, Aurora," he said. "Give it to me."

His fingers were magical. I had no idea I could feel this way beneath his touch. Slavik set me on fire, hungry and desperate for more. There was no control.

He held on to it.

Nurtured it.

Captured it all to himself.

I cried out, begging for more but not really sure what I was asking for. Slavik knew. Of course, he did. This man knew everything when it came to sex and pleasure.

He was the master.

I, his student.

I came hard, screaming his name. Slavik rewarded me by pounding into my pussy, not letting go, and damn it, he was right, there was no pain. I only focused on my need for him. On the hardness as he plunged inside me. Each thrust driving me higher and higher into need unlike anything else.

He showed me what I could take. Never holding back, and when he came, I followed him into another mini-orgasm as he stroked just the right points inside me. Each flow of his cum made me feel whole. This was what scared me.

My husband, Slavik Ivanov, had started to make me fall for him, and I had no clue how to stop it.

****

Slavik

The dresses were normally monstrosities for the bridesmaids, but the one Aurora wore suited her. A beautiful pastel pink, and it was like the dress was designed exactly for her as the arms fell away from the shoulders, covering the upper arms and hiding her bandage. The very sight always angered me, but I'd been able to keep it in check.

I sat in one of the seats as Aurora took her place at the head altar. She didn't look into the crowd as the bride began to make her way down.

The moment we'd arrived, there had been some kind of commotion. Aurora had been requested to go to the bride's quarters immediately.

I didn't get a chance to ask her what the hell was going on, but I could imagine. The younger sister didn't want to marry Andrei. Not that I blamed any woman being forced into a marriage like this. I stood with everyone and watched as the bride made her way down the aisle. The dress looked a little on the tight side. Even with the veil across her face, I noticed her huge, bulging tits that were no doubt going to pop out if she wasn't careful. The bouquet quivered slightly.

The man beside her looked angry.

Kind of reminded me of Aurora's dad. The march was slow, and I didn't know if that was the father or the bride.

Adelaide looked ready to flee.

One look at Ivan, and I saw our boss was a very happy man.

Adelaide stopped at the altar and her father lifted the veil then kissed her cheek, which looked more like a press of lips rather than an actual pucker. The fucker couldn't even be bothered to kiss his daughter goodbye. Andrei took the hand given to him, and I watched the ceremony, not listening to a word as I watched my wife.

Aurora held some roses within her hands. She'd woken this morning feeling sick. It was only going to be a matter of time before she found out about the pregnancy. So far, there was no sign of it. No swollen stomach. No tenderness of her breasts. She'd experienced some sickness in the mornings, but I helped to convince her it related to her bullet wound.

I was a complete and total bastard.

After the way she reacted to Ivan's confession, I didn't want her to jump to conclusions about why I wanted to sleep with her. I should just let her believe the worst of me. Most people did, and I was a horrible person. The truth was I would do what Ivan asked me to do for the good of the Bratva. If it meant fucking her until I knocked her up, I would. There was just a blurred line on exactly how I'd go about it.

I liked Aurora. I truly believed it was more than liking her.

In the most inconvenient times, I found myself thinking about her, curious what she was doing and wanting to be with her. I enjoyed her smile. The laughter she'd often allow to spill from her lips when she found something so funny. I liked how sweet she was. Even at the fight, surrounded by people not from our world, and yet she'd been the only person to scream for mercy.

Everything about her called to me, and I had no fucking clue how to turn this off. It couldn't be love. I was incapable of loving anyone, but Aurora, damn it. She made this hard for me.

The ceremony came to an end with a kiss.

Andrei didn't seem to mind his bride had changed at the last minute. In the way he held Adelaide and kissed her. I hadn't given Aurora the kiss.

She'd been a laughing stock at her wedding and at the time, I hadn't cared.

Like everyone else, I stood and clapped.

My woman finally looked at me, and there was a

smile. Not one that lit up her face, but a sadness.

When people started to move, Aurora came to me. There, surrounded by people, I cupped her face and kissed her, how I should have done the day of our wedding.

I finished the kiss off with a quick peck to the lips, and when I pulled back, Aurora's eyes were closed.

Slowly, they opened, and I saw the flush working its way up her body. "What was that for?" she asked.

"Because I wanted to, and I didn't want to go another second without kissing those lips." I stroked my thumb across it.

"What a way to take the spotlight away from the scared little bride," Ivan said.

I looked around to see we were the only ones standing in the church.

"They're gone," Ivan said. He put his hand on Aurora's shoulder with a smile. "I'm glad to see you're not dead."

I wanted to tear his fucking arm off for touching what was mine.

Aurora smiled. "Thank you."

Ivan walked off. Conversation terminated.

"That's good, right? He's pleased I'm not dead? I should worry if he wanted me dead?"

I laughed and kissed the top of her head. "Come on. Let's get out of here."

I'd hoped to steal my wife away to have some alone time. No such luck. The bride rushed over to us and took Aurora's hand. She didn't look my way, and my wife went, holding on to my hand in a final attempt to keep me.

The bride wrapped her arms around Aurora for some of the pictures. The bride looked to be falling apart, and my wife comforted her.

I glanced at the bridesmaids and spotted Bethany away from the small group, looking spitefully at her sister.

I didn't care as I returned my gaze to my woman.

"What do you know?" Ivan asked, coming to join me again.

"It was sloppy," I said, immediately talking about my wife's attack. We hadn't gotten a chance to talk as Aurora's father had been furious to learn she'd been shot. Not enough to come and visit her. He'd made his displeasure known to Ivan. There had even been talk of Aurora going home so they could protect her. The family couldn't even stand her and treated her like shit, but the insult was there. They'd still protect family better than us we could. There was no way I'd let my wife go back to her family.

She belonged to me. No one else. I would never allow her to go.

"How sloppy?"

"Whoever hired them was not used to doing so, or they wanted it to appear so."

"Any hunches?"

"One and you're not going to like it."

I turned to Ivan and gave him the name, and he instantly shook his head. "You're wrong."

"Look at the facts and you tell me that I'm wrong," I said. "Do you think I haven't tried to find an ulterior motive? Or one of our enemies? This is the only one that makes sense and you know it."

"Before you act, find out more."

"You know I've got physical evidence," I said. My suspicions had been raised several times, but this was the first where I knew what I was talking about.

The pictures were finished even as the bride tried to get everyone to stay. Aurora held Adelaide's hands and began to talk to her. I saw the bride begin to calm, and when Andrei approached, she went with him.

"Time for the real party to start," Ivan said. "Tell your wife I want her to save me a dance."

"Not happening," I said.

"I'm the boss."

"And she's my wife."

"Ah, but she wouldn't be your wife without me. So, I get a dance." Ivan slapped me on the back.

Not if I took all of her dances.

Aurora rushed over to me, and in front of everyone, she hugged me. "Please tell me Andrei is a good guy and won't beat her?"

"What's going on?"

Aurora blew out a breath. "When I arrived, Adelaide was having a panic attack. Bethany had said something to her, and with the dress, she'd snapped. The dress had been altered at the shop, but someone mysteriously brought the wrong size here. I imagine that was Bethany. She's been spiteful since the moment I arrived, and I bet even before then too." She blew out a breath and glanced back.

The bridesmaids were all getting into the back of the car, and I took Aurora's arm, leading her away from the nonsense. I agreed to my wife being part of the wedding party, but not leaving my side.

After she was shot at, I vowed to do better to protect her, and not because of her family.

"I talked her out of her panic attack. Convinced her that marriage is not so bad." She took my hands.

"How?"

"I told her that … I was petrified on my wedding night, and I got through it." She smiled up at me. "That I survived and I live to tell the tale. I also mentioned my husband isn't so bad either."

I kissed her knuckles. "We've got to get to that party."

"Yes. Adelaide could have a massive freak-out, and I don't want her to get hurt."

This was just another part of my wife I fucking loved.

I stopped.

Hell, no.

I didn't do love.

I liked my wife.

Liked.

Not loved.

"Is everything okay?" Aurora asked.

I cupped her face and kissed her hard. She touched my face, kissing me back and pressing her whole body against me.

"Not that I mind you kissing me, but do you want to tell me what the occasion is for?"

"Making up for lost time."

She giggled. "I like it."

I kissed her again, sliding my tongue into her mouth and reaching down to cup her ass. Let people see. I didn't care. This was my woman.

A car horn filled the air, and I broke the kiss to glance over Aurora's shoulder to see Ivan standing next to a car.

"Come on, I want a drink. Time to go and party," he said.

Damn. I forgot we were sharing a car with Ivan. Taking my wife's hand, I walked toward the car. Ivan had already climbed in, and I allowed Aurora to get in next. I closed the door and glanced at Ivan.

"This is cozy," he said.

I didn't want him anywhere near my wife.

The car pulled away from the curb as Aurora

snuggled against me. I wrapped my arm around her shoulders, and Ivan smiled wide.

"Good to see you two are getting along so well."

I was tempted to give him the bird, but instead, I kissed my wife's head. Ivan was still my boss. Best friends we may be, and we'd defied the odds of the Bratva, but I knew if he felt he needed to, he'd take me out in a heartbeat.

My loyalty was to him, and if he thought for a second it was swayed, he'd take Aurora away from me. That, I couldn't allow.

Chapter Sixteen

Aurora

I hated weddings.

I'd hated my own wedding.

When I'd been the bride, I shouldn't have been alone and yet, I had been. So alone. Always alone. At this wedding with Adelaide, I managed to still be alone. Slavik had been taken by Ivan and were currently at the table, talking. They appeared to be talking business, so I stood in the corner of the room, nursing a glass of water at Slavik's insistence. He didn't want me to get drunk. The champagne looked tempting. I couldn't deny it, but I sipped at my water, being ignored.

Adelaide kept trying to come to me. Each time she did, Andrei was by her side, holding her close. Had Slavik told him how she struggled with this entire wedding?

No one had tried to calm her down, given her points to hope for. Bethany had taken a sick kind of pleasure in taunting her little sister, and it pissed me off. The dance floor had filled up, and as it did, Bethany took Andrei, giving Adelaide the chance to leave his side. She came to me and instantly wrapped her arms around me.

I wasn't used to this.

"Thank you," Adelaide said. "Would you stay? Live with me? We could run away together."

I laughed, rubbing my good hand on her back in an effort to comfort her. "You're going to be surprised. Andrei might be an amazing man."

"Really? He swapped my sister for me. She was his first choice." She pulled back and I saw tears in her eyes.

An answering ache bloomed in my chest. "My sister is normally the first choice, but my dad … you know what, you don't need to know the details. I was given to Slavik and it has been good. He's good to me."

"I heard what happened," Adelaide said. "How he didn't kiss you at your wedding. Bethany … she said some pretty nasty things about you."

"They're not true, at least I hope not." I shrugged.

"I like you," Adelaide said. "I … I don't have any friends. Bethany tends to…" She glanced at her sister. "She likes to take them, you know? She's the most popular one. The person everyone likes. I'm just me."

I took her hand. "I can't stay here. I've got a life with Slavik, but you can call me anytime."

Adelaide nodded and took a deep breath. "Bethany said Andrei beats his women. I'm … I don't like pain, and I'm a virgin. I don't think I could … I feel sick."

I took Adelaide to the bathroom. She did indeed throw up. I pulled her hair back as she emptied out whatever was in her stomach.

I felt for this woman. Her life as she knew it was over. I had no idea about Andrei.

"I'll be right back, honey."

"Please, don't leave."

There was no way I could let her feel this way. "Trust me, okay."

"Aurora."

I let her go. There was only going to be one way to solve this.

Entering the main dance floor again, I saw Bethany all over Andrei. This wasn't my business, but I wasn't about to have another woman feel in any way like I did during a marriage.

I walked onto the dance floor and grabbed Andrei's arm. "Can I have a word?"

He immediately let go of Bethany, who protested.

Without looking her way, I took Andrei off the dance floor toward the bathroom.

My hands were clammy now that I had him alone.

"Do you beat your women?" I asked.

The smile on Andrei's face disappeared. "Does Slavik know what you're doing?"

"Your wife is currently in the bathroom throwing up. Bethany has been whispering lies or truths into her ear, and I don't know what they are. You can hate me, and to be honest, I don't care. She's petrified you're going to hurt her, and this is all Bethany's fault. All she is doing is following orders."

Andrei looked toward the bathroom. "She should come to me."

"Try being a young, virginal woman who has been swapped for her sister. I'm sure you'd go and tell your intended exactly how scared you are." Sarcasm dripped from my tone.

His jaw clenched. "Thank you," Andrei said.

I didn't trust him.

He brushed past me and entered the bathroom. Had I just fucked up?

I stayed. Holding the bathroom door slightly open and listening.

They … talked.

Andrei asked her what Bethany had said and she answered. I heard his responses.

When they left the bathroom, I made sure to hide in the shadows.

Adelaide spotted me and gave me a smile. I followed them out, going to stand in my secluded section of the dance floor. Bethany approached me, and I tensed up, waiting for the impending fight.

"You think you're so smart, don't you?" Bethany

asked.

"No. I think I'm kind and you're cruel."

"Oh, please, you saved me. Andrei is an old fossil. If you think I can't have him again, you're wrong. I can. Men are so easy. They like pretty women, Aurora." She scoffed. "But then, you wouldn't have the first clue about that. You're the pity fuck. The one who was given away by her own family because they couldn't stand to send their special one. No wonder you and my sister get along. She's a monstrosity."

"You tried to ruin your sister's day." I turned to look at Bethany. "And you failed. Go away. No one wants a spiteful bitch."

Bethany smiled. "Let's see what you're saying when your husband can't get enough of me."

She spun on her heel and left.

My hands clenched into fists. Deep in my heart, I knew she was a nasty piece of work. The way she flirted with Slavik drove a pain deep and sharp into my heart, making me feel sick.

Tears filled my eyes and I tried to hold them in. There was no reason to cry. So she said some horrible things. They were the truth.

This was my life, all my life. Second best. Hated. Pushed aside. Forgotten. Unloved. I glanced down at my hands, trying not to let the emotion overwhelm me.

It was too much.

I felt like I was drowning.

Why did I feel this way?

These were not new feelings but old ones.

Slavik stood up, and I watched with horror as he escorted Bethany onto the dance floor.

Sinking my teeth into my lip, I couldn't stand it. Turning on my heel, I headed off the dance floor, going straight to the gardens out back. There was a small patio area and while we'd been inside, rain had started to fall thick and fast.

My stomach recoiled. I put a hand on my stomach as my eyes swam with tears. I was going to be sick.

Gripping the edge of the rail, overlooking the garden, the rawness of the stone bit into my fingertips.

I closed my eyes, the first droplets of tears spilling out.

"Don't," I said.

I took deep breaths, but it was no good. They opened a flood of pain. This was not the time or the place to be crying, but I couldn't stop them. I sobbed into the air, slowly sinking down to my knees, still holding on to the stone, trying not to let anything get to me, but it was no good.

This … hurt.

Slavik's arms around Bethany. Slavik being inside her. If what she said was true, would he fall for her charms?

Arms surrounded me, and I gasped.

"I've got you," Ivan said.

This scared the crap out of me, and I scrambled out of his arms, keeping my back to him, trying to hide my tears.

"I'm so sorry," I said. This was … a nightmare.

"You don't have to hide from me," Ivan said.

I stayed tense, swiping left and right at my cheeks, trying to gain control. Nothing was happening, and I gritted my teeth. Anger rushed through me. This was … not right.

"Am I needed inside?"

"No," Ivan said. "Andrei won't leave his wife's side. They're dancing now."

"Good. That's good." I had no idea what to say.

Silence fell between us. Ivan didn't leave.

"You weren't supposed to see that."

"I'm glad I did. Is Slavik hurting you?"

"No." I turned to Ivan and shook my head. "Of course not."

"I didn't think so, and now I can look into your face."

Shame washed over me. "I'm fine."

"No, you're not. What did Bethany say to you?" Ivan asked, arms folded.

"It was nothing. Just silly girl talk."

"Silly girl talk has you crying at weddings?" he asked.

"I know, right? It must be all the emotions flying around. It's fine." I nodded my head.

"You know, Aurora, many people hate how I came to power. I was a no one. I was a fucked-up mess." He took a step toward me. "People underestimate me."

I recalled Cara's words. She'd told me what happened. "Cara told me. She said how you and Slavik and she worked from the ground up."

"Did she?" Ivan tapped his fingers on the stone railing. "Well, she's not wrong. I was the stuttering bastard of the original Bratva. An embarrassment and a disappointment." He chuckled. "He was far from those things when I killed him. I'm not like previous men in my place. I don't follow the rules or the setup. I'm my own man."

"Why are you telling me this?" I asked.

"I see the way Slavik looks at you."

I paused, not sure what to say or do. How did he look at me? Hopefully not like he wanted to kill me.

I tried not to panic. "He's loyal to you."

"I know what he is. I also know he will do anything within his power to keep you safe. You're not alone anymore, Aurora."

"You don't have to say this to me."

Ivan closed the distance between us. He was a giant of a man. As tall as Slavik and as muscular, but there was a reason he was the boss. This man was scary as fuck. I'd feel sorry for any person who captured his attention.

Was I judging him?

He once had a stutter. He'd been cast aside.

"I know what it's like to be thrown away as if you mean nothing. This treaty was never about your sister. You were not our second choice."

"You're lying. My father made his choice."

Ivan chuckled. "I've killed people for less of an insult."

I tensed up as he reached out to touch me. I didn't know what he planned to do, but he merely put a hand on his arm. "I knew immediately who he'd give to me, and I didn't want a fickle bitch in my camp. I wanted a woman who'd been cast aside her whole life. Who had a reputation for being nice and kind, and loyal. I'm not a stupid man, Aurora. I take care of my men, and you were perfect for him."

With that, he turned on his heel and left.

What the hell just happened?

****

Slavik

Bethany was a viperous bitch.

Her claws were out.

"I can't believe Aurora would lie about me. I'm a good woman. A much better match to Andrei than my sister. She doesn't have what it takes to please a man like him. I know how to." She tried to press her body against mine. "I can do things that will blow your mind, Slavik. There is nothing I won't do for you."

For the past five minutes, she'd been offering her

body up to me. "You'd like that, wouldn't you? To think you won. That you took Aurora's husband from her. I know who you are, Bethany, and to be honest, I don't like what I see or what I hear." I glared at her. I was done playing nice. "If I ever hear you talk about my woman, or you hurt her like you did the last time, I will fucking kill you. Do you understand me?"

"I have no idea what you're talking about. Aurora is a liar. She can't stand to have friends, and her aim is to make everyone feel sorry for her."

This time, I smiled. "You're wrong, and do you know how I know this? She heard you, Bethany. At the last lunch you shared together. She heard the nasty shit you said about her. I'm telling you to be glad you're a guest at this wedding, and I've promised to be on my good behavior. For insulting my wife, I'd make you pay for that. I'd make you scream and beg, and I wouldn't stop until I carved up your face and tore you to pieces."

With that, I released her and went out of the room to where I saw my wife disappear.

Ivan came back through the door.

No sign of my woman.

"Aurora's outside. You do know she's in a great deal of pain," Ivan said. "The shit that happened long before you ever met her. It plagues her."

"Stay away from my wife," I said.

"Or what? You're going to keep more secrets from me?" Ivan asked. "Like … the baby?"

I glanced over his shoulder. "It's not a secret."

"She has no idea she's carrying your baby."

"She's not ready to know and you know she thinks I do everything out of duty."

Ivan chuckled. "If you do everything out of duty, then follow this order. Tell your woman how you feel and end this misery between the two of you. She's yours,

Slavik, you just have to take her."

He brushed past me, and I turned toward him. "I can't kill her."

Ivan smiled. "I never said you had to."

He walked away, and I left the building, finding my wife on the porch, her body pressed against the stone railing. I stepped behind her, wrapping my arms around her waist. I heard her sniffle and knew she'd been crying.

"Do you want me to kill him?" I asked, brushing my fingers against her shoulder.

"No. He didn't make me cry. How was your dance with Bethany?"

"I made you cry?"

"No, not really. I guess you did. Seeing you with her hurt."

"I never want to cause you pain."

She sighed. "You can't make promises like that. I'm … I've got a lot of … issues."

I chuckled. "We all have a lot of issues."

"All my life, all I've ever been told was that I don't measure up. I am second best. I am not liked. I'm unlovable, and seeing you with Bethany after she said that you will be with her, that you'd make love to her, it hurt." Aurora turned toward me, tears glistening in her eyes. "I … I can't stand the thought of her or any other woman being with you. I know I'm not perfect."

"Don't," I said. "I don't want to hear another word out of that mouth of yours that makes the claim you're not good enough. Screw them, Aurora. You think I don't know how you feel? I was left to rot in the dirt for years. I fought my way. That fight you witnessed, that was fucking clean compared to the shit I've put up with. I am loyal to Ivan, but I'm also loyal to you. There isn't going to be another woman. I have no desire to screw around."

I ran my fingers through my hair. Talking like this didn't come naturally to me, and seeing the pain in her eyes renewed my rage. "I can't promise your life is going to be easy, but I will do everything I can to make you love this life."

"Will you be happy?" Aurora asked.

I was confused. "Me?"

"Yes. Will you be happy with me?"

"Have I given you the impression I'm not?"

She smiled and shook her head. "No."

"Then I'm going to be happy." I kissed her head. "Are you okay?"

"I think so. I just, I don't know what came over me. I've been getting so emotional lately for no reason at all. I don't understand it." She shrugged. "This … wedding. I don't know what it's doing to me, but it's like I can't stop the pain, and it's morphing into anger. I've never felt this way before."

There was no one around, and the last thing I wanted to do was join the wedding party again. Adelaide had stuck by my wife, pulling her away from me. I'd never thought I was the jealous type until Aurora. "Talk to me."

She sighed. "You know most of it. My dad offering me in place of my sister. Not even asking me what I wanted. Years and years of not measuring up. Of being second best." Tears swam in her eyes, but I recognized another emotion, anger. I'd rarely seen it in Aurora's eyes. "Adelaide feels something similar. It's not exact, but it's close. The pain is like more than she can bear. She doesn't know if she's terrified of her new husband, or angry that she is just a replacement for Bethany."

Her teeth sank into her bottom lip. "All my life, all I've ever been is second best to my sister to everyone around me, including my own family. I've been gone nearly ten months and other than one dinner, no calls. No celebration. Nothing." Tears fell from her eyes, and she spun away from me. "Just ignore me. I don't know what's wrong. This is all too much."

I knew what to do.

Taking her hand, I led her out of the wedding party, away from any prying eyes. I pulled my cell phone out of my pocket and called Ivan.

"We're leaving the party early."

"Did I give you permission for it?" Ivan asked.

I didn't even hesitate. I kept on walking. "My woman needs me."

I hung up my cell phone but sent a quick text to my men waiting at the hotel.

"Wait, what about Adelaide?"

"She's got people. I'm taking you. No questions asked."

The driver was smoking as we approached, leaning on the car, glancing down at his cell phone. He laughed before looking up, and the cigarette was gone, cell phone away, and the door was held open for us.

I told him to take us to our hotel.

"Slavik, what's going on?"

"Trust me." I took her hands, kissing the knuckles.

My cell phone went off, and I pulled it from my pocket.

Ivan: Tell her about the baby.

I didn't know why my boss was meddling. Ivan rarely interfered. This was the first time I'd kept anything from him.

"Are you okay?" Aurora asked.

She'd been having a meltdown but asked about my well-being. This woman, she was … I had no words.

Cupping her face, I tilted her head toward me and brushed my lips against hers.

She moaned my name, kissing me back, and damn it, when did a kiss have to be so addictive? I licked across her lips, sucking the bottom one into my mouth, using my teeth to pull it from between hers.

"Slavik," she said, moaning louder. Her hand landed on my chest, right above my heart.

Staring into her eyes, I was struck by every single part of her.

The driver came to a stop, and I exited the car. Opening the door, I held her hand, and together, we walked to the elevator.

I wasn't touching her enough. I tugged her close, wrapping an arm around her waist, keeping her tight to me as was physically possible. Kissing the top of her head, I watched the elevator descend rather than go up.

"Slavik, we're not going to our room."

"I know."

"What's happening?"

"Trust me."

She rested against my side, and in the reflection of the doors, I saw her snuggle up against me. No smile teased her lips. She looked sad. I hated it and was about to wipe it from her face.

The doors opened and I stepped out.

As per my instructions to my men, the gym was bare. No one was around.

"Slavik?"

I moved her past the running machines, the weights, toward the far part of the room. A punching bag hung, looking a little worse for wear, but durable.

Mitts waited, and I picked them up, securing them to my wife's hands.

"I'm not going to fight you. I'd lose."

"This is not about you fighting me," I said. "You think I don't know a thing or two about pain? About rejection? About not measuring up?"

"Slavik—"

"I do." I'd never spoken these feelings to another living soul. "I use it to help make me a better leader. I don't need people to like me or to care about me. They have to respect me. There is no shame in being who you are. They don't like you, that's on them, because, Aurora, when I look at you, I see no fault, no flaw. I see a woman who is worthy of my attention, and everyone else around here can go get fucked before I let them treat you like that. The Bethanys of this world, they're everywhere. I can find a hundred of them right here in this building, but I can only find one Aurora. You don't need to compare yourself to them. There's nothing wrong with you. You're one of a kind, and that makes you fucking special."

I cupped her face, tilting her head back to kiss her. "Now, all of that pain, the anger. Feed it. Channel it. Throw it at this, and let it leave you, knowing you're a better person than most. You don't need all of that other crap."

I slammed my fist against the bag, and it swung. "Just unleash it."

I moved to stand behind the bag, holding it into place.

"This feels silly."

"It's not. You're afraid. Don't be. I'm here. I've got you. I'm the only one that can see."

She licked her lips and held her hands up.

The first jab at the bag was pitiful. There was no real fight to her, and I got it. She'd never given in.

All these years, she had no choice but to swallow the bitter pill and look the other way. To hide it deep,

deep down. She couldn't do that. If she did, it was only going to make her feel worse.

"There is no shame in this, Aurora. Trust me to help you through this. Remember, I wasn't surrounded by family. I had to earn my place here. I was kicked out. Ignored. Rejected. I worked the streets for every single crumb. This is my life now. I will never allow another person to treat me like trash. I will crush them. You're worth everything, Aurora. One day, we're going to have children. If we have two girls, or three, would you let one or two feel like they didn't matter because of the most beautiful?"

"No!" She slammed her fist against the punching bag.

It was harder than before. This time, she didn't need any more encouragement from me. With each hit, I watched the anger come to the surface, the sheer agony of everything she'd been through.

All of it manifested as she took it out on the punching bag. Her hits got harder. The pain clearly starting to morph into something else as she finally let loose. This time, rather than use her fist, she lifted her leg and kicked the bag hard. The dress was so loose that it didn't constrict her movement.

Perspiration dotted her brow, and after she finished, she came to me, wrapping her arms around my neck, holding me close. "Thank you."

"You don't need to thank me. This was all on you."

I ran my hands down her back, my dick hardening as her soft body brushed against mine.

Chapter Seventeen

Aurora

I floated.

Staring up at the ceiling, the water carried me as if I was weightless. With my hands resting on my stomach, my mind started to wander.

After attacking the punching bag, Slavik had taken me to our room and made love to me for the remainder of the night. It had been glorious. I smiled at the memory alone. His hands all over my body. His lips on mine. His dick filling me.

Each time even better than the last. I hadn't wanted him to stop.

When the morning came, we had no choice but to leave the hotel room and head back to his city.

We'd been back a week. My birthday was next week, and he'd given no mention of even knowing. Did he know?

My birthday had never been a big deal back home with my family. There were usually some presents and a few cards. Never a party. No one wanted to celebrate my birthday.

Taking a deep breath, I spread my arms out, allowing the feeling to completely consume me.

This morning, I'd woken up and vomited. Slavik had been there to rub my back. He'd promised to spend the day with me, but a call had him leaving. Something big was going down at work, and I knew it caused him great concern, but he refused to talk about it. I was there for him regardless. Whatever it was, he could handle it.

Left alone with nothing to do, with my thoughts, my attention had caught on the calendar. As my sickness started to abate, realization dawned. The morning sickness, the sensitivity to smells. It was all related.

Pregnant.

I had to be. It was the only logical explanation.

Only, I didn't know how to go about getting a pregnancy test without alerting my guard or my husband.

I needed to know the answer.

Would Slavik be happy? Would he stop being attentive? Was this new closeness with him a ploy to get into my pants more often?

My mind was ruining everything in my head, driving me crazy with not knowing. I couldn't stand the thought of Slavik only using me for sex. I knew he had a duty to get me pregnant, but for now, I did feel selfish in only wanting to enjoy the two of us together.

A baby though.

My hands returned to my stomach. I'd be able to have a child to love and to cherish it in every single way my parents had failed me. I'd never fail my child. If it was a boy, would Slavik allow me to … be there? Would he take our son away from me? My daughter?

Tears filled my eyes, and I gritted my teeth.

I needed to clarify our position, or at the very least, my position in our child's future. This shouldn't be something I found out now. There was no way I wasn't pregnant. The sickness had to be explained that way.

Releasing my arms, I stared up at the ceiling. I couldn't spend all day floating my troubles away.

Arms wrapped around me, dragging me down into the water. I screamed, water filling my mouth.

I flailed against the arms, but they let me go the moment I started to struggle. Breaking free of the water, I turned to find Slavik, a smile on his face.

Coughing out the water, I slapped him on the chest. "Don't do that again."

"I couldn't help it. You didn't even hear me come in, did you?"

"No."

I pushed my hair back, glancing around to find the guard who'd recently been assigned to me gone.

"Any news on Gus?" I asked.

"He's recovering still." Due to the extent of his wounds, a short stint in rehab had been needed. I'd been unaware he'd been shot in the hip, and the damage alone meant he was having to learn to walk again. The surgery had gone well in repairing him. Slavik usually gave me updates.

"Good. That's good. Do you think we should send him a gift basket?" I hated that someone was hurt because of me.

"I've taken care of it. A man like Gus doesn't want a gift basket."

"What did you get him?"

Slavik's brow rose. "Do you really need me to say it?"

"No." *Women*.

Slavik smiled, and it wasn't an I'm-about-to-murder-you smile. This was an actual, genuine smile. Not scary. He wrapped his arms around me, and I didn't fight him as he pulled me close. "Do you want to tell me why you're all alone in the pool?"

"You'd be pissed if I took my new guy."

"True." He ran his hands down my back to my waist. I didn't notice a difference in my stomach. He pulled me close, and I felt the hard ridge of his cock. "Do you have any idea how much I've thought about you today?"

He went to the strap of my one-piece bathing suit. My mouth went dry as he lowered it. I didn't put up a fight as he pushed it past my breasts, going down my body until it was at my waist. He guided it past my hips. Once in the water, it fell slowly to the pool bottom, and I stepped out of it. Slavik dipped beneath, picking it up, and threw it across the pool for it to land on the edge. "You can put that back on later."

Glancing in the water, I saw he was already naked.

"How did you get in?"

"I'm trained to go undetected." He lifted me up in the water. "Put me inside you."

Even as my face heated, I reached between us, holding his cock. I placed it at my entrance like he'd shown me to do recently. He sank me onto his cock, and we both groaned. The sounds echoed around the room.

With each inch, I gripped his shoulders, holding on as he took me.

"Look at me," he said with a growl.

Opening my eyes, I gave him my full attention with a moan.

"Fuck, yes. I love the way your cunt feels around my dick. I can't get enough of you, Aurora. I'm tempted to start taking you back to work with me so I can have you whenever I damn well choose."

I wrapped my legs around his waist as he pounded inside me.

Pleasure rushed through me, and I kissed him, not wanting this to end.

All my troubles faded as I focused on my husband. The impossible man I was falling for. No doubt about it in my mind. I was loving this man in ways I didn't think possible. He wasn't nice, nor was he easy. He infuriated me, and at times I knew I hated him, but I couldn't get enough of him.

Up and down, he guided me over his length.

"I want to feel you come all over my cock." He moved us through the waves until my back pressed up against the side of the pool. "Touch your pussy. Let me feel you come all over my dick."

This always made me feel a little embarrassed. I slid my hand between us, touching my clit. I stroked the bud and gasped.

Slavik's moan was deep, guttural, turning me on as his cock seemed to pulse and get bigger within me.

"That's it, baby, fuck, yeah, finger your pussy. Let me feel you come. You like my cock, don't you?"

"Yes," I said, moaning.

"That's right."

As I played with my pussy, he started to shallowly stroke within my body. Each thrust driving my arousal higher.

I fingered my clit, staring into his eyes. Held by his gaze, not wanting to move as I worked my body, bringing myself closer and closer to that glorious peak. When I came, Slavik held my hips, slamming deep inside me. It was like my pussy had something to hold on to and he fed it.

Driving in deep, fucking me, taking me.

I couldn't get enough. I didn't want him to stop. The pleasure was out of this world.

The moment I stopped, Slavik turned into an animal, fucking me with all his might, driving in deep, consuming me, taking me. Each hard thrust of his cock turned me on. I had no choice but to hold on as he took me.

I wanted this more than anything.

He slammed inside me. His grip was so tight it would leave bruises. I felt his hardness kick as he filled me with more of his cum.

This was why I knew I had to be pregnant. We didn't use protection. We never had.

Slavik kissed my lips. "I've been thinking about doing that all day."

"In the pool?"

"No. I imagined you in our bed."

My heart fluttered whenever he would talk about us. *We*, *our*. I liked it.

"We got the pool dirty."

"I own the building. I can pay for them to clean it."

"I don't know if people are going to like us constantly closing off rooms to them." The other day, Slavik had found me in the gym. My weight-loss goal had come back in full force since we returned. He'd distracted me by taking me over the bench, on my knees. There had been a full mirror in front of us, and as he took me, he made me watch.

"Do I need to remind you not to care about what people think?" he asked. "I'm the only one who matters in your world."

I touched his cheek. "You are the only one that matters."

****

Slavik

With everything kicking off around me, I didn't have time to spend with my wife. Another attack on two of my businesses, another brothel, not as high maintenance as Cara's, as well as a casino, had my men stretched. We were doing constant patrols. There had also been another attempt on Ivan's life. The bastard hadn't managed it, but he'd been paid a small fortune with promises to the Volkov Bratva if he succeeded. This required me to fly out to Ivan to check on him.

Much to Ivan's annoyance, I put him on twenty-four-seven protection. All the brigadiers had supplied men to stay with him at all times. He hated this level of fuss. The bastard who tried to kill him hadn't succeeded, but it had been close. One wrong move, and Ivan would have been dead. As much as Ivan pissed me off, he was the only person in this world who was like a brother to me. I'd die for him. The only other person I'd die for was currently lying naked beside me, sated.

All day, I'd been making love and fucking my wife.

This time was a luxury to me. Stolen to have what I wanted. With all the shit going down, and me putting more people into play, the less time I had for this woman. The less time I had, the more I wanted to spend with her.

"You're thinking again," she said. "How can you be thinking?"

"I've got lots of thoughts." I ran my fingers up the curve of her back. Each time I caught sight of her naked, I found myself looking at her stomach.

This morning, she'd vomited again. I held her hair back, soothing her, trying to distract her. After her sickness abated, I'd often leave to return to work. This time, I'd stuck around, feeding her dry toast. I'd sent my man off, and Aurora started the morning curled up against me, watching a movie.

It had been some action movie with a very hot sex scene. We watched together, and I sensed the change in her. The way she turned toward me, almost as if begging for me to touch her, to fuck her, to take her.

I'd started by running my fingers up her thigh, slowly at first, gradually building until I cupped her between the thighs. The sweatpants she wore were gone within an instant. While the movie played on, I fingered her to a screaming orgasm, and to reward me for my patience, I'd positioned her across my lap, driving her down onto my dick. Her shirt was gone, as was her bra, and there on the sofa, I'd gotten my wife to fuck me. Her tits bouncing, sinking down on my dick, taking me all the way into her cunt. When I came, I'd sat her back and watched my cum spilling out of her pussy. I couldn't resist pushing it back in.

That was our first time.

We'd enjoyed a light lunch, then I finished by eating her pussy and fucking her across the table.

A shower together, and I'd driven inside her until the water had run cold.

Now, as we lay in bed, her on her stomach, the tempting globes of her ass stuck in the air, I had an idea.

"Aurora, do you trust me?" I asked.

"Yes."

"Good."

I pressed a kiss to her shoulder and climbed off the bed. When she went to move, I placed a hand on her shoulder, telling her to stay still.

"You're making me curious now."

"Good." Another kiss to the shoulder, and I went to my private drawer inside my closet, taking out the tube of lubricant.

Returning to the bedroom, I saw my wife being the good girl that she was, not moving an inch, and this made me smile.

"You're so good, Aurora. Such a good woman."

She glanced at me, her gaze falling to the tube in my hand. I climbed on the bed and reached for some of the cushions, stuffing them beneath her waist, lifting her ass to my gaze.

I slid my fingers into her pussy. She was so wet, but then today I'd been very greedy. She was already pregnant, and now my cum didn't have to just fill her pussy, I could have my fill of every single part of her body, and right now, all I wanted to do was fuck her ass.

Leaning forward, I brushed my lips against her ear. "Do you trust me?"

"Yes."

I smiled.

Plunging two fingers inside her, I stretched her pussy. She rocked back, lifting herself onto my fingers, trying to make herself come.

I opened the tube of lubricant and eased my fingers out of her pussy, tracing that thin piece of flesh between her cunt and asshole, and coated my slick digits against her anus. At the same time, I squeeze some of the lube out of the tube, getting her nice and wet.

She gasped. “Slavik?”

“Trust me. Remember.”

My virginal wife knew exactly what I was doing. I’d slipped into her library in the spare bedroom. The book she’d been reading had been left on the sofa, the pages spread open. I’d picked it up, realizing my dirty wife had been reading an anal sex scene. I didn’t mind. I had avoided her asshole for fear I’d traumatize her.

That one scene got me curious. Aurora had a system in her library. I’d watched her organize, and I noticed the books I saw her reading were on one side, with those she had yet to read on another. I’d picked out a couple of her books, flicked through, and saw my wife liked to read romance books with an erotic edge.

I had no problems exploring my wife’s desires.

“What are you doing?” she asked.

To answer, I pressed a single finger against her asshole. Her tight ring of muscles was stubborn, keeping me out. “You know what I’m doing. Relax. You know how it goes.”

Aurora glanced over her shoulder. “How?”

“I can read too.”

Her eyes went wide. “You’ve read my books?”

“No. I got curious. I’m a little disappointed in you, Aurora. You knew you could come to me. There was nothing for you to hide.” I kept on teasing her anus, stroking her. Sliding my other hand between her thighs, I touched her clit, and this made her moan.

"Now, you get to play out whatever you fantasized about." With two fingers either side of her clit, I rubbed her and stroked. I pressed the finger at her anus, teasing her tight hole. Distracting her.

She began to rock against my hand, and this time as I pushed against her anus, I didn't let up. I made her take a single finger.

Aurora gasped, but she didn't tell me to stop.

My cock was so hard, and all I wanted to do was fuck her hard, but first, I wanted to prepare her, to spread her open.

When she was close to orgasm, I stopped fingering her pussy. Spreading her left ass cheek, I began to push in a second finger, opening her up. She gasped.

"Does it hurt?" I asked.

"No. It … it's weird." She panted out the word.

I'd applied plenty of lube to her anus. Letting go of her ass cheek, I pushed some more, working it into her anus as I got both of my fingers inside her. Holding her ass cheek, I spread her open, and she thrust back against my fingers. The action was so slight, but I felt it. My sexy wife wanted this. She wasn't saying no.

I stretched her ass out until she drove back on the fingers, begging for me to make her come. I wasn't ready to give in just yet.

With my third finger, I slid it between the two and began to open her up even more. A whimper escaped her, and I paused, allowing her to get used to the feel of the three.

"Please," she said.

"Do you want my cock?" I asked.

"Yes."

I didn't give her my dick straight away. My cock

was already slick with pre-cum, and I worked my fingers into her ass, getting her accustomed to it. She was mindless on the pleasure. Her ass was a beacon, calling to me to take it.

I'd been a gentleman up until now, by my patience would only last so long. I removed my fingers, grabbed the lube, soaked my cock, and then I had the tip at her tight entrance which had closed up after my fingers left it.

She'd open for me.

I was rock-hard.

Aurora tensed up, and I ordered her to play with her pussy. This time, as I sank inch by tight glorious inch into her ass, she could bring herself to orgasm. The moment she had more of my cock in her ass, I grabbed her ass cheeks, spreading them wide so I could watch as she took it all.

The sight alone was enough to make me spunk, but I gained control. I sank to the hilt, my balls slapping against her cunt. Her moans filled the air. I counted to ten before I began to rock. Going in and out, slow easy strokes.

"How does it feel?"

A moan. "Amazing, I think."

I smiled.

Each stroke on her clit had her ass tightening around me. My balls were so heavy. I wanted to come, but I took my time, allowing her to get accustomed to my dick in her ass. This wasn't easy.

She was fucking glorious. Tight, hot, virginal, giving. Aurora was everything.

"Please!"

That one word was all I needed.

I began to harden my strokes, going a little harder, driving inside her, fucking her, taking her.

I heard Aurora come, and I felt it around my cock as her asshole became even tighter. My orgasm was so close, and as I filled her ass, it spilled from the tip, filling her asshole. I didn't pull out even after the pleasure faded. I stayed deep inside her. Collapsing over her, but not giving her all of my weight, I kissed her neck.

"Have I ever told you how amazing you are?" I asked.

"No." She giggled. "I can't believe we just did that." She pushed her hair from her face. "I loved doing that."

"All you've got to do is ask."

"Sure, because asking for you to give me … anal is a random conversation piece."

This time, I chuckled. "I know from what I read in those dirty books this is not all that you want, is it?"

She laughed. "You're right. I can't believe you read my books. Don't you have anything more interesting to do with your time?"

"Lots." But all I'd wanted was to know more about my wife, what made her tick. "And now as per your books, I think it's only fair that I clean you."

She groaned, and I laughed as I pulled out of her but lifted her in my arms, carrying her through to the bedroom.

Chapter Eighteen

Aurora

I watched Slavik across the dining room table. Today was my birthday, and after spending the week waking up to his kisses and making love, he hadn't been there. Already dressed and ready for work. I stood before him in my night shirt and shorts, which I pulled on in a hurry.

"Morning," I said, sipping at my tea. Coffee still made me feel sick

He looked up from his cell phone. "Hey, baby, good morning."

I smiled. I loved it when he used sweet words like that. "Busy morning?"

"Yeah, I've got to head into the office early."

"Right."

Still no mention.

I wasn't about to tell him it was my birthday and see the horrible realization that he'd forgotten. This was kind of like any other breakfast back at home. No one cared. They all went about their own business.

Pressing my lips together, I took another sip of my tea. I refused to be sad on this day. I'd spent a lot of birthdays alone. Today would be another one in a long list.

Thinking about the day and how we'd been the past week, I turned toward my husband and watched him. He clicked away at his cell phone, and I put my tea down. I walked toward him and leaned against the table.

"Slavik, there is something I always wanted to try." My hands shook as nerves took over.

He put his phone down and looked up. "There is?"

I nodded. "Do you trust me?"

"Yes."

His response surprised me. At first, I hesitated, shocked by his word, then I did no more than sink to my knees in front of his chair. There was enough space for me to fit. Putting my hands on his knees, I slid them up until I got to his zipper.

His hands were on the outside of his legs, and he made no move to help me as I worked the zip down.

"Tell me what you want," he said.

My heart raced. Heat pooled between my thighs. Nerves hit me hard. "I want to … suck your cock."

Did that sound corny? Porn star-ish? I had no idea, but this was what I'd been thinking about each time he went down on me. I loved his mouth on my pussy. The pleasure of his tongue as it danced across my clit. For a while now, I'd been thinking about reciprocating the offer, only, nothing had come up.

"You want to suck my cock?"

"Yes." Insecurity rushed through me as I sat back. "Unless you don't want me to." I'd assumed he would. Rejection was a hard thing to swallow, but it was my birthday, just another thing to add to my bad memories.

Slavik opened his belt, then his button, before taking out his cock. He wasn't completely hard, but as he worked from the tip down to the root and back again, I looked into his eyes. "Babe, I've got no problems with you wanting to suck on my cock. Why today? Is it a special occasion?"

I kept the smile on my lips even as his words cut me to the core. Rather than voice my feelings, I wrapped my fingers around his length. "You're going to have to tell me what to do." Every time I brought up my lack of experience, it seemed to drive him crazy, and I enjoyed it.

"First, you're going to want to lick it. Use your tongue, taste me."

I moved forward, shuffling on my knees. With Slavik holding his cock up for me, I licked from the root down to the tip. The taste and feel of him were so strange. Hard as he was getting, so the more he held himself, and soft at the same time. A hint of salt hit my tongue as I flicked across the little slit in the top of his cock.

Gliding down the opposite side, I licked his cock.

"Now, put your lips on the tip, and slowly sink your mouth on my dick."

With my gaze on him, I wrapped my lips around the head. He was even harder now, and I tucked my hair behind my ear, taking his cock into my mouth, feeling him go down until he hit the back of my throat. I stopped and quickly eased back, coming off his length.

"Keep doing it." He held himself still, and I worked his cock with my mouth, sucking him to the back of my throat.

After a few seconds, he released his length and I took hold of him. He wrapped his fingers in my hair and began to guide me over his length, making me take more of him. Even as I gagged, he held my head in place and started to thrust up into my mouth.

I moaned.

With each thrust, the taste of him got stronger in my mouth.

"Fuck. Yes. Fuck. That feels so fucking good." In and out he pumped, and I couldn't resist looking at him.

His gaze was on me.

"You're going to have to stop or you're going to get a mouthful of cum."

I kept my lips on his cock, and as he came, I was shocked by the jerk of his release as it filled my mouth.

On instinct, I swallowed him down, relishing the taste of him as he hit the back of my throat.

His tight grip on my hair pulled me off his length, and I sat back, wiping at my wet lips to dry them.

Slavik had closed his eyes as he came. Finally, he opened his eyes, and I smiled at him. He stroked my face, and no words were needed.

The moment was interrupted by the shrill of his cell phone. I stayed on the floor, kneeling as he answered.

I saw the sudden change in him.

"On my way." He got to his feet.

I shuffled out of my spot and followed him. "What is it? What's the matter?" Worry filled me.

"It's Ivan. His home was attacked last night. He's in the hospital. They don't know if he's going to make it."

"Oh, no."

"I've got to head out there," Slavik said.

"Let me come with you."

"No! You're staying here. Don't argue with me. I can't take care of you and do my job. Just stay here."

He stormed out of the penthouse suite, and I stood alone.

No one was around. I wrapped my arms around my waist.

The door opened, and in walked one of my bodyguards. He averted his gaze, and I glanced down to see I was still dressed in my pajamas.

I left the corridor, going to the bedroom. The bed was made as I'd done it after I got up. A force of habit. Sitting on the edge, I stare at the door. My birthday. Yay.

Tears filled my eyes, and the taste of Slavik was bitter on my tongue. Getting to my feet, I rushed into the bathroom. I grabbed the nearest toothbrush, dolloped on a good amount of paste, and got to work on my teeth, trying to wipe the memory from my mind. With my gaze on my reflection, I couldn't help but look at my stomach.

I finished brushing my teeth and lifted my shirt, turning to the side. I had to be going crazy.

There was a bump. Not a huge noticeable one, but I saw it. The bump was there.

Slavik had distracted me from finding out the truth. I needed to know if I was going to be a mom, or what any of this meant.

Dropping my hands, I changed into a pair of jeans and a large shirt. I slipped on a pair of pumps and left the bedroom.

"I need you to take me to a pharmacy," I said to the guard. I couldn't remember his name, I thought it was David or something. After everything that happened with Sergei, I didn't get close to the men who guarded me. It was safer for me to just be who I was, away from it all.

He pulled out his cell phone.

"There is no reason to call my husband. He doesn't need to know his wife requires lady products."

The man … paled.

What was it with men and lady products? It was as natural as breastfeeding.

"You're going to drive me to the pharmacy. I can go in and be out in a flash. No big deal." I forced a smile to my lips.

"Mr. Ivanov needs to know."

"I know, and you can tell him after, okay? He is busy at the moment, as I'm sure you're aware. Do you want to be known as the guard who interrupted my husband's journey with details of his wife's purchases at a pharmacy?"

I talked really fast, trying to get my point across.

This could backfire.

I wanted to find out if I was pregnant before I even let Slavik know I was. If I wasn't, no big deal. If the stick read *yes*, then my life was about to change.

The guard hesitated, and my patience ran thin.

"Okay." The guard went to grab my arm, but I stepped forward, rushing out of the apartment. My hands shook as we waited for the elevator.

At the ground parking, he held my door open for me, and I slid inside.

Once outside in the open air, I took a deep breath, trying not to think about what all of this could mean.

The first pharmacy we came to was still closed. The second one had a line outside, and at the third, my nerves were frayed.

He parked the car and as he made to get out, I put a hand on his shoulder. "Keep an eye on me from the car. I promise I'm just going in to buy lady products. I don't need an entourage."

"Mrs. Ivanov."

"I will tell my husband lies if you don't do this," I said. I never threatened anyone in my life. After what my sister did, I always tried to be a nice charge. Today was not the day. It was my birthday. I was all alone. My husband had taken off. I was at the end of my patience.

Without another word, I climbed out and entered the pharmacy. I went immediately to the pregnancy tests then to the lady products, picking the brand I liked and the style.

At the counter, I paid with what change I had and offered the man behind the counter a smile.

"I hope congratulations are in order," he said.

I smiled. "Me too."

He winked at me, and I took my bag, exiting the pharmacy to get back into the car. The driver ignored me. I'd angered him. Guilt rushed through me, but I didn't apologize. He took me straight to the apartment. Back inside, I ignored him and went to the bathroom.

With still shaking hands, I read the instructions on the back of the box. Sickness coiled in my gut. It was just peeing on a stick.

Minutes later, hands washed, I stared at the stick, watching as it changed, and my life as I knew it would follow suit.

I was pregnant. Slavik had done what the boss had ordered.

My son or daughter would inherit this legacy, would one day stand in Slavik's place. Actually, no, just my son. If I had a boy.

Collapsing to the floor, I put both of my hands to my stomach.

Slavik and I were only just getting along, finding a life with each other. Was it all a trick for this baby?

Closing my eyes, I leaned my head against the wall.

My birthday. I should have known it wasn't going to be a good day.

When the bedroom door slammed open, I jolted to my feet, throwing the test into the trash bin as the guard who now hated me pushed the bathroom door open. He held a phone.

He didn't say a word as I took it.

Holding the phone, I put it to my ear. "Hello," I said.

"Aurora, it's me."

It was Slavik.

I breathed a sigh of relief. "How are you? How is Ivan?"

"Ivan Volkov is dead."

Those very words rang in my ear. I dropped the phone.

What did this mean?

Fear rushed through my body.

Someone had tried and succeeded in taking out the Volkov Bratva leader. This had ramifications.

Tears filled my eyes. My hands went to my stomach. I dropped the cell phone in the process, trying to understand what I'd just heard. None of it made any sense.

The guard picked up the cell phone, but I didn't hear what he said to Slavik. Nothing mattered to me right now. How had we gone from the happiness of what seemed like a few hours ago to the chaos of now?

Sinking to my knees, I put my hands against my head. The dull throbbing made me feel sick.

I was pregnant.

My husband's boss had just been killed.

My baby stood no chance of coming into a happy home.

I had to tell Slavik we were going to have a baby.

****

Slavik never came home.

The day passed, turning into a second, then a third. He didn't call. No messages came through from his guards. They changed. One man coming, another leaving. For a week, this happened.

My birthday had to have been the worst on record.

I stood at the kitchen counter, a hand on my stomach. I found myself doing this more often than I should.

Wondering. Trying to figure out about the future.

My family hadn't called. My parents sent no condolences to me, no birthday wishes either.

With a drink of water in hand, I walked toward the window and stared out across the city. I hated this window. The view. The heights.

People walked around without a single care in the world. There was no pain waiting for them. They could have children and be happy to raise them in this world. They heard about the terror and violence on the news, but it rarely reached them at their front door.

"Hey, little one. I … I will protect you and love you. I promise." I whispered the words so the guard didn't hear.

They had amazing hearing.

The silence from Slavik made me feel sick. Ivan Volkov was dead. I had no doubt Slavik would take over, lead the other brigadiers through this time. What my husband inherited, I shuddered to think. If I allowed myself even a moment to consider what was at stake, I questioned my position at his side.

Would he even want me?

I wasn't … the kind of wife the boss would have. Ivan didn't even have a wife nor a girlfriend, or an intended.

Sipping at my water, I wondered where I stood. Since Slavik had gone silent, I had to wonder if he was planning on getting rid of me. Ivan started our marriage. The peace treaty lasted between my family and his. I was the ordered bride. The consolation prize.

My hands shook.

Would I be kicked out?

My family would never take me back. People would look at me and laugh.

Stop it, Aurora. You have no idea what you're talking about.

Slavik and I weren't a love match. I rubbed at my chest. The piercing pain was more than I could bear. My stomach knotted.

Over the months, my feelings for my husband had

changed. This silence between us only confirmed what I knew. I loved him and I hated it. I loved a man who might never love me back.

Tears filled my eyes and I closed them, trying not to allow them to fall back.

Not happening. I was not going to cry. I would stay strong. Nothing would make me weak.

I loved my husband, and after all this time, I would learn to love him even as he hated me.

A sudden knock at my front door made me pause. The guard turned and walked toward the door. I remained near the window, basking in self-pity. Pregnant. Alone. Miserable and in love.

Just kill me now.

Rubbing at my temples, I looked up to see Cara.

"Hi, darling!" She rushed toward me and pulled me into my arms. The action caused my water to spill over the edge. "I've been so busy with work. Utterly swamped." She let out a sniffle. "I came over as soon as I could. Slavik, he has been … this is tough for the two of us."

"You're not with him?"

"No. Someone had to be here. You know how it goes."

I stared at Cara. Her face wasn't puffy or red. Her eyes glistened, but they were not bloodshot. I spent a lot of time crying, especially these past few days, and I looked a mess. My eyes were swollen, bloodshot. Even around my eyes was sore from wiping away the tears. I hadn't known Ivan Volkov for a long time, not even intimately as a friend, but I still mourned his loss. Bad man or not, he'd only shown me nothing but kindness.

"You must be hurting?" I asked.

"I am. It … it has been a struggle to get up in the mornings. If it wasn't for Slavik giving me work. He knows what I need to get me through this trying time." She put a hand to her stomach and took a breath. "I loved Ivan so very much." The same hand went to her mouth and she turned away.

"I'm so sorry for your loss." I felt … numb.

"I'd have been here sooner. With Slavik off dealing with the funeral arrangements and of course bringing those responsible to justice. We will not let this stand. We will fight." Cara's face turned into a frown. Her hand clenched into a fist.

"I agree."

I sipped at my water, noting the spillage on the floor. Brushing past Cara, I went to the kitchen, acting on autopilot as I grabbed a cloth and returned to clean up the mess.

"Honey, are you okay?" Cara said.

"I'm fine."

"You don't seem fine. You're acting really strange."

I rubbed the floor until it was dry. I didn't know if the few lunch dates Cara and I had been on constituted us as friends. My baby was currently my top priority. I loved my child so much already.

Talking to Cara about my pregnancy was not high on my list. "You talked to Slavik?"

"Yes. He is struggling, as I'm sure you can imagine," Cara said.

I glanced at Cara, and she watched me. Head tilted to the side. Her voice sounded strange to me.

"I wouldn't know."

"What do you mean?"

"He hasn't called me. I don't know what he's going through." I stood, taking the towel to the sink as my words sank in to my own ears.

Slavik, my husband, had called Cara before he'd

even talked to me. Had our time together meant nothing? I knew the truth, and it hurt more than all the other rejections I ever felt.

"You know, it's not a big deal. Vik is a complicated guy."

Vik. The name some of his friends called him. "I guess."

"You know what, we're going out to lunch. No questions asked. My treat."

"I don't feel like it."

Cara tutted. "Come on. I'll talk to your guard. He can drive us. It'll be fun."

So that was how I ended up in the back seat of a car, dressed in a pair of jeans and a shirt, sitting next to a really beautiful woman, being driven across town to a quaint little café.

"I will say I need to make a pit stop first. It won't be long." She gave directions to my guard, and I sat back, hands on my stomach. "Are you feeling okay?"

"I'm fine."

"Good. Good. We're getting so close to Christmas. It's always a busy time, the festive holidays. Men cannot stand being at home with their women and they come to see me and my girls."

Cara continued to chat incessantly. I stopped listening, staring out the window at the passing scenery.

The car came to a stop, and I didn't notice or recognize any of the buildings. Slavik had taken me all over the city to his different venues and enterprises. He was a very rich man and an astute businessman.

"Where are we?" I asked.

"Come on." Cara climbed out of the car.

My guard followed suit as we walked toward the old rundown factory. It wasn't large, perhaps a two-story building, but on a small scale. The sign on the side had decayed and the paint had chipped away from years of neglect.

Cara opened the door and we entered. The scent of dust filled the air. I spotted a couple of rats up ahead, and I screamed.

The unmistakable sound of a gunshot filled the air, and I spun around to see Cara holding a gun. My guard was dead. The wound to the head had sprayed all over the walls. My stomach instantly recoiled, and I bent forward, vomiting.

"So fucking disgusting."

I finished throwing up, and Cara grabbed me by my long hair and dragged me through the factory.

"What are you doing?" I asked.

Pain rushed through my head at the grip she had on my skull. None of this made any sense.

Why had she killed my guard?

Had Slavik sent her to kill me?

She threw me across the room, and I hit the side of a table, using my hands to take more of the impact so I didn't catch my stomach.

"I can't believe it was so difficult to get to you," Cara said. "I mean, why you?" She tutted.

Glancing at Cara, I saw she'd led us into a large open space. Several tables looked modern, and I saw paperwork sprawled out. Boards were hung, and I caught pictures of myself, Slavik, and Ivan. Along with notes of locations, times, and then I saw the images of the man who had attacked me the night of the banquet.

Cara smiled. "Yes, look your fill. You really should. After all, your husband is going to find this and everyone is going to know how I stopped you. Of course it will mean an end to the treaty with the Italians, which is fine. They're easy to stop, and we'll soon be taking over their turf." She clicked her fingers.

"What is all of this?" I asked.

"This … this is twenty-plus years of being kept on the bottom. Twenty years of being overlooked. Twenty years of allowing dicks to rule. Not anymore it's not."

"You did this?" I asked.

"No, darling, you did. You and your traitorous family. All along, it was a ploy and a game to infiltrate Ivan's Bratva. To weaken them from within. You, my sweet, arranged for all of the killings. All of the attacks, and you paid for them until you got the one you wanted, Ivan Volkov. Son of a bitch never saw it coming." Cara tutted. "He should have known not to deal with me, but what can I say? They're fucking brain dead when it comes to a woman in charge."

I stood up and looked at all the planning. There was so much detail. After all this time, Cara hadn't been loyal to them. She'd bided her time until the right moment where she could take them out.

"You were always going to kill Ivan?" I asked.

"Seeing as you're going to be dead soon, I suppose I can tell you that I never planned to kill Ivan. Not in the beginning. He was a sweet guy, deadly, vicious, and all that, but I liked him. I don't do love. We had a business arrangement, and I have to say, for the most part, he kept to his side of the bargain."

"What changed? You got the life you wanted."

"What changed?" Cara rushed toward me. Her hand suddenly wrapped around my neck. She was so strong, and I held on to her wrist, trying to stop her from choking me to death. "You changed fucking everything. My rightful place was by Ivan's side. If not his, then Slavik's. That's my place, but you, you came along and ruined everything. Then Ivan, he thinks he can marry his men off one by one and nothing would come of it. I saved them on those fucking streets, and now, they're going to be mine. I'm going to show Slavik what a nasty cunt you are. He'll want me, and then I'll be by his side ruling this place as it was meant to be. The new order is not for now. I don't believe in peace. I want war."

The Cara I thought I knew was an act. She changed right before my eyes. The violence simmered within her.

"Slavik will never believe you."

"No?" she asked. "You think he'd believe you after how long he's known me? You don't stand a chance, Aurora. I am sorry for all of this. You are a means to an end."

I stared at Cara, shocked as she raised the gun at me.

She tensed, and I closed my eyes. No bullet came.

"Fuck!"

I had no time to move as the sound of the door being broken in filled the air. Within a matter of seconds, Slavik and his men were there.

****

Slavik

I listened to Cara's accusations. My wife on her knees, tears filling her eyes as she looked at me.

All the while, a perfect story painted for all to hear. I saw my men and Ivan's, and their anger grew with each word spoken.

My wife.

The woman I'd fallen in love with was a traitor?

"You see, Slavik, we can't let her leave here. Look at the damage she has caused. I told Ivan he never should have done the treaty. You, yourself, fought against it."

I stared at Aurora. She made no sound. No defense.

"Do you trust me?" I asked.

"Of course, I trust you," Cara said. Her hands touched my shoulder. "How could I not? I brought her to you. I knew you'd follow me to protect me. You love me."

The buzz in my pocket alerted me to the next step, and I turned to Cara. I dropped the gun and stroked her cheek. She was a good friend, the best. Through thick and thin, she'd been there for me and for Ivan.

"I wasn't talking to you," I said, grabbing her head and shoving her down to the ground as she screamed.

My men tensed up.

"Do you really think bringing my wife to this factory was all it was going to take? All this information gathered together, pointing the finger of blame at my woman?" I asked.

"I don't know what you're talking about. She has polluted your mind, Vik. This is not you. Please, someone, stop him. He's a traitor to Ivan. Kill him. Please, kill him."

I pointed my gun at Cara's head.

"You thought you could get away with it, but Cara, the moment you started to steal from Ivan, I knew. I knew the funds being taken, the men who started to attack. You're not the brightest woman. All you've ever been able to sell is your cunt. Sex is all you know and you think you could take this from Ivan? From me!"

Out of the corner of my eye, I saw one of my men approach my wife, and I raised my gun. "You touch her, and I will fucking kill you."

"She's a traitor, boss."

I shot him in the leg and turned to look at all of my men. "Now would be a good time for you to come out."

"I rather like the suspense and drama," Ivan Volkov said, removing the hat and scarf he'd used to cover himself so I could get him on a plane and back to my city.

Cara gasped. "Ivan. I knew it. I knew you were alive. Please, tell him to stop. You know I would never hurt you."

"Oh, honey. You were sloppy, darling," Ivan said. He looked around at the information Cara had left.

I'd known from the start of the attacks she had something to do with it. At first, I wasn't sure why. The little crumbs she'd left me to work with didn't give anything away. The money she stole was used to take Ivan out, but as she did, she got sloppy.

Cara was never much of a thinker or a planner.

"This is all Aurora and those Italian bastards!"

Ivan moved toward my wife and offered her a hand. "I am so very sorry for all of this mess."

My wife continued to shake.

I'd pointed a gun at her to play along, to draw Cara away from my wife so she'd be out of harm's way. I still held a firm grip on Cara's hair, but all I wanted to do was go to my woman, to pull her into my arms, to kiss her, to tell her it was going to be okay.

Tears fell from her cheeks.

"Oh, Cara, you were doing so well. I have to say when Slavik told me of your involvement in this months ago, I told him he was lying. There was no way you'd hurt me or the Bratva."

"I wouldn't. You know this. You know me."

"Exactly. I know you and I told him to get the proof. Until I happened to overhear this." He lifted his cell phone and played the recording he got.

"Remember, do not come back until Ivan is dead. I want him gone. Send me a picture if you have to, and I will

make sure your debt is removed. You will not owe me a thing. The Bratva will be mine, Cara's."

Ivan clicked off his cell phone. "I'm a cautious guy. Men can be bought, as can women. Nothing is ever sacred anymore, so I designed my own security system. I know when people are in my house, Cara. Your guy was dead before he even finished the call. You finished that conversation with me."

Cara's face went pale.

Ivan had called me. Told me exactly what to do and so I did. I left my wife and immediately went to his side. I made the final announcement of his death, and with it, we waited, making our way back to my city where Cara refused to leave. I knew something was going down today the moment I watched her enter my apartment building. Aurora's guard had called me as soon as Cara entered. His call had stayed with me until the moment he died. His family would be taken care of.

"No. No. No," Cara said. "You're lying. You're bluffing. It's all that whore's fault." She started to cry, but the tears never made an appearance.

Ivan crouched down to be on her level. "You want to tell me what is going on?"

Cara went silent. "You think I don't know about *her*? You think I didn't know when you changed our plans?"

Ivan's jaw clenched.

"You're never going to be happy with her. I won't allow it. I will hunt you down, and I will kill you," Cara said. "You and Slavik, you're both mine, and you gave him away. It was supposed to be us three against the world."

"Cara, you had the job you wanted. You had everything you wanted. I offered you more power and you refused."

I'd been there when Ivan had told her to take any city or cities as her own. She'd told him no. All she wanted was her own brothel. To control men. To help him from the ground. We'd always accepted that. I put as much protection on her as Ivan did.

We grew up together. Our lives were bound with one another, but Cara, she wasn't the same person.

"I know what you have to do," Cara said. "Do it. You think I won't do it again? Next time, I'll be better. Next time I'll make sure every single person you love is dead long before I put a bullet in your head. I'll make you all suffer. This … this will be a party in comparison."

Ivan pulled out his gun as Cara continued to rant, pressed the muzzle against her head, and pulled the trigger. I let her go.

Her corpse lay on the ground.

I looked at Ivan for a split second before I went to my woman. Aurora collapsed against me with a sob. Her body shook in my arms, and I ran my hands all over her, trying to make sure she was okay. To find any sign that she was hurt.

"She was crazy," Aurora said. "You were going to kill me."

I cupped her face. "No. I was never going to kill you. I've seen how Cara is, and I knew she'd hurt you. She would have killed you, Aurora. All I did was get her away from you."

I slammed my lips down on her lips, not caring about the men who surrounded us. They were already following Ivan's orders, dealing with the body and the cleanup. All the information Cara had gathered would be destroyed. Breaking the kiss, I stared into my woman's eyes. "I love you." I spoke the words slowly so she wouldn't have any room for doubt.

The amazement on her face made me laugh. "What?"

"I'm in love with you." I could have lost her. One wrong move today and she … no, there was no way I'd let it happen. I refused to even think of losing her. "I will never hurt you, Aurora. Never. You are my fucking life, and not just because of the baby."

"You know?"

I groaned. "I've known since the attack at the restaurant. I know you heard Ivan. I didn't want you to think I knocked you up on command. I got you pregnant because I can't take my hands off you. I'm in love with you, Aurora. So much so, you drive me crazy." Reaching into my back pocket, I pulled out the folded tickets I had stored there. Cara had messed with my plans. "I wanted to give you this on your birthday, but Cara, she … you know how it is."

Aurora looked up with tears in her eyes. "You remembered my birthday?"

"I never forgot it. How could I forget one of the best days? You were born on it."

"Fucking gross. You're supposed to be my fucking beast, and here you are spilling your heart out." Ivan made a vomiting noise.

I kissed my wife before turning toward my best friends. He looked sad. Our men were all gone. "You okay?"

"The cleaning crew is outside. I figured I'd let you finish your little declaration before I brought you in." He turned to Aurora. "It's nothing special he's gotten you. A month alone with him on a honeymoon vacation. In the meantime, I get to step in here and deal with his shit."

"You're babysitting," I said. "Nothing more."

Ivan rolled his eyes. "Let's get out of here."

He looked pissed off. Not that I could blame him. Cara, Ivan, and I went back a lifetime. We were each other's best friend. The one person in the whole world we could rely on.

Leaving the building, I put Aurora in my car and told her to stay. I walked to Ivan, who stood watching as the building began to burn.

"I thought you said the cleaning crew was here?" I asked.

"It is. They're doing what I told them."

I glanced over at the building. The flames were engulfing it, taking up all of Cara's betrayal in smoke. "You okay?"

"Yeah. It just goes to show you never really know anyone, right? Cara was supposed to be on our team."

"Who did she mean?" I asked.

"What?"

"It sounded to me like she thought you betrayed her. Who was the woman?"

Ivan smirked. "There is no woman."

The lie was easy to detect.

"Remember who we are, Slavik," Ivan said, putting his sunglasses on. "And if you ever betray me, your wife will belong to me. I'll keep you alive just to make me watch you hurt her."

"I won't ever betray you."

He looked at the house. "Funny, Cara once said the same thing."

There was a difference between me and Cara. I wasn't in love with Ivan, and I didn't feel cheated.

I watched as Ivan climbed into his car, and he snapped his fingers for his driver to start moving.

I went back to Aurora.

"Is everything okay?" she asked.

"For us, yes. For Ivan, that I can't tell." I cupped

her cheek, drawing her in close. “I’m sorry I didn’t get to wish you a happy birthday.”

She smiled. A true, honest, full-faced smile, and I was smitten.

“I wanted to hate you,” I said.

“And now you love me?”

“Yes. You always told me that you were second best, but I promise you, Aurora, you’ll always be my first.” I took possession of her mouth, holding her tight to me. The building in flames faded behind us.

I was never going to let this woman go. She never stood a chance.

I loved her. There was no denying that, and I never intended to hold back. Aurora would have all of me, the parts I didn’t let anyone else see.

“Slavik,” Aurora said.

“Yeah.”

“I love you.”

I smiled. “Call me Vik.”

Epilogue

Aurora

Five years later

We'd left the penthouse apartment after my first pregnancy, and Vik found us a country home. It was a modest seven-bedroom set back in the countryside with a nice expanse of garden. He made sure to have a pool as well as a gym installed on the grounds. There was always plenty of guards.

Ever since Cara's betrayal, Ivan stopped allowing anyone to get close to him. He didn't accept visitors, and he'd even kept Vik at arm's length. We wouldn't let him break off his friendship. Even though he terrified me, I always extended dinner invitations as well as special invites for him to come. He kept most of them.

Christmas was the only time I saw the real man, not the boss, the man in charge. Our kids loved him.

Our firstborn we'd named Slavik Ivan Ivanov. When we told Ivan his name, he'd burst out laughing, but we'd seen the joy in his face.

Our little girl came a year later. It would seem Slavik was addicted to getting me pregnant. We named our daughter Hope. Last year, I'd given birth to another son, and true to my husband's nature, he'd named him Ivan Slavik Ivanov. Yeah, I wasn't exactly sure about that one, but he wouldn't budge. Strong names for his boys.

Glancing out the garden, I saw the barbeque was already going and Ivan controlled the grill.

We had Andrei and Adelaide coming, and they were on their way, as well as a few other Brigadiers.

Slavik came up behind me, wrapping his arms

around my thickening waist.

"How are my two girls?" he asked, kissing my neck.

"I'm pregnant again. My ankles feel huge, but the doctor has told me I'm healthy." I leaned back against him.

"You love having my children," Slavik said.

"If we have another boy, you've got to promise me you'll find another name." I looked out at the garden. We had two Slaviks and two Ivans in our presence. I chuckled to myself. Baby Ivan was too young to recognize his name.

Our son Slavik kept on going to adult Ivan to see what he wanted.

"Never going to happen. We're going to have girls from now on, you will see."

I sighed. Leaning against him. "And what makes you think that?"

"Simple, I'm the boss and your body, it knows this. It will do as it's told."

This did make me laugh. "You're kidding, right?"

"Nope." He crouched down, his mouth near my swollen stomach. "You hear that, baby girl? You're going to do as you're told. Only girls can reside here."

I kept on laughing, and when he pressed a kiss right on my pussy, I looked around the garden to see if anyone saw. Vik protected me from others, and he glanced up at me with a wicked glint in his eye.

"And this, my pretty cunt, knows what I want." He kissed me again, and this time, I couldn't help but close my eyes.

"How did I get so lucky?" I asked.

He got to his feet. There was no answer as he stroked my hair back from my face and I tilted my head back to look at him.

I always hoped for happiness.

Never did I think I'd get it.

Slavik kissed me, and I knew there was no need for any reason or answer. I loved him and he loved me, and against all the odds, we'd found each other and this happiness I'd protect and treasure.

****

Slavik

I was a monster.

A bastard.

A brute.

The thing nightmares feared.

After some of the things I'd done, I never deserved happiness. To feel that, you had to be a good person. I wasn't good. I was evil to the core, but with Aurora, I knew peace. I knew happiness, and above all, I knew love.

I loved my wife more than anything.

Holding on to her hands, I took the pain as she screamed through the labor, giving birth to our fourth child.

I hated hearing her screams. My instinct was always to protect her, to stop the bad things from happening. I held on to her as the doctor told her to push. As per my instructions, the doctor was a woman. There was no way I would allow a man between my wife's thighs, even to deliver my baby.

I was that fucking possessive of her. She was all mine. I didn't share. There were times it was a struggle to share her with our kids.

Aurora collapsed to the bed. "It hurts." She cried out.

"I know. I know. You've got this, babe. You've got this. I love you so damn much." A day never went by that I didn't tell her how I felt.

After all the shit with Cara, I'd learned my lesson. There was no room to wait. Aurora could have been taken from me, and I made sure I never took a single moment for granted. My life was devoted to this woman.

Aurora gripped my hands and squeezed, pushing our baby out. I heard the screams, and I kissed my wife's head, staring at her.

"Are you okay?" I asked.

She sighed. "Yeah, I'm okay." She turned to kiss my knuckles. "Are you?"

She knew watching her in labor was always a struggle for me. The first time, I'd nearly killed her male doctor and the tension in the room hadn't been great, which was why I requested, no, demanded, a female doctor. Also, most of the staff had to be female.

My wife smiled at me.

"I'm good."

I hated when men talked to my woman. All her life she'd been passed over, treated like she was second best, but to me, I knew the truth. She was first, the best, and now, she was all mine. Others already had their chance. I wasn't giving her back.

Our baby girl was given to us, and I looked down, falling in love all over again. Our children were a fucking joy. I'd never wanted to be a dad. After only knowing pain and rejection from my own father, I'd vowed never to be one myself, but Aurora gave me the strength to be a better person.

"I guess you're right," Aurora said.

I chuckled. "About what?"

"My body does follow your orders."

I kissed the top of her head. "I love you, and I don't care if it's a boy or girl. I just want you both to be healthy."

It was a good thing I told her that, as within two

years, she gave birth to another boy, and now, I had to figure out what to name him.

The End

SAM CRESCENT

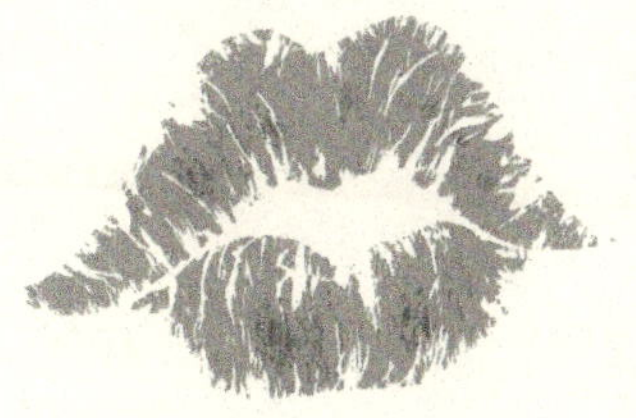

EVERNIGHT PUBLISHING ®

www.evernightpublishing.com

Made in the USA
Las Vegas, NV
24 June 2024

91449874R00173